GOT ME HOPING

VET SHOP BOYS BOOK 1

CASEY COX

Cover Design: Wicked By Design
Editing: Mary-Anne Hinkle
Proofreading: Lori Parks

THANK YOU

This book would not be what it is today without the help of some incredible people.

Thank you - K.M. Neuhold, Eden Finley, Briar Prescott, N.R. Walker, and Lucy Lennox for so kindly and graciously providing the best feedback an author could ever hope for. I'm still pinching myself!

Thank you - Mia Monroe for your excellent advice, support, and all-round amazingness. Let's have margaritas sometime. First round's on me.

Finally, thank you to my "fab four" - Tammy, Brady, Lauren, and Rachael for being there from the very beginning.

1

NOAH

"Whoa, whoa, whoa. Back it up. You've never had a one-night stand?"

Three sets of eyes land on me like laser beams. The last thing I expected to be doing tonight is admitting *this* to my friends and colleagues, especially during a drinking game I haven't played since my days in vet school.

"Why are we even playing Never Have I Ever?" I complain-grumble. "It's a stupid game that always devolves into sex."

"Uh, you just answered your own question there." Gus smirks at me. He's the boss and owner of Vet Shop Boys, the veterinary clinic Fulton, Chase, and I work at.

"No. I've never had a one-night stand," I admit. I try to play it off casually, like it's no big deal, but I can feel my cheeks heating up. I'm thirty-four and single, so why haven't I had one? I scratch the back of my neck. "Is that weird?"

Fulton's hand lands on my shoulder, his friendly eyes meeting mine. "No, it's not weird. You're just not wired that way, that's all."

Thankfully, that was our third and final shot for the evening. It's a Tuesday night, and all four of us are on the other side of thirty, so we know our limits. I downed two out of three drinks, revealing that I'd both skinny-dipped and had sex on a beach. So not a total prude.

"*Should* I have a one-night stand?" My eyes bulge. Dammit. I hadn't meant to ask that out loud.

"It's up to you, man." Chase shrugs before taking a sip of his drink. "I had a few in college before I met Julie and settled down. Some guys need to get that shit outta their system, you know?"

Gus nods. "There's no harm in trying, right? I mean, you don't want to be ninety, on your rocking chair with your husband by your side, and wondering what a one-night stand *could* have been like. Besides, it's just some simple, no-strings fun."

"Exactly," Chase chips in. "Nothing more. Nothing less."

I take a sip of bourbon and let their words settle over me. Gus resumes his conversation with Chase, who's telling him all about

Miles the turtle who was brought in today with a small crack in his shell. Turns out the best thing to patch it up with is epoxy resin. Who knew?

I finish off my bourbon as my eyes sweep around the bar. It's pretty busy for a weeknight. We're sitting in what's become our usual booth, tucked away in the corner behind the pool table. The dance floor in the distance is silhouetted with bodies.

I guess you could say we're regulars here. Being a vet is the best job in the world, but sometimes it can get tough. It's not all cute puppies and cuddly kittens. So having a few drinks and socializing with one another is a good way to decompress and blow off some steam at the end of a long day.

"What's it really like?" I mutter to Fulton, who's sitting beside me.

He stops scrolling through his phone and squints at me, running the silver, thin-rimmed glasses back up his nose. "What's *what* really like?"

"A one-night stand." I reach for a glass of water and drain half of it in one go.

"Meh. Overrated if you ask me. Kinda like jerking off with your non-dominant hand."

I snort. "What does that mean?"

Fulton places his phone on the table and turns to me. "Well, it's familiar and feels okay-ish. It's also not that great and a little awkward, but it gets you the desired outcome."

"Which is?"

"You tell me."

I blow out a heavy breath. "It's been two years."

Fulton fiddles with his red and yellow polka-dot bow tie. "Two years since..." He stops himself as soon as he realizes what I'm referring to. "Oh."

"Yeah."

"And there's been no one since?"

"Nope." My voice is small, barely audible over the music.

He adjusts his glasses. "And you're still not on any of the apps, are you?"

"Apps?"

"Yeah. You know, like Grindr, Scruff, Tinder, Woof, Growl, Squawk, Oink, Yay or..." Fulton throws his head back before letting out a very horsey, "Neiggggh."

"Okay, now you're just making animal noises."

He lowers his head. "True. But when did you realize?"

"Meaning?"

"Meaning that in two years of being single, you haven't used a single dating app. There's gotta be a reason for that."

My fingers circle the top of my glass as I think it over. Why aren't I on dating apps or having one-night stands? I've had three long-term relationships and been left with a broken heart each time. Fulton says it's because I give too much of myself. I treat my boyfriends too well. But isn't that how love is supposed to work? At their core, aren't relationships based on a foundation of *I treat him well, he treats me well?* That hasn't exactly worked out that great for me so far. It takes two to tango, and I've been left solo on the dance floor more times than I care to remember.

I can't deny that the lonely pull in my heart has been getting stronger lately. A gentle curiosity stirs in my stomach. Maybe some simple, no-strings fun might actually be the thing I need right now.

A pool game is starting up between a bunch of guys in front of us. I notice one of the guys who's just walked in, he's tall and has shoulder-length blond hair. I crane my head a little to get a better look, but one of his friends shoves a pool cue in his hands and blocks my view.

"What if I want to do it?" I say. "Have a one-night stand, that is."

Fulton sits up a little taller and clears his throat. "Well, then. As your best friend, fashionista with exquisite taste, and one of the best veterinarians in all of Brookhaven, Virginia, let me offer you some sage advice, should you choose to resign from your position as President of the Blue Balls Society."

I let out a low chuckle. Fulton is quirky as fuck. He likes wearing funky colorful outfits, he celebrates his half-birthday since his actual birthday is on Christmas Day, and he listens to Mariah Carey Christmas carols...in June. He also happens to be the best friend a guy could ever hope to have.

I drain the remaining water. "Lay it on me."

"First, set your expectations to low."

"Okay."

"Once you've done that...lower them again."

"Geez, you're really selling it."

Fulton's mouth slips into a smile. "I'm a realist. Besides, like the guys said, it's just one night of no-strings fun."

"Fair enough."

"Now before I give you the four golden rules for any one-night stand, I'm going to preface this by stating, for the record, that there is nothing wrong with you never having had a one-night stand. That borders on reverse sex shaming, and you know how I feel about any sort of shaming."

"Roger that." I tip my fingers in salute, grinning. I love when Fulton goes on one of his mini-rants.

"The rules, like all things to do with men and sex are, unsurprisingly, very simple."

"I'm all ears."

Fulton lifts a finger as he spouts each of them off. "Don't spend the night. Don't see him again. Don't share anything personal. Don't fall in love with him. That's it. Stick to these four rules, and you're golden."

I quirk a cheeky eyebrow. "That's an awful lot of *don't-ing* for something that's meant to be fun."

"It is what it is." Fulton shrugs, his face growing more serious. "Ultimately, sex is about connecting. But how you choose to connect, whether it's with the one and only person you love and want to be with for the rest of your life, or a random stranger whose path crosses yours for a few hours, there's no right or wrong way."

He takes a breath and looks like he's about to say something else, when Gus' voice drifts over to us.

"Has anyone seen my fiancé?" he asks with an exaggerated hand flourish. Even in the dim lighting, it's hard to miss the dazzling bling on his ring finger. "My fiancé seems to have disappeared. Do you think I should go and look for my fiancé?"

Gus recently got engaged to Marco. He's just a *teeny* bit excited about it.

"Geez, anyone would think you're getting married or something," Fulton teases, but Gus doesn't bite. He's got groomzilla written all over him in big bright neon letters, but after what that man's been through, no one deserves to find true love more than him. I'm happy for the guy, even if it means we'll no doubt have to endure months of wedding planning torture.

"I haven't seen him." Chase cranes his neck on the lookout for said missing fiancé. "He mentioned something about going to the bathroom, but that was a good ten minutes ago."

Fulton lets out a yawn. "I might take off, you guys."

Chase nods and reaches for his jacket. "Yeah. Me, too."

We all get to our feet. Gus is still searching for Marco as we exchange a round of hugs.

"I gotta pee. I'll see you tomorrow at work. I've got the late shift," I announce to the group as I leave.

As I approach the men's room, Marco stumbles out. He looks a little disheveled, his shirt's hanging out, and if I didn't know any better, I'd say his lips were swollen.

"Hey, Marco. You okay?"

"Uh, yeah." He averts my gaze.

"We're all leaving. Gus is looking for you."

"Oh, okay. Cool." He ambles past me without so much as a wave. Hmm, that was weird.

I take care of my business and hustle toward the exit when I stumble into a six-foot-plus vision blocking my way. Breath escapes my lungs as two hazel eyes with shards of gray pierce right into me.

"Why, hello."

A twinge spikes in my chest. "Uh, hi."

He drags his hand through his wavy shoulder-length blond hair that's pulled into a messy bun, a few loose strands falling and framing his angular face. A sweet rosy hue fills his cheeks, contrasting nicely with his broody stubble.

A glimmer of a smile plays on his lips. "Having a good night?" His voice is calm despite the flurry of people and sounds around us.

I give a quick nod. Words would be useful at this point, I know, but my mouth seems to have lost its ability to articulate them. My eyes, on the other hand, are in overdrive, roaming up and down this man's body.

He's wearing a white crewneck, and the flimsy shirt material is clearly fighting an uphill battle confining all that soft skin and supple muscle, the outline of his strong, well-defined chest and abs clearly visible. Ripped, faded jeans stretch over miles and miles of muscled legs, and the outfit is finished off with a pair of dusty brown cowboy boots, bringing just the right amount of swag to his stance.

Oh, and the man smells good. Damn good. I close my eyes for just a second and inhale the spicy citrus scent wafting off him. It's not a cologne or an artificial smell. It's something natural, and it seems to be short-circuiting my brain.

He's smiling at me, looking all flirty and inviting. He hands back the pool cue to one of his friends. That's when I notice he's wearing four or five different colored bands around his left wrist. One silver, a few dark and tan leather, and a couple of bright colors thrown in there, too.

"I'm Haze." He reaches his hand to mine.

"Noah," I reply. We shake hands. "Can I... I'd like to... I mean, would you like..." Oh, fuck. I really suck at this. It's been a while since I've done the whole *talking to a cute guy* thing.

Luckily for me, Haze interjects. With a mischievous twinkle in his eye, he asks, "Drink or dick?"

I blink. Excuse me, but did he just say—

"It seems like you want to ask me something." Haze speaks slowly, measuring me with his deep eyes. "And I'm guessing it's you'd either like to buy me a drink, or you'd like to see my dick."

"Drink," I squeak, before clearing my throat so that I don't sound like a prepubescent teen. "Drink. I'd like to buy you a drink."

He chuckles, his warm breath dancing over my face. "Too bad, Noah." He leans forward, the citrus scent enveloping me. "Because I have a *spectacular* cock."

We make our way to the bar and slide onto a couple of barstools. I order drinks—a beer for him and a soda for me—while trying my best to avoid visualizing his cock. I mean, how great can it really be? A dick's a dick, right? So why is my heart thudding so hard against my ribs every time I think about it?

As our drinks arrive, my brain and mouth both thankfully decide to come back online. "I've never seen you here before," I say, taking a sip.

"My housemate dragged me out. Don't come here a lot, even though we only live a few blocks away. I'm glad I came."

A heat flushes through my chest. "Same."

Haze lifts his glass, his bright eyes measuring me as he takes a sip. "You know, I spotted you the second my friends and I started playing pool. You were sitting in the corner booth, talking to your friends, looking all Henry Cavill-like."

"Is he the one who plays Batman?"

"Uh, no." A gentle smile pulls at Haze's lips. He licks it away and says, "You might be thinking of Ben Affleck."

"Right."

"Henry Cavill is way hotter."

"Uh, thanks." The heat from my chest rises up my neck. "I noticed you earlier, too, when you walked in and started playing pool with your friends."

Haze's smile deepens. "What brings you out on a Tuesday night?"

"After-work drinks," I explain. "Any reason in particular your housemate dragged you out tonight?"

Haze gives a slight shake of his head and I watch as a few loose golden strands bounce around his face. "Student life."

"Oh, what are you studying?"

"Acting at the Brookhaven Performing Acts Academy."

"Very cool. I'll keep an eye out for you on the big screen."

He clasps his hand over mine, but says nothing. Our eyes stay locked as we share a comfortable silence. Haze seems nice. And not just because he looks great and smells divine—there's something else about him. An ease that I can't help but find appealing. An energy crackles between us. I can feel it.

The conversation I was having with my friends earlier in the night crashes into my mind. Here I am, sitting at a bar with a cute guy who has just told me he's got a great cock. Is this what perfect one-night stand material looks, talks, and smells like?

I chew down on my lower lip before asking, "Have you ever had a one-night stand?"

Clearly not what Haze was expecting me to say, judging by how high both of his sandy-colored eyebrows shoot up. "Why do I feel like this is a trick question?" he answers with a nervous giggle.

"Not a trick question. I promise. My friends and I were talking about it earlier tonight, and it turns out I'm the only one from my crew who hasn't had one."

Haze's eyes narrow. "I find that hard to believe. You're freaking gorgeous." He glides a hand over my bicep, and when he looks up at me, the desire in his eyes is hard to miss. "Is this your way of asking me to be your first one-night stand?"

Haze pulls out his bun and reties his hair as he waits for me to respond. My breathing gets heavy, and I'm overcome with a feeling I haven't felt in years.

Desire.

I consider his question. Is that what's happening here? Is this what I want?

Deciding to take a chance, I place my hand on his knee, gently toying with a loose thread below the rip. The warmth of his body radiates through the denim.

"Yeah. I guess it is."

He runs his fingers down his stubbled jaw. My heart's beating out of my throat as I wait for his response. God, I hope I haven't completely misread the situation.

"In that case, I would be honored to be your first time."

A rush of relief sweeps through me. "First one-night stand," I clarify. "I'm not a virgin."

"Good." Haze leans in even closer and smirks against my ear. "My spectacular cock and I are very happy to hear that."

He gets to his feet, and I do the same. "So how do we do this? Whose place do we go back to?" I ask.

Haze reaches across the bar and chugs the rest of his beer. He wipes the back of his hand against his lips. "Has your place got walls?"

There's something sleek and graceful about the way he moves, and I find my eyes drifting again to the bracelets that adorn his wrists. I'm so distracted I could have sworn he'd asked me if my place has walls.

I lift my eyes to his face. "Sorry? Missed that."

He blinks and repeats, "Does your place have walls?"

Nope, didn't mishear him. "Uh... Yeah, it does. Doors and windows, too, if that helps," I throw in with a snicker.

"Great. It's settled then." He shrugs his jacket on and flashes me a wide grin. "Your place it is."

2

HAZE

I didn't plan on going out tonight.

I was perfectly happy working on a new batch of patchouli and lemongrass soaps to leave for my housemates, bopping away to Beyoncé's *Crazy in Love* blasting through my headphones.

I thought the highlight of my evening would've been ordering the killer san choy bau from our local Chinese restaurant. But see, the thing about living in a place with no walls—and having a housemate who doesn't take no for an answer—is that...well, I somehow ended up playing pool with Tate and a couple of our friends at a local bar instead. From the moment Tate lifted the headphones off my head, eyebrows raised and blue eyes sparkling, it was a done deal.

A pre-send-off send-off, Tate called it on the short walk over from the converted loft he and I shared with two other housemates. I moved in three years ago, right as I was starting my second degree. Apparently, the guys had trouble finding a roommate, mainly due to Tate's line of work. He's a cam model on 4FansOnly. A top one percent cam model, he'll be quick to point out. I've got literally zero issues with that at all. It's just the, you know, no walls thing. Gives us all front row seats to whatever crazy shenanigans the guy gets up to. Funnily enough, I'll probably miss it once I leave.

"How was your day?" I ask as we step into the bar. It's busier than normal for a Tuesday night.

Tate and I shrug off our coats. "Nothing too out of the ordinary," he replies casually. "A guy watched me crawl around on my bed with an anal wand hanging out of my ass, a bi couple wanted me to watch them while they fucked, and a guy looked at my feet while he jacked off."

"Standard workday, then," I quip as Tate raises his hand and waves to our friends. "You should write a book about all your sexcapades."

"I probably should, you know," he says over his shoulder.

We head over to the pool table, where our friends are waiting for us. I'm thrust into the game straight away, making the first shot easily.

After a while, my gaze drifts to a group of guys sitting in the corner booth behind us. Well, one guy in particular. I don't know if it's his dark hair, the set of his square jaw, or the massive biceps bulging through the tight black T-shirt he's wearing, but my eyes are drawn to him like magnets. Even with music playing and conversations bubbling all around me, the man is an oasis of gorgeous.

He's engrossed in a conversation with a guy wearing a yellow and red polka-dot bow tie. When I spot his friends getting up and leaving a few minutes later, hope rises in my chest that he'll walk past the pool table so I can get a closer look at him. Instead, he swerves left for the men's room.

It's my turn again, so I aim the green ball into the corner pocket, but my angle is slightly off, and I just miss. Guess my mind is on other things. Like the fact that I'm leaving on Saturday to spend six months in London. Or the fact that I'm approaching thirty and still not sure about what I want to do with the rest of my life. Or that I can't get my ex's words out of my head. They seem to have burrowed themselves in there.

I don't know who you are. You don't even know who you are. You're a fucking chameleon, Haze.

The bitterness of Daniel's sentiment has lost none of its sting since he ended things just over a year ago. We were together for almost five years. The real sad part? As much as I hate to admit it, he's probably right.

I guess I am a chameleon, a laid-back, "go with the flow" kinda person. On the good side, it means I can adapt and adjust to any situation I find myself in. The diverse and eclectic group of friends I have attests to that, or sharing a no-walls loft with three other guys and not batting an eyelid. On the negative side, it also means that I'm now on my second degree and becoming increasingly uncertain if acting really is the career path I want to pursue.

Daniel taunted me for it and used it against me. He said I tried too hard to fit in and please others. Funny how he never seemed to mind when I did things to please him and go with *his* flow. And boy, did I do some things for him.

My thoughts screech to a halt when the guy I've been subtly ogling all evening practically bowls me over. Okay, I admit, I *may* have strategically positioned myself near the hallway that leads to the men's room so that we'd maybe bump into each other as he left. I wasn't expecting it to happen quite so literally, though.

He seems a little nervous, and it's cute as hell. Maybe that's why it unleashes a cheekiness in me. As we settle at the bar and have a drink, I'm struck by his eyes. Yes, he's got the whole Henry Cavill thing going on, and seriously, those biceps are beyond ridiculous, but it's his eyes that pull me in. They're a rich, mossy green, but more than that, they're kind. You can tell a lot about a person by their eyes, and his tell me he's a decent guy.

Even as we're chatting away, I can see that he's a little on edge. It's endearing, though, and when he tells me he's never had a one-night stand, the pieces fall perfectly into place.

He's still a little skittish as we wait for an Uber outside the bar. I zip my bomber jacket all the way up and blow out a puff of steam into the cold night air. "I've only had four drinks," Noah tells me, eyeing the road, on the lookout for the car. "I'm just erring on the side of caution, is all."

"It's okay," I assure him, gripping his forearm. He's got that irresistible hard-jaw, soft-eyes combination that makes *everything* okay.

The ride back to his place is a silent one. Our fingers play with each other across the middle of the backseat, threads that tangle, then loosen. His thumb caresses the top of my hand. We smile at each other, and his eyes gleam under the passing streetlights.

Once we step onto his porch, Noah turns to me with a serious look. "Now, I have to warn you about something."

My pulse ticks up a notch. I wasn't getting any weird serial killer vibes from the guy, but hey, you never know. Serial killers can live in nice, quiet suburban neighborhoods.

His expression softens. "You're in for a licking."

"Excuse me?"

"Hear that?"

He points to the front door, and I lean toward it. Muffled pants are coming from the other side.

"That's Buddy," Noah says with a grin. "He's a golden retriever I rescued a few years back. He's starting to go blind, but he likes to lick everything...and everyone."

"Got it." The tension in my shoulders evaporates. I reach out and run the back of my fingers against Noah's cheeks. "I'm down for a good licking."

Noah closes the space between us and cups my face in his big hands. Our mouths press together, softly at first. The tenderness surprises me in the best way possible. He's being polite, which I find charming.

His tongue flicks past my lips and begins to explore the inside of my mouth. He's taking his time, like he's savoring me. I don't mind one bit. I wrap my arms around his waist to draw him in even closer. A low growl rumbles its way from the back of his throat, escaping through the tiny sliver of space between our lips. I can feel his erection pressing against mine. Also very charming.

A torrent of heat ripples through my body, negating the chilly night air, as our kiss deepens. Any hesitation he may have had disappears as he drags his fingers through my hair and claims my mouth with his tongue. Unfortunately, we're interrupted by the sounds of an impatient retriever scratching away at the inside of the front door.

Noah smiles against my mouth. "You ready for the Buddy onslaught?"

"Bring it on."

Noah opens the door, and boy, he wasn't kidding. Seventy pounds of golden-haired fuzz leaps out onto the porch. Buddy licks

Noah first. His face, his ears, his hands. When he's done, he turns to me. Without any hesitation, he bounds straight on top of me, smattering me with a waterfall of wet licks.

We make our way inside. Noah closes the door behind me before helping me take my jacket off. "It's bedtime," I hear him say. Thankfully, it's aimed at Buddy and not me.

I'm impressed to see Buddy respond immediately, turning around and scampering down the hallway. "He sleeps in the laundry room," Noah tells me as he presses another kiss to my lips. "Which just so happens to be on the way to my bedroom."

"Well, what are we waiting for?"

We hustle down the hall, Noah deftly closing the door to the laundry room as we pass it. He grabs my hand and peppers it with a few featherlight kisses as we enter his bedroom. I don't take any time to notice the details of the room because as soon as the door closes, Noah and I wrap ourselves up in each other. Bodies pressed together, we kiss. It's a long, deep, passionate kiss and I soak up every delicious drop of it.

My hands travel across the hard planes of his back. As much as I don't want to pull away, we're still wearing clothes. Way too many clothes. I tug his shirt up. He gets the hint and he helps me take it all the way off. And damn, if I thought he was beautiful at the bar, Noah standing shirtless in front of me is truly a sight to behold.

He's muscular in the way men are from doing manual labor, not because he's spent countless hours at the gym. His arms are huge, and they bulge and flex with every movement he makes, but nothing about him feels forced or posey. A light dusting of dark hair covers his chest and trails down. No six-pack, but his stomach looks firm as fuck.

Noah motions for me to take my shirt off, so I do. He hums appreciatively, and I can feel the heat of his gaze as his eyes rove over my torso. I close the small distance between us, our lips finding each other softly. He threads his thick fingers through my hair and it feels divine.

We inch our way to the bed. When we get there, I pull back slightly. I can see his eyes have darkened. "What's wrong?" I ask, picking up on his hesitancy.

We sit down at the edge of the bed. "It's been a while since I've done this."

I frown, confused. "I thought you said you've never had a one-night stand before?"

"I haven't." He plays with a loose thread on my jeans, averting my gaze. "I mean sex. I haven't had sex in...two years."

"At all?"

Shit. I didn't mean to blurt it out like that. Before I can say anything to let him know there's nothing wrong with not having had sex in a while, he juts his chin out.

"There is Max, I guess."

My brows crease. "Max?"

Noah tips his head toward the nightstand.

"Wait. You killed a guy called Max and stuffed him into your bedside table?"

His head falls back, and he laughs. Noah's laughter is warm and breathy, and I'm happy my attempt to lighten the mood seems to have worked.

"Max is my dildo."

My hand finds Noah's thigh. "Well, no offense to Max, but he's no match for my cock."

"Is that so?"

"Yeah. You want me to prove it?" I tease.

Noah licks his lips, nodding. I curl my fingers around the back of his neck and pull him in, our mouths melding. As we kiss, I make a promise to myself. This is Noah's first one-night stand, his first sex in two freaking years—I'm going to make this good for him.

I manage to wrestle my lips away from his for a moment and jolt my head. "Let's move up. Oh, and let's lose the pants." We scramble a little, taking off our trousers and briefs. I'm not gonna lie, a happy warmth spreads through my chest when Noah's eyes widen as he takes me in. Hey, I wasn't lying about my cock.

With an appreciative huff, his pants join my jeans on the floor as we make our way up the bed. With Noah on his back, his green eyes dart about, probing me. I can't tell what he's thinking, obviously, but I feel something between us. More than just innocent flirting or physical attraction. I shove those thoughts aside and remind myself that this is a one-time thing only as I lick my way across his furry chest and down his stomach.

A sigh escapes his lips as my tongue swirls over his hip bone. The heat coming off his granite-hard cock is intense, but I ignore it as I probe my way further down...and around. I scoop my hands behind his thighs and lift Noah's muscular legs into the air.

Noah makes a startled sound. He's peering down at me, his eyes bursting with interest. "Is this okay?" I ask.

He nods, and the tips of his hair clump against the sides of his face. As if to tell me that it really is okay, he hooks his elbows behind his knees, giving me exactly what I'm wanting. Access.

With Noah holding his legs in position, I lower myself, ghosting my lips over his meaty ass cheeks. I don't know why I'm starting here, with this. I realize how intimate eating someone out is, and yet it feels right. There's something about Noah that makes me feel like I can just do whatever I want to.

I delicately dig my fingers into his flesh to stretch his ass open a little. Noah buries his head in the pillows as I gently blow a current of warm air toward his entrance. That's it. That's all I do. No direct contact, just my breath.

"Oh god," he cries out. "Haze, I have no idea what you're doing, but that feels amazing."

I smile. I haven't even really begun, and Noah's already quivering beneath me. I can't wait to see what happens when I introduce him to my spectacular cock.

3

NOAH

Last Tuesday night, I went a little wild and treated myself to a small tub of low-fat ice cream while binging last season's *This Pet's Got Talent* for the hundredth time. Tonight, I'm holding my legs up in the air for a stranger I met at the bar who's about to start tongue-fucking my hole.

This Tuesday night wins.

Haze seems to be blowing nothing more than air against me, and it feels so damn good. If this is what all one-night stands are like, I can't believe I waited thirty-four years to have my first.

A low, deep moan tears from my chest as I feel something warm against my entrance. I glance down the length of my body, but all I can see is the ashy blond top of Haze's hair. He's pulled it out of its bun, so now the strands dance loosely whenever he moves his head. Speaking of head movements, his are slow and deliberate and igniting my body like nothing else.

I feel an inviting wetness, and then...he inhales me with a loud and filthy slurp. Holy shit. If the guy's scent short-circuited my brain, his tongue lapping against my ass is enough to positively sear my nerve endings. My head falls back onto the soft pillows as I lift my hips, overcome with a burning need for more of what he's giving me.

"Is this okay?" he asks for the second time.

"Yes." I pant. "Don't stop. Please."

His fingers stretch my ass open wider, and he dives in once more. His stubble grazes my taint, prickling the sensitive skin with the best kind of burn. He's slurping greedily, hungrily. I can see the top of his head bobbing about, like he's trying to plunge even deeper into me.

Rimming someone is so intimate. I find myself touched by it in a way that feels deeper than what I expected from a one-night stand. Fulton's warnings to set my expectations low fly out the window as I hear a carnal spitting sound. It's quickly followed by the touch of a moist fingertip pressing against me.

"I'm going to slide a finger in," Haze says. "Is that okay?"

"Yes."

I hiss as the initial sting hits me. Fucking myself with a dildo doesn't come anywhere near Haze's tender touch. My body wraps around him as he carefully glides in and out of me, slowly and so carefully.

He looks up and throws me a crooked grin. "Don't suppose you have any lube?"

"As a matter of fact, I do." With his finger still inside me, I twist around to reach into my nightstand drawer and pull it out.

Haze's eyes bulge. "Holy shit," he exclaims. "That's like a gallon jumbo-size bottle."

I nod sheepishly. "It's more economical this way."

I hand him the bottle, which is not a gallon, by the way—he was exaggerating. He slicks two fingers with the stuff and works them into me.

The steady, almost melodic rhythm he settles into relaxes me. Any thoughts I have scatter before drifting away. I'm floating on a cloud as pleasure rolls through my body. The vulnerability of surrendering like this to a stranger's touch doesn't scare me like I thought it might. Haze knows what he's doing, and he's doing it incredibly well.

He pulls away from me to sheath his dick with a condom he must have had on him. The very same dick he hyped up at the bar. Yes, it's long, and yes, it's girthy, but the thing that stands out the most about Haze's cock is that it's so fucking pretty. Spectacular doesn't do the thing justice, and as he readies himself, I can't help but get giddy with anticipation.

It's been long, *sooo* long, since I've been with someone. A deep well of need rises up inside of me. I didn't realize just how much I needed this sort of touch and connection until this very moment.

"Fuck me, Haze."

There's a desperate pleading underpinning my tone, but I don't care. I want this so much. I'm normally the one looking after people, putting everyone's needs before my own. It's nice that, for even a brief moment like this, someone else is taking care of me.

Haze looks up at me and smiles. His long fingers continue to stroke up and down his cock, lathering it with lube. "That's exactly what I intend to do."

He crashes over me, his long hair dangling just out of my reach, his palms fisted into the bed beside me. "Wait. How are you going to—"

Before I can finish asking how he's going to enter me, I feel the crown of his cock pressing against my ass. The corners of his mouth twist in a smirk. "I told you I had an amazing cock."

"Oh, yeah?"

"Yeah. It comes with its own navigation system. I paid extra for the guaranteed hole-in-one feature."

Before I can come up with my own cheeky retort to that, my brain turns to goop as holy shit, his cock expertly—*and hands free*—plunges into me. My lower back arches off the mattress as my body takes him in. A bead of sweat trickles down the side of his face and drops onto my chin. Haze's face is all concentration as he pushes deeper into me.

I focus on my breathing, drawing steady even breaths until finally he bottoms out. The fullness is on the cusp of being too much. But before the feeling overwhelms me, a joyous bliss takes over. "Fuck." My voice is so coarse I barely recognize it.

"Is this okay?" Haze asks, and seriously, those are fast becoming my three favorite words in the English language.

I interlace my fingers behind his neck and nod. "It's perfect."

Haze's gaze lingers on me as he slowly begins to rock his hips, thrusting in and out of me, my body tuning itself to the movement. Our eyes stay connected the whole time as his pace quickens. Once he's got a steady rhythm going, he adjusts his body weight to free up a hand. He licks the palm of that hand and encases it over my shaft, fisting it up and down in time with his movements.

My senses explode as I succumb to the pleasure this man seems to be so effortlessly drawing out of me. It's like he's found a way to shine a light on parts of me that have been hidden away in the dark.

I grab at his chest hungrily. A loud groan slips from his mouth as I run my hands across his pecs, tweaking his nipples. "You like that?"

His eyes are ablaze. "Uh-huh. I've got *very* sensitive nipples."

I latch onto the pinky-purple nubs, rolling them between my fingertips. Haze throws his head back, producing more strangled-sounding moans as he thrusts harder, further, deeper inside of me.

"I want you to come for me," he grits out.

His grip tightens around my cock. My balls clench and slap against his abdomen. My fingers pinch, squeeze, and twist his nipples. He fists my cock furiously. I scream and almost black out as my orgasm thunders into me so hard it feels like it's going to tear me in two. As I'm writhing underneath him, Haze's face scrunches up as he bellows out a whopping, "Holy fuck!" His whole body twitches and shudders as he comes, too.

We stay still for a few moments, catching our breath. A sigh heaves out of him. "I'm going to pull out of you. Slowly. Is that okay?"

"Very okay." I brush a strand of loose hair off his face, pinning it behind his ear. "Thank you."

The care and attention he's showering me with throws me for a loop. This isn't something I'm used to. He pulls out of me more delicately than anyone I've ever been with. With the grace of a panther, he escapes into the en suite. I hear water running, and a few seconds later, he returns with a washcloth to clean me up. His tongue pokes out of the corner of his mouth as he makes sure not to miss a single spot. He then takes the towel, lube, and condom into the bathroom before returning to the room and collapsing onto the bed beside me.

I nestle into the nape of his shoulder. "Thank you," I repeat.

"Why are you thanking me?"

My fingers absently slide across his smooth chest. "For being so kind and gentle."

He presses a kiss to my forehead as I continue, "For having a spectacular cock."

His chest vibrates as he lets out a low laugh. "For being the best first one-night stand a guy could hope for."

"It was my pleasure. Believe me. You were incredible."

"Well, you weren't so bad yourself," I grin back. "What you did to my ass with just your tongue..." Words float away from me at the memory.

"Does my cock get an honorable mention in any of this?"

I snicker. "I don't know if honorable is the right word, but it was pretty fan-fucking-tastic."

"And man, what you did to my nipples. Holy hell. I know this is just a one-night stand and all, but that was...incredible." He pauses for a moment. "*You're* incredible, Noah."

My insides go all gooey at the compliment. I rub my feet against his as we fall into a comfortable silence. I'm feeling relaxed and dreamy until it hits me. This is the first and last time we'll ever see each other. It doesn't seem fair, even though we were both upfront about what this was. A one-time thing only. Still, I can't deny that a part of me does want more.

We continue to lie in silence as my mind wanders back to Fulton and his four rules. Rule one was "Don't spend the night." But we're at my place, not Haze's, so I wonder if I can use that loophole to ask Haze to stay the night. His warm body feels so good against mine. There's no way I'm ready to let him go just yet. It's just one silly little rule, after all.

I look up at Haze's face, his features soft and imbued with a golden post-orgasmic glow. "I don't know if this is an appropriate thing to ask, but...do you want to stay the night?"

He beams down at me. "Yeah. I'd love that."

And with a gentle kiss on my forehead and a huge smile on my face, we fall asleep.

~

Since I technically broke one teensy tiny rule by spending the night with Haze, I don't see any harm in cooking the guy breakfast the next day. Right? He would've worked up an appetite last night. I wouldn't want to be rude or run the risk of having him faint from exhaustion on the way back to his place. Besides, I only broke one silly little rule. I'll stick to the other three. Promise.

After letting Buddy outside so he can take care of his morning business, I find myself pottering around quietly in the kitchen, trying to think what kind of a breakfast guy Haze is. Coffee's a sure thing, but what else?

I open up the pantry and tap my fingers against my chin. Cereal seems boring. Bacon and eggs is a risk. He could be vegetarian. I settle on pancakes. The mixture I've got is gluten and dairy-free so it seems like the safest option.

As I walk over to the cupboard to grab a pan, I smile at the dull ache I can feel as I move. I really have been in a sex drought. Two years. Two freaking years with just me and Max. I smile as I flick on the coffee machine. It was worth the wait, though.

The sex last night was the best sex I've ever had. The way Haze looked after me, kept checking in on me to make sure I was okay— man, that's some mind-blowing shit right there. I've been in three long-term relationships and never felt that cared for. Which I guess says a lot.

Rather than lowering my expectations, Haze has set them sky high. How will any other one-night stand ever be able to compete with that? A twinge pulls in my chest at that thought. Maybe it's a sign. I should quit while I'm ahead. Maybe I got lucky on my first go and should drop out of the race now.

Yeah. That feels better. As amazing as sex with Haze was, I'm not really a one-night stand kinda guy. It's weird to think that last night, the guy was inside me, and in a few short minutes, we'll say our goodbyes and never see each other again.

I throw a pod into the coffee machine and set it to percolate. No-strings fun, that's what the guys had called it. Nothing more. Nothing less. But for a reason that I can't put into words, Haze has got me hoping for something...more. It's a silly thought, I know. One meal and then we'll never see each other again. That's what we both signed up for.

A sad sigh escapes me as I grab my favorite blue mug, pour in some coffee, and continue getting breakfast ready.

4

HAZE

I usually sleep like a baby after good sex, so the only surprise after the mind, body, and soul-shattering sex Noah and I had last night is that I haven't slipped into a six-month coma. But if I had to get woken up, I suppose there's no better way than with...neck licks?

I hum in amusement as Noah glides his tongue up and down the side of my neck. His surprisingly big, sloppy tongue. Hmm, guess I must have missed that minor detail about him, although in fairness, it was my tongue doing most of the work last night. Maybe this is his idea of evening the score. Not complaining one bit.

"Mmm," I murmur. I have no idea what time it is, but I'm sure it's still too early for words. Plus, you know, morning breath.

Noah shuffles down the bed, making me flop around on the mattress as he repositions himself...at my feet. Uh, okay, so he's into feet? Before I know it, he's lapping sloppily at my toes. Okay, he's *really* into feet. It's not really my thing, but it feels kinda good, so I guess I could try and go along with it.

I decide to crack an eye open. "Good morn——aargh!"

I jackknife and leap off the bed. "Buddy! What are you doing?"

I scrub a palm down the side of my face as I realize my early morning lick-fest was courtesy of one adorable golden retriever. Buddy's head jerks around the room, and I remember Noah telling me about the poor fella starting to lose his sight. There's no way I can be mad at him. He's too damn cute.

I plop back down onto the bed, and Buddy edges over to me. I give him a few pats, which he responds to by snuggling in even closer to me, almost toppling me onto the floor. "You're a good boy, aren't you?" I scratch behind his ear, which he absolutely loves, as I let out a series of yawns.

The room is empty. No sign of Noah. I stretch my neck, left and right, and as I turn to the semi-open door, a delicious smell wafts in and hits my nostrils. Mmm, coffee.

I help Buddy off the bed and take a quick shower, shrugging on my boxers and white crewneck when I'm done. I check my face in the bathroom mirror one last time and tie my hair back in a loose ponytail. It's time to follow my nose.

It leads me down the hallway and into the kitchen. Noah doesn't hear me approach, so I lean against the wall and take him in for a moment. He's hovering over the stove, wearing a pair of tight fitting black sweatpants and a navy blue tank top. A coffee machine percolates in the corner. He takes a sip from a blue mug before returning to flip over...ah, pancakes. Nice.

I smile as sparks tingle throughout my body. I can't remember the last time I felt like this. So peaceful and...content. But is it really any wonder? Noah is gorgeous, loves animals, has a nice place, and he's making me breakfast. If that doesn't scream perfect, what does?

There's a part of me that wants this. A life with a guy who's happy doing his own thing. A house with walls. A future where I know what I'm doing. And someone to share it all with.

You're a chameleon, Haze. You don't even know what you want.

The words ring in my ears, not even giving me a momentary reprieve to slip away into a fantasy that won't ever come true anyway. Before my thoughts turn too dark, Buddy bounds past me and into the kitchen. As soon as Noah turns around to give him a pat, he notices me standing in the corner. His face lights up. "G'morning."

I smile, liking the way he combines the two words, making the greeting his own. "Good morning."

I step into the kitchen. I'm a little unsure as to what the etiquette here is. Sure, I've had a few one-night stands before, but staying the night? That's a whole new thing. Do we kiss? Hug? Handshake? No, definitely not that. Noah eyes me standing in the middle of the room, like a deer caught in headlights, but doesn't say anything. I solve the physical contact dilemma by opting to avoid it entirely. Instead, I amble over to the counter and take a seat in one of the high-backed stools.

"Would you like a coffee?" His eyes glimmer in the morning light, and it makes my breath catch in my throat.

"Please," I manage to get out.

Noah pours a cup and hands it to me. Our fingers meet briefly. There. That feels like the appropriate level of contact. I have no idea why the grazing of our fingertips sends electric pulses shooting up my spine. Then again, my whole life is a total calamity, so what do I know about anything?

"There's cream and sugar, if you like," Noah says, tipping his head toward the counter.

"I'm good, thanks."

I don't know if he's sensing my nervousness, or if he's just giving me some time for the caffeine to kick in, but I appreciate the silence. As I watch him stack a pile of pancakes, I can't help but think how nice this is. How normal. How much I want something like this...for more than one night.

Not that this is going to be that.

The guy wanted to experience his first one-night stand. That's it. That's all this is. There's also no way for this to become anything more since I am leaving the country in a few days. No. This is just a one-time thing with a gorgeous, friendly guy who was thoughtful enough to cook me some amazing-smelling breakfast. Our story finishes, our paths uncross, at the end of this meal.

"Shall we eat at the table?" Noah suggests as he walks past me and places the plate of pancakes onto a small wooden table. I nod, sliding off the stool and straight into him.

"Well, hello." He braces my shoulders, his hair tousled and falling over his forehead. He smiles. God, that smile. It's so fucking wide and happy it makes me want to smile.

I shuffle on my feet. "Hi."

All my bravado from the bar last night is gone. All that's left are memories of an incredible night colliding with the bleary morning light of the day after. His eyes soften, and he leans in toward me right as I glance over at the table. Oh, shit. Noah was going to kiss me. I turn, inching my lips closer to his face just as he starts to move toward the kitchen. He backs up, but trips over his feet.

Not. Awkward. At. All.

"Plates," I say, slapping my hands against my thighs way too hard. "Let me help you get some plates." Yeah, because carrying two plates a few feet is definitely a two-man operation.

A few moments later, we start eating. I ended up carrying both plates and bringing the cutlery, too...so, that's a good thing? Man, I really suck at this. There's a reason why I never spend the night.

I haven't had many hookups since Daniel broke up with me. With other guys, it's always been sex followed by a quick goodbye. I never hung around afterward. One time I showered and watched half an episode of *Unbreakable Kimmy Schmidt*, but that's about it.

But for some reason with Noah, there's a part of me that doesn't want to leave. It makes no sense. We glance up at each other every so often while we eat, sharing a silent exchange that I can't explain.

The only sound in the kitchen is us chewing and Buddy breathing loudly at Noah's feet. I liked it a whole lot more when *other* sounds were filling the space around us. But I guess that's all in the past. Once we get through the nominee for Most Awkward Breakfast at the One-Night Stand Awards, that's all this will ever be.

A memory.

My heart sinks at the thought.

"So, I broke one of the four one-night stand rules last night," Noah begins lightly.

"Oh, yeah. And what might that be?"

"Don't spend the night."

I snicker. "Yeah. I've heard of that one." After a few beats, I add, "I'm glad you asked me to stay, though."

A warm glint fills Noah's eyes. "Me, too."

"These pancakes are delicious, by the way," I say, barreling another forkful into my mouth.

Noah smiles. "Thanks. I wasn't sure what you liked for

breakfast, so I thought pancakes would be a safe bet. Oh, they're gluten and dairy-free, by the way. Shit. I should've asked if you had any allergies."

I put my fork down. "Noah, relax. Thank you, but if I had allergies to pancakes, one: I would tell you about it, and two: I don't think I'd want to live anymore."

He laughs, and it makes me feel happy. I don't think of myself as a particularly funny guy, but I find my brain scouring for anything that can draw another one of those deep, rich laughs out of him.

"So, you said there were four rules. What are the other three?"

He rolls his eyes. "It's stupid."

"Come on. Tell me. I wanna know."

As he lists them, the bottoms of his ear lobes flush a rosy pink. It's the cutest thing I've ever seen. "I told you it was dumb," he says once he finishes.

"No. Not dumb. Good to know, actually. And look, you don't have to worry about breaking any of the three remaining rules."

A few lines scatter across his forehead. "I don't?"

I shake my head. "Nope. I'm leaving for six months this Saturday. Headed to London, so rule two is a lock. You will never see me again."

His frown deepens, and I can't be sure, but something dark skirts behind his eyes. It's so brief that it makes me think I must've imagined it.

He clears his throat. "More coffee? Pancakes?"

"Yes and yes."

We both have another helping of pancakes, and the conversation remains light for the rest of the meal. We don't talk about anything much, but it just flows easily. Once we're done, I glance down at my phone. It's just after nine. On a Wednesday. I've got classes later today, but what about him?

"Don't you, like, have work to get to or something?" I ask.

Noah collects my plate and takes it to the sink. "I'm working the late shift today."

I follow him, admiring the way his back muscles flex as he starts to wash the dishes. I open my mouth to ask him what he does for a living before clamping it shut. What's the point of knowing that? In five, ten, maybe fifteen minutes, we'll be saying goodbye forever.

I lean my hip against the counter. His face tightens in the way it does whenever someone realizes they're being watched. He finishes rinsing the plates and turns the faucet off.

His eyes flick up to meet mine. "Yes?"

"Here. I want you to have this."

I unpin the thin tan leather bracelet from my left wrist and hand it to him. I'd like to say it has some cool story behind it, but the truth is, I don't even remember where I got it. Probably from one of the markets Tate's always dragging me to.

Noah finishes wiping his hands on a dish cloth. "I—I can't take that."

"Why not? It's not breaking any of the four rules, is it?" I tease with a smirk.

He doesn't smile back. Instead, he takes the bracelet from me and lifts it in front of his face, inspecting it like it's a priceless jewel and not something that probably cost me less than five bucks.

"Consider it a token," I say, doing my best to keep my tone breezy. "A congratulatory one. On your first one-night stand."

His eyes cloud, and he swallows hard. "Thank you, Haze. This is really nice of you."

"Don't mention it."

Noah tries to put it on his wrist, but it's a little fiddly to do with only one hand. "Here, let me help you with that."

He stretches his arm out, and my fingers travel along the dark hairs that line his forearm before reaching his wrist. I bring the two pieces of thin leather together and tie them up.

"Is that okay?" I ask, and for some reason, Noah's whole face lights up. "What? Why are you smiling at me like that?"

"No reason." He lifts his arm to appreciate the adornment. "I really like it. Thank you."

After a few moments, he turns to me. "Wait. I feel like I should give you something in return."

I grin like a Cheshire Cat. "Yeah. You can give me something."

"Anything. What would you like?"

I clutch his hand, holding it in my own, and tip my head toward the hallway that leads to his bedroom door. "Round two."

5

NOAH

Six months later...

Molly is one gorgeous kitten. To be fair, I'm probably slightly biased because I think all animals are beautiful, even the ones most people think are ugly or scary. Molly's a long-haired Maine Coon cat with a stunning coat of rich caramel, silver, and pure white. I always check in on animals after I operate, but I'll be sure to find an excuse to spend a few extra minutes fussing over her. She's that adorable.

The pre-op medication is making her sleepy. I can tell because her third eyelids are showing. All cats and dogs have a pale, pinkish third eyelid that moves across the eye rather than up and down, but when they're awake and alert, it's not usually visible.

Molly cuddles into my chest as I carry her into the prep area and put her down gently on the table. Megan, one of the amazing vet nurses, swoops into action while I move into the theater and commence the usual preoperative procedure—getting changed into a pair of light blue scrubs and thoroughly washing my hands.

Spaying a cat is a relatively simple procedure, and it's best to do it before they come into season and start calling. That's when a cat becomes very flirtatious with everyone—and everything. I get to work, and a few minutes later, it's all over, and Molly is taken to the recovery ward.

That was the first and only procedure I have booked today. The rest of my early morning shift is made up of consults. That's one of the things I love most about being a vet—the variety. As animal science advances, more and more of the younger vets are choosing to specialize and focus on only one area. I wouldn't be able to do that. Since I was a kid, I've loved all animals, and it keeps me excited and passionate about my work to be able to treat all the kinds we have coming into the clinic.

I've been working at Vet Shop Boys for the last five years. Fulton got a placement here right out of vet school, and as my best friend, felt it was his duty to constantly be on my case to apply for a position here as well. But I was intrigued by farm animals and accepted a position with a clinic on the outskirts of the city. After a few years, I'd had my fill of cows and sheep and goats. I finally gave in to Fulton's incessant nagging and met with Gus. It took all of sixty seconds for Gus to convince me to join.

Anyone who works with animals is crazy about them. But what makes Gus unique is that he also cares deeply about the people who look after the animals. So while Vet Shop Boys has all the basic building blocks you'd expect to see in any mid-sized veterinary practice—a reception, a few consult and prep rooms, a surgical theater, and an adjoining pharmacy—Gus has gone above and beyond as well.

We're one of the few clinics in Brookhaven that operate from four in the morning to ten at night. That gives pet owners more flexibility to bring their animals to see us, especially if they have to juggle work and family commitments. Gus also pays well, and all employees enjoy the best health insurance and retirement benefits on offer. Being a vet won't make me a millionaire—I knew that going in—but a healthy pay package is a nice way to get recognized for the hard work and long hours we put in.

I finish getting changed in the staff changing room. Another thoughtful perk. When Gus bought the building with his partner at the time sixteen years ago, they renovated and extended it, demolishing a few old rooms into a custom-designed theater, adding a pharmacy beside the main building and creating staff-only spaces such as a changing room and a lounge, where we can all hang out and take a break when we need it.

I shrug on a white medical coat over my checkered red and black long-sleeve shirt. Beige pants complete the outfit. Typical vet garb, I know, but I've always liked it. I've wanted to be a vet since I was a kid, and to me, this is what vets look like. I still pinch myself sometimes that I get to actually do my dream job. I know how rare that is.

I pull out the last piece of my outfit from my locker, fiddling with the tan leather bracelet as I slide it over my left wrist. Yeah, *that* bracelet. Yeah, the one from *him*. I haven't heard a word from Haze in the six months since we, uh, met, but that's to be expected. After breakfast and an incredible round two—the guy has got one seriously talented tongue on him; seriously, if there was a Tonguing Olympics, he'd win the gold medal in every category—we said our goodbyes, and he left. We didn't exchange numbers since he was leaving the country, and something about sticking to the three remaining rules?

My face glows like it always does whenever I look at the bracelet. It's the only one I've ever worn in my life. It's not something I'd ever buy for myself, but it's a nice reminder of Haze and our short time together. Silly and sentimental, I know, I know.

I wander over to the staff lounge at the end of the corridor. Fulton is sitting in one of the couches by the large bay windows, the late summer sunlight streaming through.

"G'morning."

He peeks up from his phone. Before making myself a coffee, I walk over to get a glimpse of what he's got on. He often wears a funny shirt under his lab coat. It's kinda his thing.

"Hey," he says as I approach. He puts his phone down beside him and opens his arms. He knows what I'm here for. I glance down at the black shirt. Scrawled across the front in large white letters is, ***I kissed a pug and I liked it—Kitty Purry.***

Despite myself, I snicker. "Nice one."

He beams proudly. "Twenty bucks on Etsy. How could I resist?"

I grin and shake my head, saying nothing. His face turns serious as he asks, "How did it go?"

We always check in with each other after any surgical procedure, even the most rote ones. It only happens rarely, but even something routine can go horribly pear-shaped. And even if nothing goes wrong, sometimes operations can simply bring up emotions. I mean, you literally have an animal's life in your hands.

Mental health issues are rife in the veterinary world, so we always make a point to follow up with each other.

"It went well." I make my way over to the kitchen area in the corner of the room. "Molly's in recovery, and I don't foresee any complications or need to worry about anything. She'll be back to her *purrfect* self in a few weeks."

He smiles. "Glad to hear it."

Fulton is obsessed with cats and on his way to becoming a crazy cat dude. His words, not mine. At last count, he was the proud paw-rent of seven cats. All rescues, of course.

I tap the coffee machine to get it going. "Wanna cup?" I ask over my shoulder.

"It's Thursday," Fulton answers.

"Oh, right. Of course." It's been a busy week, and I have a knack for forgetting what day it is.

Despite being the owner and possibly best boss in the world, Gus also has a weekly tradition of buying all staff on shift a cup of coffee––or tea, for those that are that way inclined––every Thursday morning. It's a sage piece of advice he picked up from his grandmother, and it's a habit that's been with him his entire career.

Right on cue, the familiar jingle of the front door opening rings out. It's followed by Gus' usual, "Hello, beautiful people" greeting. He never checks to see whether the waiting room is full of people or not. He just trudges in and bellows it out. It never fails to bring a smile to even the most anxious animal owner's face. I chuckle, too.

His footsteps thunder down the hall until he walks into the room, drink tray in hand. "It's Thirsty Thursday," he declares with a wide smile, handing Fulton and me our drinks.

"Thank you," I say with a wry smile. "And also, Thirsty Thursday is not what you think it means."

"It means what *I* think it means," he counters cheerfully. "One of the many pearls of wisdom Nanna imparted on me was this: if you want to endear yourself to others, remember how they like their tea or coffee. You guys know I started doing it as a student, memorizing every vet, nurse, and staff member's favorite drink, and bringing it in for them every Thursday. Never steered me wrong. *That's* the true meaning of Thirsty Thursday."

"That's a beautiful story," Fulton says smiling, even though we've both heard it a million times. Fulton opens the lid of his tea to let it cool a bit. "Just whatever you do, don't type Thirsty Thursday into Instagram. You'll get quite the shock."

Fulton and I chortle. "Joke's on you," Gus replies with a smirk. "I'm forty-seven years old. I'm not even allowed on Instagram."

The three of us laugh. Gus plonks himself down on the couch. "There are two things we need to talk about." He's looking straight at me as he says it.

I take a sip of coffee. "Yeah?"

"One, you haven't confirmed your plus-one for my wedding. It's next month," he reminds me. Like he's been reminding me weekly for the past five months, daily for the last four weeks.

"That's where you're wrong because I *have* confirmed that I *won't* be bringing a plus-one to your wedding."

"Have sadder words ever been spoken?"

"Shut up, Fulton," I grumble, and he smirks. He picks up his phone and continues reading.

Gus puffs his cheeks out in that pitying way he does whenever he's got bad news to deliver. My coat suddenly feels tight and itchy around my shoulders.

"Noah, seriously," Gus continues. "Marco and I were going over the seating arrangements last night. You're one of my closest friends, so I feel like it's my duty to give you fair warning." He pauses for dramatic effect. "The singles table is bad. Real bad. Mainly from Marco's side, of course. His relatives and friends are even more tragic than mine, if you can believe it."

"I can," Fulton deadpans into his tea.

"Shut up, Fulton," Gus and I say at the same time.

Gus turns back to me. "I do have a slutty third cousin coming in from Georgia that I can sit you next to, but I can't guarantee that he'll stay with you for the whole time."

"Is that the best you got?" I joke.

Gus throws a serious look my way. "It is. It really, *really* is."

"Fine." I scratch the side of my face. "I'll find someone. I still have a few weeks."

"Twenty-seven days." Gus lifts his index finger. "You have twenty-seven days to find a date to the most perfect day of my life, Noah Walters."

I sigh and nod. We all thought Gus was going to be a nightmare groomzilla from hell, but he's been surprisingly low-key about the wedding planning. This is the thing he's bugging me about the most, so I guess the least I can do is scrounge up a date to bring with me.

I take another sip. "And the other thing you wanted to talk to me about?"

Gus gets up and yanks me by the hand. Good thing I've got sharp reflexes. Otherwise, I'd be wearing my coffee right about now.

"Where are we going?" I ask as he drags me out of the room.

"You had a day off yesterday, so you haven't met our new receptionist."

"We have a new receptionist? But I saw Harmony behind the desk when I got in this morning."

"Harmony wants to reduce her hours, spend more time with her kids. So he's only going to be working a few days a week."

"He?"

Gus stops mid-stride and faces me in the narrow corridor. "Yes, *he*." Gus emphasizes the word. "And he is mighty fine. Not for me of course because I have an amazing, wonderful, and charming fiancé." He cups the back of his hand over his mouth. "Who, just between us squirrel friends, is a devil in the sack."

I wince. "Too much information."

We start walking toward the reception area, slower this time.

Gus lowers his voice as he says, "I have no problem with staff dating staff."

"Huh?" What is he getting at?

"This guy would look amazing in a suit and in my wedding photos. Hint. Hint."

I roll my eyes. "You are too much. There is no way I'd ever take—"

We reach the front desk as a familiar, intoxicating spicy citrus scent hits me. The last time I smelled anything like it was with— Oh my god... No, it couldn't be.

The receptionist's shoulder-length blond hair is tied in a neat ponytail, his long fingers tapping away at the edge of the counter. My eyes fall out of my head as I heave back. The new receptionist spins around in his chair to face us. His eyes join mine, ballooning to the size of saucers.

"Oh my god! Noah."

"Haze."

Gus' eyes dart between us like he's got front row seats at the US Open. "Wait. You two know each other?"

6

HAZE

Noah!?

I blink a few times. I'm looking at Noah. Those friendly green eyes. That classically handsome face and square jaw. Those bulging biceps straining the fabric of his coat.

What on Earth is Noah doing here?

A few seconds pass until my brain snaps into gear. He's wearing a white overcoat, and he's with the owner so, duh, it's pretty obvious what's happening. Noah is a vet, and he works here.

"We, uh...we've met." His words stumble out, but he hasn't stopped looking at me since I turned around to face him. Come to think of it, my eyes haven't left him either.

"Great, then," Gus says, his head still swinging between the two of us.

Harmony, the receptionist who has been training me, walks up to us. "So I see you've met Noah. He's the best."

"One of the best," another vet chimes in behind Gus and Noah. I can't remember his name, but underneath his white coat, he's wearing a T-shirt that's made me giggle every time I've walked past him this morning. He looks oddly familiar, like I've seen him somewhere before, but I can't place where.

"Oh, Fulton," Harmony says with a giggle in her voice. "You know you're really my favorite."

"I'm standing right here, you guys." Gus lets out a pretend exasperated sigh.

This is only my second day here, and already, it's one of the friendliest places I've ever worked at. I'm perched on the edge of the chair, my eyes still trained on Noah. He's still taking me in, his face a mixture of shock and...something else that I can't quite make out.

The bell above the front door chimes. "Mrs. Patterson," Harmony sings out brightly. "How are you? How's little Moozey doing?" I hear a cat let out a loud and very unimpressed-sounding *meow*. Fulton escorts Mrs. Patterson and her cat into a consult room.

Everything that's happening is occurring on the periphery because Noah and I haven't taken our eyes off one another for even a second. The phone rings, and I hear Harmony answer it with a cheerful, "Good morning. This is Vet Shop Boys. You're speaking with Harmony."

"Well, I might head off, too. I've got some wedding planning stuff to sort out this morning," I hear Gus say.

"Uh-huh," Noah replies absently.

"We might need to do a last-minute venue change. We're thinking of flying guests to the moon for the reception."

"That sounds good," Noah replies.

"You know, that whole intergalactic craze is, like, so on trend for weddings right now. We're thinking of serving alien sashimi with sides of moon dust."

"Sounds tasty," Noah mutters, and I giggle. Gotta be honest, I can't help but feel a little happy about the effect I seem to be having on the man.

I hear an exasperated sigh—a real one this time—as Gus flings his arms in the air and turns on his heel to leave.

With his eyes still pinning me, Noah leans forward. "Can I... Can we...talk for a second?"

I spin around. Harmony is on the phone, but she nods her head anyway. That's some good multi-tasking-slash-eavesdropping skills she's got going on there. I follow Noah down the hallway to the staff lounge. Ribbons of light stream through the windows into the empty room. We're standing face to face.

"I had no idea you worked here," I blurt out right as Noah asks, "When did you get back?"

We smile at each other. It's a little awkward, but it's also a little nice, too. "You first," we say in unison to each other. More smiling.

I shake my head. "I swear, I didn't plan this. You never told me what you did for a living, so I never expected—"

"It's okay," he cuts in. His smile has been growing on his face the whole time we've been standing here. At some point, one of us, or both of us, have edged closer, and we're less than a foot apart.

"When did you get back?" he repeats.

"Five days ago." Everything's happened so fast, I can barely believe it myself. "My housemate, Tate, found a job listing online the day after I arrived," I explain.

"Is this the housemate you share a house with no walls with?"

I grin, distracted by the light catching the green in Noah's eyes. A fluttery feeling lands in my belly that he remembers such a small detail from the night we met. "Yep, that's the one."

Noah cocks his head as I go on. "I submitted my application that same day. Two days later, I'm being interviewed in Gus' office. The next day, Gus offered me the job. I started yesterday." I pause, chewing on my lip nervously. "Is this okay?"

If Noah was smiling before, he's positively beaming now. "Totally okay," he assures me.

For some reason, I babble on about how the job suits me so well because it's part-time, which means I'll be able to fit it around my final year studies, how the pay and benefits are great, and how nice and friendly everyone here is. That's when I notice Noah's eyes have fallen to my lips.

I stop talking. I can't think of anything else to say. Luckily, I don't have to. Noah's fingers interlace around my neck as he draws my mouth to his. Without thinking, my hands wrap around his waist, pulling him in closer to me.

Our tongues tangle as a wave of bliss washes over me. The kiss deepens, his hands running through my hair, mine pressing into his lower back. It dawns on me that Noah's the last person I kissed. Yep. Despite being a sucker for a cute British accent, no one caught my eye while I was over there. No one's even come close, really. Not since...him.

"Whoa." Noah rears back. "I'm so sorry. I don't... I've never... I mean, I shouldn't have done that."

I step in closer to him, smoothing my hand down the front of his white coat and reveling in the firmness underneath the fabric. I need to ask Tate if vet porn is a thing because if it's not, it sure as fuck needs to be. Noah's outfit is everything a vet's outfit should be, all clean and wholesome-like. But the body underneath it? Holy hell. The memories of Noah lying naked under me drain my brain of all blood, shooting it south to my cock.

"It's okay. I like kissing you."

His face stays blank, like he's holding in a breath. After a few beats, he smiles, his eyes crinkling at the edges. "I like kissing you, too." He leans in and inhales, his eyelids fluttering. "You smell amazing."

"You look amazing."

We stop talking, and our eyes lock. It's like we're both taking a moment to process the surprise of seeing each other again. I bet I was the last person he expected to run into today. I sure as heck never thought I'd be seeing him ever again.

Noah reaches out, brushing my stubbled jaw with the back of his hand. My chest floods with warmth. I smile when I spot the bracelet he's wearing. The bracelet I gave him that he's *still* wearing after all these months.

"Nice bling," I remark.

His smile fizzles. "Oh, do you—do you want it back?"

I laugh, gently tracing my fingers over his left wrist. "No. I'm glad you're still wearing it." I am. I don't know why, but it makes me happy knowing he liked it enough to be wearing it more than half a year after we were supposed to never see each other again.

Oh, shit. *That.* His four rules about having a one-night stand.

I can't remember all of them. All I know is that we broke the first one by spending the night together, and then I told him he wouldn't have to worry about breaking any more because we'd never see each other again. Guess that one's shot to shit now as well.

I swallow hard. "I can find another job," I offer, even though I don't really want to. But I'd do it. If he takes me up on it and says that's what he'd prefer, I'd quit and find work someplace else. "I don't want this to be awkward for you, and if you'd prefer that I—"

His thick fingers cover my lips. "No." His voice is firm. "I would never make you quit your job. That's ridiculous."

I bite into my lower lip. I can still taste him there. "Are you sure? I mean, this is breaking one of the four golden rules, isn't it?"

His eyebrows knit together. "Rules?"

"Yeah. You told me about how your friends said there were four rules for a one-night stand. Wasn't one of them something about never seeing each other again? Kinda hard to do that if I'm working here."

His hand finds its way to mine, and he squeezes around my fingers. "I can't believe you remember that."

"I remember everything about that night." I suck in a breath, wishing there's some way to vacuum those words back in. I have no idea why I just revealed that to him.

Noah's eyes are searing into me. He tightens his grip around my hand, but says nothing.

"I don't want to make things difficult for you. Is me working here really okay with you?"

He smiles, his green eyes sparkling as he replies, "Yeah, it really is."

∽

I spin around in my Aunt Jocelyn's desk chair, admiring the view of the river and the downtown office tower tops from her corner office. She's the CEO of the family's law firm, Adams & Daughters. The glass door opens, and she strides in, her face exploding like fireworks when she sees me. We haven't had a chance to catch up since I've been back. She's on the phone and gives me the yapping signal with her hand, rolling her eyes as she does it.

I mouth back, "Take your time." I'm assuming it's a work call, so I don't want her to rush on my account.

Aunt Jocelyn is a badass. Well traveled. Has a degree and a double master's. Legendary sharp tongue and quick wit. Takes crap from no one. So, life goals, basically.

One of the things I love most about her is the way she came through for her brother—my dad—after Mom died. My birth turned from being a day of joy to a horrific day of mourning. Mom went into cardiac arrest right after giving birth to me. It turns out she had an undiagnosed high blood pressure condition called preeclampsia. Mom and I only shared a few short minutes on this earth. She died in the same hour I was born.

Both sets of grandparents and my two other aunts, Jane and Stephanie, rallied around us. But Dad's always been closest with Jocelyn. Aunt Jocelyn had been living in Europe at the time. She moved back home, took over the family firm, and has basically been like a mom to me my entire life. She even created a bedroom for me at her house for when I stayed over, which was a lot. Even though it doesn't make up for the loss of my own mom, I feel lucky to have a dad and an aunt who did everything they could to make me feel so loved.

She kicks off her Louboutins. I flash her the sign for, *Wanna drink?*

She brings her fingers to the edge of her mouth in the sign for, *Gotta toke?*

I clutch at my chest, feigning shock. Her call ends a few moments later, and she leaps over to me. "Hazey baby!" I inhale a mouthful of her long auburn hair as we embrace. "It's so good to see you, honey. I've missed you so much."

"I've missed you too, Aunt Jocelyn."

We pull apart. "I can't wait to hear all about London. But first, seriously"—she quirks an immaculately groomed eyebrow at me—"you got any weed?"

"Aunt Jocelyn!"

"What?" She shrugs. "Medical cannabis is legal."

"There's nothing wrong with you," I point out.

"That's not true," she says with a playful smirk. "I happen to suffer from an affliction known as ADS."

It's my turn to lift a brow. "And what, pray tell, is ADS?"

"Associated Dick Syndrome," she deadpans right back at me, and I laugh. "Seriously, honey. It's a very common condition that affects many female CEOs and managers who have to spend their whole lives working twice as hard as men in similar positions. Just because they have a dick doesn't mean they're entitled to act like one."

She doesn't wait for a response from me, even though frankly, I have no idea what to say to that. Instead, she marches over to the cabinet and pours two glasses of whiskey. She hands me one, and with a merry *clink*, we sit down next to each other on one of the brown Chesterfield couches in the middle of the room. "I spoke to your father last night." She brings the glass to her bright red lips. "I want to hear all about London, but he mentioned you've started a new job."

I scratch the back of my head. "Uh. Yeah..."

I know Aunt Jocelyn won't let me get away with a non-answer, so I fill her in on how Tate found the job ad, a bit about the clinic, and how great everyone who works there is. Okay, maybe not *everyone* who works there. I do my best to skirt around any mention of Noah, mainly because I don't really know what to say.

After we kissed and talked briefly in the staff lounge, we kept it professional for the rest of our shift. It's only my second day there, so I still have a ton to learn. Seeing Noah popping into the waiting room as he calls owners and their pets in for their appointment is enough of a distraction. The thoughts that play on repeat in my mind of how I'd like to lock us into one of those consult rooms and tongue-fuck the life out of that sweet ass of his don't help, either.

"Haze? Hello? Earth to Haze."

Aunt Jocelyn's bright red fingernails snap in front of my face, jolting me out of my Noah-inspired fantasy.

"Are you okay, honey?"

I'm fidgeting with my fingers, so I jam them into the pockets of my jeans. "Still a bit jet-lagged, I guess."

"Honey." Aunt Jocelyn places her hand on my knee, her tone soft and sweet. "Don't bullshit a bullshit artist."

I glance up to find her smirking at me. "Jet lag doesn't make someone smile and look like... Wait. I know that look." She straightens up, shimmying her shoulders like a contestant on a game show who's sure they've got the right answer. "You met someone in London, didn't you?"

"No." I should leave it at that. It'd be the smart thing to do, so of course I don't. "Not in London."

Aunt Jocelyn drums her fingers against my knee, and I can see the cogs spinning in her mind. "At your new job?" she guesses correctly.

Dammit. I wince, and that just seals the deal. "Wasn't today only your second day?"

"It's a little more complicated than that." A torrent of words tumbles out of me as I explain meeting Noah half a year ago, before launching into what's probably only a semi-coherent blur about one-night stands, and the four rules, and bracelets, and a hot kiss in the staff lounge. I don't know how much sense I'm making with any of this. I actually am still jet-lagged, and I haven't had a proper night's sleep since I got back. I must be making at least some sense because Aunt Jocelyn simply nods along to what I'm saying, humming to herself every once in a while.

I brace myself for a barrage of questions to be hurled at me, but she just smiles softly and, for whatever reason, decides to take it easy on me and changes the topic. "So tell me about London. How were the workshops? Are you a fully-fledged performer now?"

Panic roils in my gut, but I do my best to suppress it. I plaster a smile onto my face. "It was good. Great. I mean, amazing." With each word I utter, my voice goes up an octave.

Aunt Jocelyn knows how much I've struggled to "find my path." I'm closing in on thirty and onto my second degree, and yet still it doesn't feel like the right thing for me. My heart sinks. I don't want to revisit any of that for the millionth time, so I tell her about my student exchange at the London College of Performing Arts and the bunch of acting workshops I took over the summer.

She then fills me in on what's been happening at home. We talk for a while longer before I get up to leave. She pulls me in for a hug. As she's holding me in close, she says something cryptic. "Figuring out what you *don't* want, Hazey, is just as important as figuring out what you *do* want."

Aunt Jocelyn's words stay with me all night, and I alternate thinking about what she may have meant and... Noah. Seeing him again. Kissing him again. Knowing that we'll be seeing each other a whole lot more now. Having all these thoughts swirling around in my head is enough to leave my poor jet-lagged brain more than a little sore.

I brush my teeth before bed when my gaze drops to the bracelets I'm wearing. I smile around my toothbrush, warmed by the fact Noah's been wearing a reminder of me on his wrist all this time. I drift off with thoughts of Noah playing behind my eyelids.

7

NOAH

As was the case yesterday and the day before, I can smell Haze before I see him.

Okay, that sounds way creepier than I intended it. What I mean is, as soon as I swing the front door of the clinic open, Haze's scent overwhelms the air in the office. The day I first saw him here, it was spicy citrus. Yesterday, it was peppermint. Today, it's something more earthy. Sandalwood, maybe? I've narrowed it down to the guy having the world's best collection of either body wash or shampoo. The smells are too enticing, too natural, to be anything synthetic like cologne or deodorant. Not that I've spent every waking minute thinking about him since he started working at the clinic three days ago or anything.

As I step into the reception area, Haze peers up at me through thick, sandy-colored lashes and shoots me a smile. My breath hitches in my throat. I know he hasn't orchestrated it with the sun gods, but morning light is filtering in on him and showering him in an almost ethereal glow. His hair has gotten a few shades lighter over the summer, but man, that smile of his is as irresistible as it was the night we first met. I move forward, inhaling him with every step I take.

Working weekends sucks, but it's a thousand times better having Haze here. Unfortunately, he only does the early morning shift. It's four hours long, while my shifts can stretch out to twelve, fourteen hours. It's been crazy busy lately, and apart from the few minutes we snagged alone together in the staff lounge, we haven't had a chance to properly talk. Just seeing him is nice, though.

"Fuck me with your BBC. Yeah, fuck me. Fuck me," cuts through the air.

I've been so busy drinking in our new thirst-quenching receptionist that I completely missed a client sitting in the corner. A bright red and blue eclectus parrot sits in a gold cage beside a middle-aged and very embarrassed woman. She is visibly mortified by the X-rated commentary her bird is squawking into the thankfully empty waiting room.

"Noah, you're here. Great." Haze leaps out of his chair and strides over to me. Each step he takes envelops me even deeper in his intoxicating fragrance. He's wearing a long-sleeved black button-up shirt, and it brings out the silver flecks in his hazel eyes.

I manage to pull my gaze away from him for a moment and eye the woman sitting in the waiting room, frantically shushing the bird every time it lets rip with another stream of expletives. "What is going on here?"

Haze grabs me by the arm and leads me a few steps away from the woman and her misbehaving bird. He leans in closer and whispers, "That's Mrs. MacPherson. She came back from a business trip late last night to find her parrot—"

"It's an eclectus," I interrupt and squint past Haze's shoulder to get a better look at the brightly colored bird. "A female, judging by its black beak. The males tend to have orange noses."

"Right, okay, whatever."

I look back at Haze. We're standing only a few inches apart, his hand still holding onto my arm. Not complaining about that. We haven't touched, or been this close to one another, since my *I don't know what came over me* moment when I kissed him three days ago. Although, in fairness, he did kiss me right back.

There's a slight tremor in Haze's voice. That's when I notice he's trying to keep a straight face. "Noah, that bird is one foulmouthed animal. You should hear some of the stuff coming out of her mouth."

I swing my face right in front of Haze's to block it from Mrs. MacPherson's line of sight. I wouldn't want her to catch the smile now pulling at my lips, either.

"She has no idea where the bird—Ruffles, her name is—where Ruffles has picked up any of this stuff from."

I bite the inside of my cheek and compose myself, reminding myself that we're at work and I need to be professional. You see a lot of things as a vet, but as they say, there's a first time for everything. I usher Mrs. MacPherson and Ruffles into the nearest consult room. Before I step in, I peer over my shoulder at Haze. He's sitting back at the front desk now. Our eyes meet for a moment, his still sparkling with the unexpected humor of the whole Ruffles situation.

Warmth spreads like a long-burning log inside of me. I want to kiss him again. I want to be with him again, feel his body on top of me, inside of me. I could spend the rest of the day staring at him, and he doesn't seem to be moving, either.

"Come on me. Come on my face, motherfucker."

Ruffles, it seems, has other ideas.

"Holy shit, that's hysterical," Fulton cries, wiping a tear from his eye. I've just finished telling him about my encounter with the foul-mouthed parrot the previous morning. It was a much-needed comedic respite in an onslaught of otherwise long and exhausting days. Yesterday, I did a twelve-hour shift. Today, I worked just over fourteen hours. In addition to my usual round of consults, I operated on a cat that fell out of a window and on a German Shepherd that got brought in after being hit by a car.

I let out a yawn and slump further into the seat at our usual corner booth, at our usual bar, in the very same place where I first laid eyes on Haze. Sitting here, I remember something I'd forgotten about that night. We bumped into each other when I came out of the men's room, but I actually noticed him before that, when he first arrived and started playing pool with his friends. He caught my interest from the moment I laid eyes on him. He's kept it the entire time since. And now, we're colleagues, and who knows what will happen?

As if reading my mind, Fulton nudges into me. "So what's it like working with Haze?"

"Good question," I mutter. "It's one I've been asking myself a lot."

Fulton smiles warmly at me. I told him, and only him, about who Haze is and how we met all those months ago. Fulton's great to talk to about stuff like this. There's never any pressure or judgment from him, and I know that all he wants is the best for me.

"Come up with any answers yet?"

I let out a breath. "I know it's too soon to make anything out of it, but..."

Fulton sits, waiting patiently for me to find my words. "I've been thinking about him. A lot. I never expected to see him again."

"Has there been any more kissing?"

I chuckle. Yeah, I told him about that, too. "No. I've barely seen him. It's been so busy these past few days."

Fulton nods in agreement. "It's been crazy hectic."

"Haze had a day off today, and I'm off tomorrow. I haven't looked at my roster for the rest of the week, so I don't know when I'll see him next."

"Do you like him?"

Before I can answer Fulton's question, I spot Gus, Chase, and Harmony approaching. Fulton changes the subject, wasting no time telling them about my encounter with Ruffles yesterday. "I'll get us a round of drinks," Chase offers, while Gus and Harmony are still laughing, shaking their heads in disbelief.

"We'll talk later," Fulton turns and whispers to me, and I nod. I try to push thoughts of Haze aside for a while, at least, and focus on what's right in front of me. Which just so happens to be a pair of shoes.

"So...blue suede shoes. Whaddya think?" Gus announces with a dramatic flair, plopping a pair of shoes into the middle of the table that are not only blue and suede, but bedazzled, too.

"They're wonderful," Harmony answers diplomatically. "What are they for?"

"Marco's great-grandfather was Elvis Presley's tailor's best friend," Gus begins, and it takes me a second to catch up with what he's said. Like I mentioned, it's been a long day.

I nod. "Got it. And?"

"Well, Marco thought it'd be fun if we both wore these shoes. They go well with our tuxes. Plus, you can never have too much blue at a wedding, right?" He crosses his fingers and chuckles.

Chase returns with our drinks, and I take a sip. Gus didn't turn out to be the groomzilla from hell some of us were expecting, although some of his choices, like blue suede shoes, are a little on the interesting side of the good taste spectrum.

Out of seemingly nowhere, Fulton, who's sitting beside me, pulls out three ties and lays them out onto the table.

"Geez, guys, if I'd known this was going to turn into a fashion show, I would've gotten dressed up," Harmony jokes.

"I had an inkling we'd be talking about weddings," Fulton says, raising an eyebrow at Gus. "I'd like to get group consensus on these."

Chase scrunches his nose. "What are they?"

"Knitted ties," Fulton replies. "I kinda like them. They're old-school and were popular back in the 1950s, so I'm thinking...new trend alert?"

He's laid out three colors on the table: burgundy, red, and green. I pick up the green tie and thread the material through my fingers. "It feels nice," I comment.

Gus leans over to inspect them, squinting. "Yes to the style. No to the colors. The palette clashes. If you can find something in gray, black, or blue, you're good."

Okay...so maybe Gus has a *teeny* bit of groomzilla lurking within him. Fulton seems happy with Gus' response, though, and carefully folds and packs the ties away.

Harmony uses the temporary lull in conversation to change the topic. To me. "So, Noah." Her lips curve into a smirk. "What's going on with you and Haze?"

"I have no idea what you mean." I take a pull of my drink. "And I have no idea why you're smirking like that, either."

"Uh-huh." She's full-on grinning now. "So tell me, why is it that

I can practically hear Haze's neck snap every time you walk into the reception area?"

"It does?" I bring the glass to my lips to conceal my smile. At least no one can feel the fluttering in my chest right now.

Chase's phone buzzes, and a frown crosses his forehead. "Julie," he offers by way of explanation. "I need to go."

Harmony looks at the time, sighs, and starts to get up. "It's getting late, and I've got children and a husband to feed. I should go, too." Before Harmony leaves, she turns back to me and wags her finger in my face. "That boy likes you."

I try to play it off, saying nothing, and give a noncommittal shrug in response. But inside, butterflies are flying around in my stomach like their parents are out of town for the weekend and they're throwing a massive party.

"So, you and Haze, huh?" Gus nudges into me with a shit-eating grin on his face once Harmony and Chase have left.

It's only him, me, and Fulton left, and I haven't had the chance to fill Gus in on how Haze and I know each other. With a sigh, I decide to just get it out into the open. "Haze is the guy I had a one-night stand with six months ago."

Gus' eyes go wide. "Wait. You had a one-night stand? How did I not know about this?"

I clutch my chest. "Oh, I'm sorry. Did I not send out a memo to the entire office detailing my sex life?"

Gus rubs his hands in glee. "This round's on me. I want all the juicy details when I get back."

We wait until he returns. Gus' tongue is practically hanging out of his mouth as he places the drinks in front of us. "This is going to be good. Now spill."

I lift the glass to my lips. "Remember that time we were playing Never Have I Ever and it turned out I was the only one who had never had a one-night stand?"

Gus nods.

"Well, after you guys left that night, I ran into someone. Haze. We got to talking, and one thing led to another..."

Gus claps his hands in glee. "I am *very* impressed."

"Why? I had a one-night stand. I didn't cure cancer."

"That's true, but I'm impressed that you stepped out of your comfort zone." Gus' voice goes soft, and he places his hand over mine. "How long has it been since, you know..."

I know exactly what he's talking about. "Two years," I say, taking a gulp of my drink.

"Actually, it's two and a half years now," Fulton chips in.

"Shut up, Fulton," Gus and I say at the same time. It's something we do out of habit. There's no malice behind it. We all smile at each other for a minute.

"But yeah, it's been two and a half years since Graham..."

I trail off, not wanting to say the words "cheated on me" out loud. Graham and I were together for eighteen months. Call me old-fashioned, but I kinda have a thing about not cheating on someone... Then lying about it... Then giving your partner an infection and, somehow, blaming them for it. Thankfully, I was able to treat what he gave me with a shampoo, and my skin recovered two weeks later. My heart, on the other hand...

"Hey." Gus places his hand over mine. "You're an amazing guy. You just haven't found someone that's equally as amazing as you."

"That's right," Fulton jumps in. "It's great that you're so giving and loving and understanding, but Noah, all of those things are a two-way street in a relationship."

"I know, I know." I sound resigned and tired because I am, the truth of their words and the long shifts I've been working finally catching up with me. Everything Gus and Fulton are saying makes perfect sense, and I agree with them. It's just I seem to have this bad habit of falling for guys who, no matter how well I treat them, end up leaving me.

"So what are you going to do about it?" Fulton asks. He can tell I've been in my head so he prompts, "About Haze, I mean."

I shrug. "I don't know. What can I do? I've now broken two out of the four one-night stand rules, right?"

Gus looks confused, so Fulton does a quick recap for him. "Don't spend the night. Don't see him again. Don't share anything personal. Don't fall in love with him."

"Right. Well, like I said to you before, I have no problem with staff dating. Or inviting them as plus-ones to, say, I don't know, your amazing boss' wedding that's coming up in a few short weeks."

Fulton chuckles. "You never quit, do you, Gus?"

His head slants to the side, smiling. "You know it." Gus turns to me. "But seriously, I just want you to be happy. If you think it could be with Haze, I say go for it."

Fulton speaks up. "As cute as I think it would be for you to invite Haze to Gus' wedding—and I'd even be willing to share a color-approved knitted tie with him—I think there's something you need to do first."

"What's that?"

"Talk to him. I mean, the two of you working together must be a surprise for him as well. He probably never expected to see you again either. You're also good friends with his boss, and he's the new guy. And by the sound of things, there may be some feelings involved. So all of that could all be a lot for him to deal with."

I scrub my hand down the side of my face. I do want to talk to Haze—it's been killing me that we haven't had a chance to be alone again. Now that the initial shock of seeing each other has worn off, I'm curious to know how he's feeling. "Any suggestions about what I should do?"

Fulton thinks about it for a moment. "Maybe go have lunch with him and talk to him about what's happening and how you're feeling. Assure him that you're cool with working together." Fulton pauses. "You are cool working together?"

I smile stupidly, and that seems to be all the answer Fulton needs.

"Oh, yeah. He's definitely cool with it," Gus teases before making a bunch of kissy noises.

Fulton joins in by wrapping his arms around his shoulders and making all sorts of weird moaning noises while panting out, "Ooh, yeah, Haze."

I lean back in my seat, chuckling at my two stupid friends, as I remind myself that we're meant to be grown-ass men.

8

HAZE

"I've been doing some investigative googling," I announce to Noah as I walk into the staff lounge a couple of days after the Ruffles debacle. It's just after two, and he's having what appears to be a very late lunch. The clinic has been nonstop busy all day, like it has been every day since I started, so I'm not surprised this is his first chance to take a break.

"Oh yeah?" He motions for me to join him at the table. We're not alone. We're never alone at work. There's always people scurrying around, which I guess is to be expected in a clinic that employs twelve full-time vets. Still, it kinda sucks. A couple of vet nurses are sitting on the couches, but they're far away from us so that we can talk somewhat privately. That's a good thing. We'll need a little space for the conversation we're about to have.

"It's about Ruffles," I begin as I pull up into a chair beside Noah.

He chuckles and plays with his food. "This should be good."

I lean in closer. "It is." Our eyes meet as I continue, "So BBC rang a bell to me. It's a news network in the UK, and since I've spent the last six months there, that kinda makes sense. But it didn't explain why Ruffles was adding the...uh..."

"Fuck me's?" Noah lifts an eyebrow.

I breathe out a giggle. "Yeah. That part."

I'm momentarily distracted by the way Noah's looking at me. His eyes are twinkling, but there's a stiffness in his shoulders, too. Like he's got something else on his mind. I really want to know what that is, but since he's looking at me expectantly, I go on. "I jumped online, and yes, BBC does stand for British Broadcasting Corporation..." Noah's gaze suddenly latches onto something behind me, but I continue. "But BBC also stands for..." I pause and take a deep breath. "Big black cock."

"Jesus, fuck!"

I twist around right as Fulton staggers back from us. He raises his hands by the side of his face, his eyes wide as saucers. "Sorry, sorry, sorry. I didn't mean to intrude."

"It's fine," Noah says, letting out a deep, rumbling laugh. The same kind that takes me straight back to his kitchen when he laughed at some pathetic pancake joke I made. Not that I've been replaying every single part of every single interaction we've ever had, or anything.

"We're talking about work," I inform Fulton.

He grins. "Yeah. Right. And I just discovered that Jake Gyllenhaal is my long lost brother."

Noah rolls his eyes and points to an empty seat next to me. "We're talking about Ruffles. Haze here has cracked his code."

"Oh, right."

Recognition washes over Fulton's features as he joins us and I explain my findings. "Maybe if the bird was exposed to porn that uses that kind of language, that's where she picked it up from?" I hedge, and I see Fulton nodding in agreement beside me.

Noah takes a bite of his salad. "Yeah. That makes total sense. Hey, Fulton, don't suppose you want to call Mrs. MacPherson for me and tell her the news?"

Fulton throws back a laugh. "Not a chance."

I find myself smiling along, but I can't help but be disappointed that once again, Noah and I are surrounded by people. I don't want to be rude, so I sit there as Noah and Fulton discuss various talking bird species and the different ways they pick up language.

I like Fulton. He's a really nice guy. Today, his bright orange shirt says, **Dogs have owners. Cats have staff**. I just wish I could get some alone time with Noah. We haven't spoken properly since I started working here, and I think it's time we do the whole adulting thing and use words.

I let out a sigh. Noah and I need to talk, but it won't be right now.

~

I approach the consult room and lean against the doorframe. Noah's at his desk, tapping away furiously on the keyboard. One thing I've picked up in my time working at the clinic is that vets spend a lot of time typing, checking, reading, and updating their consult notes.

My insides fill with a gooey warmth as I take a moment to take Noah in. He hasn't seen me, so I study the serious look on his face as he's staring at the screen, his rock-solid broad shoulders that gently ebb and flow as he types, the way he stops and tilts his head from time to time as he's gathering his thoughts.

I clear my throat, and he looks up. A smile caresses his lips. "Haze."

"Sorry to interrupt." I step into the room. "Your four o'clock just rang. They're running ten minutes late."

"No problem. Thanks for letting me know. Oh, and thanks for telling me about your investigative googling before. I'm pretty sure that wasn't in the job description. I really appreciate you doing that."

I shuffle on my feet. "Don't mention it."

"I've spoken to Harmony, and she's told me how quickly you're picking everything up, and I see the way you interact with everyone. You're a great addition to the team."

His words are like a match to kindling, my chest exploding with a fiery heat. "Thanks. I really appreciate you saying that." I turn on my heel and start to leave when...

"Haze?"

I spin around. Noah motions toward the empty chair opposite him. "Have you got a moment?"

"Uh, sure."

As I sit down, I feel my heart clanging in my chest. Apart from the kiss in the staff room on my first day, and the few seconds we had in the staff room when I shared the results of my investigative googling, Noah and I haven't spent any time together alone.

Until right now.

He's on one of those desk chairs with wheels because he slides away from the computer and positions himself right in front of me.

He brings his hands together, the tan bracelet I gave him peeking out from under his long-sleeve shirt. "Listen, um, do you eat? I mean, would you like to eat? Have lunch. With me?"

A crimson tinge fills Noah's cheeks, and in addition to his stammering, it's the cutest thing I've ever seen. Yep, even Mrs. Johnson's adorable brindle and white French Bulldog puppy that she brought in this morning can't compete with the way Noah's looking right now.

I stretch my arms, placing my hands palms-down on the desk. "That depends. What's on the menu? Food?" I inhale sharply before saying, "...Or you?"

Okay, now his cheeks are the color of beetroots. I giggle, and Noah grins at my cheekiness. I'm wondering if it takes him back to the very first night we met at the bar. I don't know what it is about Noah, but he brings out a different side to me. I'm not usually this flirty or funny, but when I'm with him, it's like these parts of myself that I didn't know existed come out. Luckily for me, he doesn't seem to mind. I'm hoping that a small part of him may actually like it.

"I was thinking about food." Noah settles back into his chair. The heat from his cheeks transfers to his eyes as he adds, "For now. How about lunch tomorrow? There's a nice Mexican place not too far from here."

My heart is jackhammering away, but I do my best to not show my excitement. I swallow hard and nod to confirm our...meeting? Appointment? Date? No, not that... Although... Maybe? Is Noah asking me out?

As if he's reading my mind, he chimes in. "It might be nice if you and I had a chance to talk. Privately."

"Yeah. I agree." I stare into Noah's gorgeous green eyes. "I'll see you then."

~

That evening, I lose myself in a world of colors and smells. I've laid old newspapers over the large kitchen table and assembled all the ingredients I'll be needing on it. I've got the lye and oils. Tonight, I'll be using a combination of shea butter and coconut oils, but I haven't decided on the exact fragrances yet. I've laid out my entire essential oils collection, and I'll choose whatever inspires me when I get to that point in the soapmaking process.

I'm wearing gloves and goggles and have just finished pouring the lye into water. Tate's busy working, so I don't want to disturb him. My headphones are set to low. I'm listening to Queen Bey. *Halo* is seriously one of the most beautiful ballads ever. It hits me right in the feels every single time I listen to it.

I keep stirring until the lye fully dissolves. The next step is to let it cool. This usually takes about an hour. Which is kinda good. I need some time to think. It's been a nonstop whirlwind since I got back from London. I take off my goggles and gloves and pour myself a glass of wine.

It's good to be back here. Home. It's a massive open-plan loft, but we've hung curtains along rails that are pinned to the roof, creating bedrooms. Still, curtains aren't soundproof, and I can hear moans coming from Tate's space. Our two other housemates are out for the evening.

I've missed this place. And I've missed my housemates. Especially Tate. He really is the sweetest guy ever. He insisted on paying my share of the rent while I was away, just so that I could keep my stuff here and have a place to live when I got back. That's the kind of guy he is, not that he'd ever want anyone to know that about him.

I run my fingers over the essential oils, trying to see which one of them tempts me. I open the lavender bottle and take a sniff. Aah, it really is calming. I could do with some of that right about now. I've been a bundle of nerves ever since Noah suggested a lunch...*thing*...tomorrow. I'm ninety-five percent sure he just wants to check in and perhaps establish some ground rules for working together. But it's the unknown five percent that's been driving me crazy all day.

What if he's changed his mind and says he can't work with me?

What if seeing me every day is too weird for him?

Or what if he's fine with me staying and wants to continue as "just friends?"

For some reason, that last option bums me out the most. I know it's silly. I never even expected to see him again. We're not anything to each other. But now that we're back in each other's lives, the embers he lit in me six month ago have been reignited.

I sigh gloomily into my wine. I can't help it. The truth is, I like Noah. And seeing him every day, in his element, it only makes the pangs inside ache even harder. What started off as, I'll admit, mainly a physical attraction, is morphing into something deeper now. I see how much he cares about animals, clients, and his friends. I see how hard he works, how many extra hours he puts in. And I see the way he looks at me. There's a depth to it that makes me feel like he's not just looking at me—he's trying to see me.

I turn my focus back to what I'm working on. I weigh out the shea butter and coconut oil. I've never used just these two together before. Normally, I use olive oil as a base so it'll be interesting to see how it comes out. Since I've decided on lavender as the scent, I pick out some purple coloring since lavender is often associated with purple.

I hum as I work. Soapmaking gets me in my Zen space. I get to be creative, and it soothes my mind as well. My first degree was in biochemistry, so the chemical mixing part of the process is fairly simple for me. I don't know what it is about it, but making soaps just gets me in the zone. Plus, I get a batch of great-smelling, all-natural soaps at the end of it, too.

I've been doing this as a hobby for about three years now. I can still remember my ex's face when I told him I was going to try it. Daniel rolled his eyes disparagingly. "Let's see how long this one lasts," he said dismissively.

Okay, he kinda had a point. I have tried my hand at a lot of different things. Some of them stick. Like soapmaking. Others, like candlemaking, don't—and *may* have ended with a panicked call to the fire department when I used the wrong wick and almost set fire to the apartment I was living in at the time.

It's like I just can't seem to settle on any one thing. I've been this way my whole life. I'm average-level good at a whole bunch of things, but not brilliantly great or super passionate about any one thing. Having to choose what to do with my life has been a huge source of stress and anxiety for me. But I'm on my second degree and approaching thirty, so when it comes to my career, acting and performing has to be it.

And maybe if I keep saying that over and over again, one day I'll be able to convince myself that it's true. Hopefully that day comes soon. But for now, I shove those thoughts aside. I'm in my Zen zone and determined to stay here.

From the corner of my eye, I see Tate sweep into the kitchen. He starts frantically opening and shutting every single drawer and cupboard. I take my headphones off and swivel around to face him. The clanging sounds reverberate around us. "Looking for something?" I ask after a few moments when he shows no signs of slowing down.

Tate turns to me, a serious look set on his face. "I need something smooth and shiny that's safe to shoot out of my ass because..." He pauses, then gives a little shrug. "You know, safety first."

If this were my first week or month living with Tate, my jaw might've dropped to the floor right about now. But since I've had exposure to some of the more, uh, colorful requests he's received as a cam model, I take it in my stride.

I tap my fingers along the table. "Look in the fridge," I suggest. "Try the vegetable drawer."

He darts over, but soon enough, his shoulders slump. He comes up and flops down next to me.

"No good?" I ask.

"Nah." He eyes my soaps and spots the color bottle. "Ooh. Purple. My favorite."

"You can have some when I'm done," I say.

"Thanks." Tate's eyes stay on me. "How are you doing? We've kind of been missing each other since you've been back. Everything okay?"

I give a quick nod, getting up to fetch a glass of water. "I'm all good."

"How's the new job going?"

I can't help the smile that spreads across my face. "It's great. Everyone there is so nice and friendly. The animals are cute. I mean, I only see them when they come in. I'm not exposed to any of the hard or icky stuff. And..."

My voice trails off. After a few moments, Tate prompts, "And?"

Between my work, studies, and jet lag, I haven't had a chance to tell him about Noah yet. "There's a guy who works there. He's one of the vets."

"I take it by the goofy grin on your face you like him."

"Yeah. I do. Noah and I, um, we had a one-night stand."

Tate's eyes bulge. "Geez, look at you go. You've worked there for like, a week, and you're already porking——"

"We had sex before I left for London," I cut in. "And porking, really? What are we, in junior high or something?"

Tate laughs. "Tell me all about him."

I spend the next few minutes giving Tate the rundown. How Noah and I met, went back to his place, and had the best sex of my life. I skip all the private details. I have no problem with Tate or anyone else sharing what they feel comfortable with, but I'm the kind of guy who likes to keep personal, intimate things to himself.

I also tell Tate about how I didn't hook up with anyone while I was in London. And how since I've been back and started working at the clinic, if my thoughts were a movie reel, almost all of them would be filled by Noah. Oh, and I throw in the bit about the four rules of a one-night stand that Noah's trying to follow for good measure.

"*Trying* to follow?" I pick up on the note of suspicion in Tate's voice.

"Well, yeah. That's what I'm assuming he wants to talk to me about at lunch tomorrow. We've broken the first two rules, so I'm guessing he wants to make sure we don't break any more."

"And what do you want?"

My throat tightens. That's a question I've been failing at answering properly my whole life. I've confided in Tate, so he knows all about it.

"Relax." Tate offers a warm smile. "I'm not trying to freak you out here. It's just a simple question."

"What if it's not that simple?"

"It always is," he replies straight away. "If you follow your heart, it never gets weird or complicated or hard. But find me a person who follows their heart, even half the time."

I let his words seep into me. Maybe he's right? I do tend to overthink things and work myself up into a frenzy. But following my heart? Do people do that? Does that even work? This isn't some Disney movie. It's not like the cloudy fog that I've been shrouded in will suddenly lift, and I'll have clarity about my career and a broad-shouldered, animal-loving Prince Charming to ride off into the sunset with.

"Anyway, I should probably get back to looking for something to shoot out of my butt." Tate interrupts my daydreaming. "Let's find some time to hang out soon, yeah?"

"Sure," I mutter as he moves his search to the living area.

My mind ticks back to Tate's advice. What if it really is that simple and that's what I've been doing wrong all these years? Maybe I should just follow my damn heart.

But how the hell do I do that?

9

NOAH

"The chicken quesadillas are to die for, but if you're looking for something more filling—Oh, shit," I snap my mouth shut mid-sentence.

Haze's eyebrows squish together. "What's wrong?"

"I didn't even ask if you liked Mexican food or if you have any allergies."

Haze rests the oversized menu onto the table and smiles, easing the tension that's been building in my shoulders before he even speaks. "Relax, will you? I love Mexican and share the same philosophy for it as I do for pancakes." He pauses for a moment. "If I were allergic to it, I wouldn't want to live anymore."

It takes my brain a few seconds to recognize the joke, but when I do, a smile spreads through my entire body. It's the same joke he cracked sitting in my kitchen when I'd been freaking out about not knowing what he'd like to eat for breakfast.

"I guess I'm not very good at this whole thing," I blurt out without thinking. Fuck, what the hell is that supposed to mean? I don't even know myself. I bury my face behind the laminated menu, suddenly fascinated to learn about the eight different kinds of margaritas this place serves.

Haze's fingertips curve over the top of the menu, and he slowly drags it down. "Not good at *what* whole thing?" The menu falls from my fingers onto the table.

Crap. Why have my brain cells decided to desert me all of a sudden? It's Haze. Yep, I blame him. Entirely his fault. He's armed with this intoxicating mix of confidence and shyness that short-circuits the part of my brain that makes holding a normal conversation possible. Oh, and his amazing scent that drives me crazy every time I'm near him.

"I don't, uh, *eat*, with other people very often," I offer.

Great. That's basically code for "I'm a pathetic loser who hasn't even been on a date in two, no, wait, two and a half years." Not that this is a date, but, oh god, being all cool and smooth is kinda hard without a functioning brain. Because, yeah, I'm sure that *cool* and *smooth* are totally the vibes I'm giving off right now.

I don't know how I expect Haze to react, but I'm pleasantly surprised when his fingers graze the underside of my chin, and he lifts my face to meet his. We stare at each other for a few seconds. A spike of heat pulses through me like it always does when I find myself near him, but especially when he's touching me.

Haze's lips round softly at the edges. "I don't *eat out* very often with other people either."

His words and gentle demeanor are like a thick woolly blanket on a cold winter's night, quelling the nervousness I've been feeling all morning leading up to this lunch. "In fact," he goes on. "You're the last person that I've...eaten."

I shuffle in my seat, amazed that his confession can take my cock from zero to granite-hard in less than three seconds. Not bad for thirty-four.

We place our order, which dissipates some of the sexual tension. Then we do what I came here to do. Talk. This lunch is supposed to give us a chance to discuss working together, and for me to reassure Haze that it's totally fine and to make him feel welcome and part of the team. I start off by asking, "How are you enjoying the job so far?"

"I love it." Haze's eyes sparkle like twinkle lights when he speaks. "Harmony is great to work with, so patient, and she really knows her stuff."

"She is great," I agree. "All the reception staff and nurses are. Vets may get all the glory, but we'd be lost without the people who support us."

Haze nods. "Everyone who works there is nice."

Everyone includes me, right? I feel the words forming on the edge of my tongue, but don't say them.

"I don't know a lot about animals, but I'm learning fast, and I'm keen to learn more."

I smile. "Can I ask—it's obvious you're great with people, but I'm curious what made you apply for this job?"

Haze thinks about it for a moment. "My housemate, Tate, found the listing online. The pay was good, he pointed out, but I like that it's a job where, in a very small way, I can do something to help people. And animals, too." He looks away and then adds, "I've done a lot of crazy-ass jobs, believe me."

"That sounds interesting. Like what?"

Haze brushes a loose strand of hair from his face. "Like everything. I've done the usual gigs you do when you're studying. I've been a server and worked in retail which is as horrendous as it sounds. I was a bike deliveryman for a while."

That explains the muscular thighs. I nod. "Uh-huh."

"But then some of the crazier stuff..." Haze snickers to himself. "I've delivered newspapers at midnight in the middle of winter."

"Eek. That doesn't sound like fun."

"It wasn't, but it paid surprisingly well. I was a clown at children's parties. I've done some modeling work."

Makes. Total. Sense.

"I've been a bed tester."

"A bed tester? What exactly does that entail?" I ask as my thoughts nosedive into inappropriate territory.

Haze grins. "The job name kinda says it all. You go into a lab, they hook you up to all these machines to monitor your vital signs, and they record you as you sleep. It's basically the mattress company testing their product to see if it helps people get a good night's rest."

"Wow. It sounds like you've certainly done a lot. That's really cool."

A look flashes on Haze's face, like he doesn't quite know what to make of what I just said.

"What about you?" he asks, but it sounds like he's deflecting a little. "I don't know what goes on in the consult room, or in the operating theater, but I see you in the waiting room. You're a natural with clients, you're able to calm them down and make them feel at ease almost straight away. How did you get to be so good with people?"

I chuckle to myself. "It's funny. When I joined Vet Shop Boys, the first thing Gus made me do was take a week-long course in Neuro-Linguistic Programming."

Haze's eyes narrow. "What's that?"

"It's a way of using language and behavior to interact better with others. You basically mirror people's words and actions as a way of connecting with them and establishing trust and rapport," I explain. "I thought Gus was crazy at first. I'd done my vet training, and I'd worked in a farm clinic for a few years, so I had experience with all sorts of animals under my belt. I thought to myself, *Why the hell is Gus making me take a course in dealing with people?*"

Haze leans forward, spiking an eyebrow. "And?"

"I learned a valuable lesson. While I may treat animals, I also have to spend a fair chunk of time dealing with their owners, which can be challenging at times. I mean, I get it. People usually see a vet when something's wrong with an animal they love dearly, so it's normal that they're stressed out and not thinking clearly. Doing that course has helped me to create good relationships with animal owners, as well as other staff members."

"That's awesome." Haze runs his long fingers across his stubbled jaw. "I might google it. I'm very good at googling."

I chuckle as my mind fills with memories of a certain foul-mouthed parrot. "You are a good googler, but you're also a natural with people. I've seen you the way you interact with everyone. It comes easily to you. I can tell."

A pink hue invades his cheeks. "Thanks."

Haze looks away for a few moments, biting into his lower lip in thought. "Can I ask you something?"

"Of course."

He pauses as our food arrives. "Please be honest. Is it really okay that we're working together? We were never meant to see each other again. That wasn't part of the deal, and I'm pretty sure that means that we've now broken two of your one-night stand rules. I know you said it was fine, but that was last week when I first started. Is that how you still feel now?"

I take a sip of water before answering. I've been thinking a lot about Haze and what it's like to work with him. He's asked me to be honest with him, and this is my chance to do just that. "I have to admit it was a bit of a surprise to see you sitting behind the reception desk," I start off saying.

"It was a surprise for me, too."

"I'll bet." I suck in a breath. "To be perfectly honest, it is a little hard for me to be working with you."

He drops his gaze. "Oh."

"It's hard for me because...because I like you."

"Oh," he repeats. His face lifts, and a small smile crawls over his lips.

"But like I said, I haven't...*eaten* with anyone for a long time, much less someone I work with, so I don't exactly know how to do this, or what happens next."

He snags my hand in his. "I can answer that. I know exactly what we should do next."

My breath hitches in my throat. I swallow around it. "Yeah? And what might that be?"

"Eat," he says with a giggle. "Our food's getting cold."

"And then what happened?" Fulton buzzes in the booth next to me like I'm telling him that there's been a scientific breakthrough that confirms cats really do have nine lives and not how the rest of my lunch with Haze went.

"Nothing, really. We talked and cleared the air, and we're both fine working together."

Fulton cocks his head and purses his lips. "Just...*fine?*"

He knows me too well. I bite the inside of my cheek to keep from smiling. "Okay, we're both *happy* to be working together."

"Happy?"

"Jesus, what do you want from me?" I joke. "It feels like you won't be happy until I'm professing my deep and undying love for—"

"Haze," Fulton interrupts, jabbing my shoulder.

"Ouch, what the hell was that—?" I twist to my right just in time to see Haze and Gus approaching us, drinks in hand. "Oh, thanks," I whisper to Fulton as the guys sit down.

We're having our usual after-work drinks, and it feels a tad surreal to have Haze joining us. But I also love how well he's fitting in. Everyone loves him. Harmony has been raving about how great he is to work with, and Gus has been nudging me every chance he gets to pop the big question and ask Haze to be my plus-one to his wedding.

The guys fall into a conversation, while I start reminiscing about lunch with Haze today. All in all, it went well. I'm glad we talked, and I look forward to working with him. Okay, so that was the diplomatic side of my brain talking. The other side wishes everyone would leave the bar so that Haze and I can go back to my place and I can impale myself on that spectacular cock of his.

So yeah, I've got a bit of a *Good Noah versus Naughty Noah* situation going on at the moment. If I'm being honest, I'm totally rooting for Naughty Noah to come through with the win. But like I'd told Fulton, after our lunch together, Haze and I have cleared the air, and I'm confident we'll be able to work well together. That's a good first step. Who knows what, if anything, will happen after that.

My mind circles back to Haze telling me how he hasn't been with any guys since me. I try to figure out why that is. Haze is gorgeous whatever side of the Atlantic he's on, so I'm sure he had English guys falling all over themselves to hook up with him. Why didn't he sleep with anyone while he was over there?

"So, guys," Haze asks as Fulton returns with our third, or wait, maybe it's our fourth round? My mind is starting to get a little fuzzy. I reach for the water and decide to ease up on the booze a bit.

"Can I ask, what's with the name?"

Gus nods, smiling dryly. "Glad you feel comfortable enough to ask. Yes, Fulton is a bit of a weird name. More suited to a line of vacuum cleaners than people."

"Hilarious," Fulton deadpans. "Somebody hand the man an Emmy for Best Line Spoken by A Boss With Zero Sense of Humor."

An unguarded laugh flies out of Haze's mouth. "No. I mean the name of the clinic. Vet Shop Boys. What does it mean?"

"How old are you?" Fulton turns to Haze. "If you don't mind me asking, that is."

"Not at all. I'm twenty-nine. Almost thirty."

"And you don't get the reference?" Gus leans his elbows against the edge of the table. "Vet Shop Boys." He says it slowly, adding extra emphasis on the *Vet*.

Haze stares at us blankly.

"You know, like, Pet Shop Boys?" Gus finally prompts.

Haze blinks a few more times, clearly not getting the connection. After a few moments, he says, "Is it like *The Golden Girls* or something?"

Gus huffs out a laugh. "Same era, I guess, but *The Golden Girls* was a TV show. The Pet Shop Boys was a band in the 1980s."

Haze scrunches his nose as he smirks. "Wait. They had music back then?"

We all laugh. "They did," Gus says happily. "And I am proud to say I remember most of the second half of the decade fondly. Give me Madonna over Gaga any day."

Fulton claps a hand onto Gus' shoulder. "Sad, sad man."

"Shut up, Fulton," Gus and I say together, sharing a smile.

Haze's eyes dart between the three of us, catching his first glimpse of the secret language that's formed between us over the years.

Gus' forehead crinkles. "Actually, my partner, well, my former partner, Andrew, came up with the name for the clinic."

I'm a little surprised Gus is opening up and talking about Andrew. He hardly ever mentions him. A wistful smile creeps into Gus' cheeks. "Andrew was a huge fan of the Pet Shop Boys and thought it sounded like a cute and clever name for a veterinary clinic. It took me a while to come around to it, but I always found it hard to say no to him."

"Does he still run the business with you?"

Haze realizes he's stepped on a landmine when he sees the expressions on our faces. "Ah, shit. Sorry. I don't mean to pry."

"It's okay." Gus forces a smile. "Andrew died shortly after we opened the clinic. He was killed in a car crash one rainy night as he was heading to an animal emergency."

"Oh my god, I am so sorry." Haze looks genuinely sad, the emotion pinching his features.

"It took me a long time to get over it. Over a decade. But... Now I'm getting married!"

The conversation turns lighter after that. Fulton espouses the virtues of Etsy for a while and the importance of supporting local and creative cottage industries, which then leads Gus to ask whether he's been able to find bedazzled blue shoelaces to go with his wedding shoes, which then devolves into a fiery debate between the two guys over whether the shoelaces should match the blue suede or contrast with it. All riveting stuff.

I tuned out ages ago, stealing the occasional, discreet glance Haze's way. That's much more fun. He really does fit in so well, chiming into the conversation every once in a while, pulling back at all the right times, too.

"I should get going," Gus says after draining his drink.

"Me, too," Fulton adds, shooting me a look that says, *Stay with Haze.* As if I need the encouragement.

"I'm good for drinks, but maybe we can stay a while longer?" I suggest to Haze once the guys have left. I find myself tense as I wait for him to respond, hoping he'll agree.

"Sure. I'd love to."

My shoulders relax as we slide into an effortless conversation. A contented feeling settles in my belly. I'm really glad we had a chance to talk at lunch. I don't know what the future holds, but once we get good at this whole working together thing, maybe there's a slight chance that Haze might be open to exploring something more between us as well.

Maybe it's sad and pathetic to still be broken up about being cheated on two and a half years ago, but I am. Or at least, a part of me still is. What Graham did, and how he treated me, shattered my heart into a million pieces, which means it's going to take time to rebuild from that. But the more time I spend with Haze—even if it's with other people around a booth at a bar, or in the small windows of time when I come out to the reception area to call the next client in and see him behind the front counter—there's another part of me that feels like it's ready to start to open up. I don't know what I'm opening up to, but I'm willing to take the first steps to see where it could go.

Baby steps. I'm not ready, or even able, to rush into anything. I'm perfectly fine getting to know more about Haze. How his time in London went. What hopes and aspirations he has for his career once he graduates. How many men he's loved in his life. Whether he'd like to feast on my ass again. Yeah, can't help that one. Kinda hard to push past the best sex of your life, especially when the man responsible for it is sitting so close our thighs are almost touching.

But before I get to ask him any of the questions swirling around in my head, his fingertips gently skim across my forearm, his eyes catching mine. "So, what made you decide to become a vet?"

10

HAZE

Noah settles deeper into the booth. When he starts talking, a soft smile crinkles the skin around his eyes. "I've always wanted to be a vet. I never even considered any other line of work to be honest."

"Go on. I'd love to hear all about it."

He keeps smiling. "I've always been fascinated by animals. All sorts. I was the kid that would spend all his time outside in the back garden, scurrying around, looking for insects or wildlife I could learn about. Or torment my younger sister with," he adds with a laugh.

"How many siblings do you have?"

"Just the one. Natalie. She's two years younger."

"Are you close?"

"Yeah. We try to be. She's married and lives in Phoenix. She's got two young boys now. But we talk and text all the time. What about you? Any brothers or sisters?"

I shake my head. "Nope. Just me," I reply slowly. "Keep going. I want to know how tormenting your sister with gross bugs led you to become a vet."

Noah laughs. "In my defense, I only pulled the mean big brother act very rarely. We wouldn't be close today if I was a total ass to her."

"Good point."

"We always had plenty of pets growing up. Dogs, cats, fish, rabbits. And even though animals can't talk, obviously, I always felt a close connection to them. I would pick up on signs from them and it intrigued me to see how in their own ways, animals do communicate and think and feel."

"Oh, totally," I agree.

"For as long as I can remember, I would tell my parents I wanted to work with animals when I grew up. When I was fourteen, Mom arranged for me to spend some time volunteering at a wildlife rescue center not too far from where we lived. It was eye-opening, to say the least."

"In what way?"

"The place was run by a wonderful woman named Tammy. Her passion for the place and the animals in it was unwavering. I loved the center from the moment I set foot in it." He rubs down the front of his shirt, deep in the memory.

"It was my first exposure to seeing animals hurt and in distress. That was intense. But I also got to see all the wonderful work the staff and volunteers did to help heal and rehabilitate the animals. I knew right there and then that's what I wanted to do with my life. There's no better feeling in the world than to help an animal. They're strong in their own ways of course, but they're fragile, too. They need us, and they trust us to be there for them. To me, there's something really special about that connection."

Being so close to Noah as he's talking gives me a chance to study him. Really study him. I've caught glimpses of him at the clinic of course, but I've been so focused on making a good impression and doing a good job that I've never allowed myself to get lost in him. In the way he raises his hands and shakes them when he's talking about something exciting. The way his Adam's apple gently bobs in his throat as he speaks. And the happy expression that never once leaves his face as he's talking about his love and undeniable passion for animals.

"So, yeah. That's my story. I never had a Plan B."

I feel bad about the twinge of jealousy curdling in my gut. He talks about not having a Plan B. I've never even had a Plan A. It's clear Noah's always had a clear vision for his life and what he wants to do with it. I can't help but envy people like him. Not because I don't want that for them, but because I'd like even a few teaspoons of that kind of certainty for myself.

"That's great." Despite trying to sound happy, Noah's not buying it.

He tilts his head. "What's the matter?"

"It's nothing," I say, hoping to sound like I mean it.

A few seconds slip past. "You know, for someone studying to be an actor, you're not doing a great job of making me believe you."

He's smiling, and his unspoken invitation for me to elaborate hangs between us.

I chug down some water. Fuck it. He's just shared something with me. The least I can do is the same, even if my story is pathetic by comparison. Noah will figure out I'm a driftless loser one way or the other. Might as well take the fastest route to get there. Save him the time. "I like hearing you talk about your love for animals and how you always knew you wanted to be a vet..." My voice trails off.

Noah lifts his chin. "I'm sensing a *but* coming."

I blow out a heavy breath, my shoulders slumping forward. "But I've never experienced anything like what you have. I've never had that one all-consuming passion when it comes to a career," I confess. "I've spent my whole life trying things, pulling all of these threads apart, but I'm almost thirty years old, and all I'm left with is a bunch of messy yarn and no way of weaving it back together."

I can tell I've made shit real heavy real fast by how Noah's face has grown serious. His jaw twitches tightly.

"I'm—I'm a chameleon." I practically spit *that* word out. Daniel spent years using it against me, and even though he's long gone, now I'm the one using it against myself.

Noah starts to speak, his voice low and full of caring. "Being a chameleon can be a good thing. It means you can adjust to things. You're flexible. Those are good qualities to have."

I shrug. "Yeah, it can be. Or it means I'm wishy-washy and can't settle on any one thing."

Noah's eyes roam my face. "What do you mean?"

"I mean, I completed my first degree. It took four years, I racked up a bucket load of student debt, and then what do I do once I graduate? Absolutely nothing. I didn't pursue a career. I went traveling instead."

"What was your degree in, what field of study?"

I wave my hand in the air. "It's stupid." I can feel my face flushing.

"You don't have to tell me," Noah says, and there's something about the way he says it that makes me feel that he means it.

Somehow, him being so understanding makes me want to tell him. "Biochemistry."

Noah makes a face. "Holy shit. That is literally the opposite of stupid. That's freaking hard. You have to be genius-level smart to even get accepted to study that."

"Yeah, well, not all blonds are dumb." The joke is weak, and I wince internally the second I say it.

Noah cups his hand over mine on the table. "I haven't once for a second thought you're dumb." His touch is warm and just the right kind of comfort I need right now.

"What made you want to study biochemistry?" he asks, pulling his hand away way, *way* too soon.

"Don't really know. I was good at science in high school. Looking at compounds and how they can combine to make all sorts of new things interested me, so I thought, why not? In terms of post-study career options, though, nothing really appealed to me. I don't want to teach, and I don't want to spend my life stuck in a lab. So I drifted for a couple of years, traveling, doing odd jobs..."

We both smile at that.

"So, what made you decide to go back and study performing arts, no less?"

A noisy breath whistles out of his lips. "My ex, Daniel, pushed me into it. Albeit unwillingly. He was the one who called me a chameleon. He used to joke that I was so good at being a million different people that I'd make a good actor. I performed in a few plays in high school, liked it, so again, I thought, why not?"

Noah's face has grown even more serious now. It takes me a moment to realize I'd slipped an ex into the conversation. Damn. I didn't mean to do that. I untie my hair and run my fingers through it.

Noah leans in closer, his eyes fluttering in the dim light. "How do you always smell so damn good?"

I snigger, gratefully jumping on the topic-detour-express. "I might tell you one day," I reply coyly.

He smiles again. It's warm and friendly, and it makes me realize that there's something happening between us. What it is, I don't know, but there's definitely an energy swirling around us. The more time we spend together, the stronger it gets.

"What do your parents do for a living?" he asks, taking a sip of water.

I brace against the back of the booth. "My father's a lawyer. He works for our family's legal firm, Adams & Daughters."

Noah grins. "I like that name."

"I do, too. It makes sense. The women on my dad's side of the family have always outnumbered the men. He's one of four kids and the only boy."

"Has there been any pressure on you to follow in his footsteps?"

I shake my head, feeling my hair flowing around my face. "None at all. Dad has been amazing. So supportive." I pause for a few seconds as something sharp lodges in the back of my throat. "Maybe too supportive."

Noah lifts a brow. "Oh?"

There it is again, another one of his gentle invitations, letting me know he's keen to know more, without making it feel like he's pressuring me for a response. The topic-detour-express is now passing territory that I've only ever ventured into with my very closest friends and loved ones. I trust Noah, I do, but I'm not ready to tell him about my mom just yet. So I tell him more about my father instead.

"Dad's the kind of dad that when I was a kid, if I expressed even the slightest interest in something, he'd be behind it straight away. Like this one time, we were on a family holiday in Hawaii, and I was captivated watching the surfers, so he organized for me to take surfing lessons. When I mentioned I'd like to try playing the guitar, he went out and bought me one. When I needed shoes for track practice, he got me the best, most expensive running shoes."

"It sounds like he's a great dad."

"He is," I say with a fond smile. "He really is, but—and I know I may sound like a total douchebag here—the downside of having a dad who so fervently supported anything I wanted to do was that, well, it's left me not knowing what I really want to do."

Guilt washes over me. I know how terrible what I'm saying must sound, but Noah's just sitting here, listening to me. It feels like he's trying to understand me. I'm not picking up on any judgy vibes from him.

"It's those threads I mentioned before, you know," I continue. "I'd have all of these interests or things I'd pluck at, try for a while, before moving on to something else. I never stuck with anything."

Noah sways gently, taking it all in. "What about your current studies? Do you want to be a performer?"

I shrug my shoulders. "I guess I do. I'm good-ish at it. It's fun. I suppose I should finally stick to something, right?"

Noah smiles, but his lips remain tight.

"Sometimes I wish that Dad was a bit firmer with me. Because while it's great that he always had my back and encouraged me to try new things, he never made me stick to things, either. If I got bored or lost interest in something, he was fine with that, too."

I take a breath. "I feel like a total dick for saying all of this to you because I don't even want to think about how much money he spent on me. Believe me, I know how fortunate and privileged and lucky I am to have a dad that loves me so much and was able to afford to support all my whims. But at the same time, I'm approaching thirty, and I feel lost."

A silence settles between us. I guess that was a lot to dump on the guy. More than I'd expected to reveal.

"Three things," Noah says, lifting three fingers. "One. You're not a douchebag or a dick for saying any of this. It sounds like your dad loves you very much and did his best. At the same time, it's okay for you to say that despite that, maybe he didn't give you the guidance or the discipline that you may have needed from him. It's not a negative reflection on either one of you."

I feel a bit better. "Okay."

"Two." Noah leans in closer. "No one says you can only have one dream. There are no rules about these sorts of things. Personally, I think it's good to try your hand at a range of things. It makes a person well-rounded. You've taken time to explore different things. That's never a bad thing."

"But time is running out," I counter. "I'm almost thirty years old. That's, like, Hollywood forty and gay fifty."

He chuckles. "And that brings me to my third and final point before I vacate my position atop this soapbox." He pauses, his eyes catching my small smile. "It's never too late. I don't know anything about how Hollywood works, obviously, but when I turned thirty, guess what happened the next day?"

I cock my head to the side. "What?"

"Nothing," he exclaims with an exaggerated lilt. "I woke up, and the sky hadn't fallen down. The sun was still shining. Life went on as normal. These days, thirty, forty, even fifty, aren't the old ages that maybe they used to be. I was reading an article the other day about a woman who was going to college at the age of eighty-two. You still have your whole life ahead of you. We both do."

I take some time, not saying anything, just considering his words. I can feel the rightness of them, but I can't expect one conversation to overcome years of doubt and feeling bad. It has helped, though. A lot. More than he can possibly realize.

"Thank you." It comes out quietly.

I still can't believe I told him all of this. Maybe it's my way of preempting things. The harshness of my ex's words still stings. I never want anyone to hurl them in my face again. By being upfront with Noah like this, at least he knows the weakest part of me right from the start.

He covers a yawn.

"Big day?" I ask, knowing the answer. The man's schedule has been beyond hectic.

He nods. "Big few days, actually."

"Another drink?"

I don't really feel like one, and I doubt that Noah does either, but I don't want this night to end just yet. Despite the unexpected heaviness of the conversation, I'm having a really good time being here with him.

"Thank you, but no." He palms my shoulder. "I should probably get going."

"Yeah. Of course," I reply, drawing on my acting skills to hide my disappointment.

"Come back with me," Noah says, seemingly startling himself as much as me, judging by the bewildered look crossing his face. "I mean, I'm exhausted, but we can hang out if you like. Have you ever watched *This Pet's Got Talent?*"

I shake my head. "No."

A smile lights up Noah's eyes. "It's an amazing talent competition. All done ethically and to ensure that absolutely no stress is put on the animals involved, but man, some of the things those pets can do. It's unbelievable."

You're unbelievable, I feel like saying. Instead, I nod. "I'd love to see it."

"All right, let's go."

"Wait." I grab his arm. "Before we go, there's something I need to say."

Noah stops and looks at me. "Okay?"

"I didn't say it at lunch, and I've been kicking myself all day about it."

Noah clasps his hand on mine again. "What is it?"

"When you said that you liked me over lunch, I never got a chance to tell you that...I like you, too."

I feel Noah's fingers squeeze around mine. "I'm glad."

And with a gentle desire simmering in my belly, we get up, and I follow Noah out of the bar, retracing the steps we took all those many months ago back to his place.

11

NOAH

"Now I have to warn you again," I mention as we approach my front door. "I'm not sure if you remember my overly friendly golden retriever, Buddy?"

Haze flashes me a wide grin. "How could I ever forget him? How's he doing?"

"The rate of his vision deterioration seems to be slowing, so that's a good thing."

"It is."

"But his rate of lickiness has only increased, I'm afraid."

Haze utters the same words he did last time I gave him a similar warning. "I'm down for a good licking."

This time, though, it's him closing the distance between us as he steps in to kiss me. It's soft at first, just lips on lips. I like how easy and natural this feels, but I'm taken aback by the deep well of need that it unleashes in me.

A moan oozes out of my mouth. Haze's hands find the small of my back, and he presses our bodies even closer. His hands travel up and down my arms, his grip firm as he sinks his fingers into my biceps. He seems to like them, which shoots a jolt of electricity straight to my cock. I can feel it filling out my underwear.

His tongue slides into my mouth, exploring me as his movements become more urgent. But Haze isn't the only one getting impatient. I pull away as Buddy claws at the door desperately. "Can we continue this later?" I ask.

Haze pulls back, his eyes heavy with desire, his lips kiss-swollen. "Yeah. Definitely."

I open the door, and as expected, we're greeted by a tornado of excited, happy slurps. I feel guilty Buddy spends so much time alone. I'd love to get him a companion dog, but whatever has happened in his past has left him unable to cope well in the company of other dogs. I have a few local dog sitters on rotation to take Buddy to the local park at least twice a day when I'm working crazy long hours.

We amble inside and flop down onto the couch, Buddy

positioning himself in prime position right in the middle between us. "Can I get you anything to drink? Some water, maybe?"

"I'm all good," Haze says, kicking off his shoes, leaving his socks on.

I do the same, and despite having an over-excited retriever situated between us, our feet touch. Haze smiles sweetly when I rub the top of his foot with the underside of mine. I'm glad to see him relax a bit now that we're here. The conversation at the bar took a few unexpected turns, and I can see it affected him.

I'm glad he shared what he did, even though it's brought up a slew of new questions for me. He only mentioned his dad and never once said anything about his mom. I wonder if maybe his parents divorced when he was young or if there's some other reason he didn't mention her. I never pry. That's not my style. If and when he's ready to share, I'll be here.

It also pained me to hear about the struggle he's been having choosing a career. I can't relate to that at all since my own experience has been so different, but it's clear he wants to find what he's meant to be doing with his life. I know he'll figure it out. I just hope he's kind to himself in the meantime.

I bring up the first episode of last season's *This Pet's Got Talent* and find myself explaining the rules to him. The show basically follows a bunch of vets who travel the country and visit people who have submitted their pets for consideration based on some unique or interesting talent they have. It's not like a typical reality-style TV show in that it's not really a competition and there's no manufactured drama, either.

I explain to Haze the reasons why the vets spend so much time with the owners and the animals. It's mainly to make sure the owners aren't mistreating their animals in any way to get them to do whatever cool trick they can do. Haze lets me talk, casually stroking Buddy's sandy mane and shooting me an occasional glance that sends hot sparks of desire racing through me.

After two episodes, I decide it's time to call it a night. For

Buddy, that is. I excuse myself, and we go through our usual nighttime ritual. He goes outside to potty. I bring him in and clean his face and paws with a damp washcloth before he drops onto his bed. I scratch the top of his head and behind his ears until his breathing deepens and his eyes fall shut.

When I return to the living room, Haze has slid down the couch, and if I'm not mistaken, he's fallen asleep, too. I stand there, watching his chest rise and fall, his hair messily scattered across his beautiful face. He looks so peaceful I don't want to disturb him. An excited roar from the TV stirs him, and he props himself up against the armrest.

He spots me staring at him and grins sheepishly. "Guess I'm a bit tired, too. I haven't been sleeping well since I got back."

"You're welcome to crash here tonight," I suggest. "I have a spare room."

I don't know if he realizes he's doing it, but his head shakes at the idea.

"Or you can sleep in my room." I join him on the couch. "To sleep, that is."

"Are there any other bed-related activities on offer?" All of a sudden, Haze looks wide awake.

I chuckle, weaving my fingers through my hair. "There could be."

"I'm an experienced bed tester," Haze reminds me.

I love how he makes me laugh. "I am tired, though, so you'll have to take it easy on me."

"Don't know if I can promise that."

"What can you promise?"

In seconds, he propels himself from where he was sitting to straddling me, his feet falling over the edge of the couch behind him. "This."

He cups my head in his hands and smashes our lips together. I crash into his force, our tongues tangling fiercely. Haze palms the outline of my cock, and without hesitation, I do the same to him.

"Wow," I say.

He smirks. "It's still as spectacular as ever."

"I wasn't talking about your cock." I smile against his lips.

He pulls away, his hair falling down, the silky soft tips tickling my cheeks. "What were you talking about then?"

"This. You. Me. Again."

Somehow, he understands what I mean even though I've been reduced to one-word sentences.

"It's pretty crazy, huh?"

I don't respond. Instead, I run my hand inside his shirt, up his chest until... "Oh, shit."

His eyes flare. "Uh, yeah. I got it done in London."

I trail my fingers from his left nipple to the right. "Both?"

He closes his eyes and nods as I run my fingers gently over the bar piercing. When he opens his eyes, I ask, "Is this okay?"

I feel the tremors that quiver the insides of his thighs against my own legs. I gently move him off me and position him down on the couch, peeling off his shirt in one smooth movement. His chest is as glorious as I remember it, his muscles lean and tight, his skin glowing with a late summer tan. The only discernible differences are the two silver bars pierced into his nipples.

"I've always had sensitive nipples," Haze informs me as he brings my fingers to his mouth. He sticks his tongue out and gently laps against the tips of them. He then lowers my wet fingertips to his nipples and moans at the contact. I'm transfixed by the pleasure this simple touch brings to him, as well as by the way he's using my body to make himself feel so good.

I grip his shoulders, laying him down onto the couch, and drop to my knees beside him. I smooth my hands across his chest, trailing over his hip bones, skimming the tight divots of his abs. Leaning over his chest, I form an O shape with my lips. With no warning, I gently blow at his left nipple first before moving to the right.

"Holy fuck," Haze shrieks, his head falling back. "How are you—" He jerks his head down to see what I'm doing.

A few moments later, I stop fanning his nipples to answer his unasked question. "It's something I picked up from this guy I had a one-night stand with. Do you like it?"

"Fuck yeah."

I've never heard Haze's voice sound so guttural before.

"You know, I can come just from nipple play," he reveals.

The need in his voice infuses into me, releasing fireworks in my belly.

"Is that a challenge?"

He smirks, looking down at me. "It can be. If you're not too tired, that is?"

I feel like I've just shot back ten espressos. "I'm a lot of things right now." I lower my voice, my lips hovering over his chest. "But tired is not one of them."

His long fingers wrap around the back of my neck, and he pulls me into him, my tongue lapping at his sensitive skin, aiming a series of targeted flicks at the metal bar. Haze is writhing underneath me, and it's the hottest feeling in the world, knowing I'm responsible for eliciting this response from him. I unzip my pants to free my own aching cock. I've been working so much I can't even remember the last time I jacked off. The hot, swollen flesh feels good in my hand.

"Can I bite them?" I ask.

I can see Haze's head bob up and down, but I wait for him to say yes. And hopefully provide some guidance. I've never been with a guy who has such sensitive nipples. I wonder if mine are. Up until this moment, I can't say I've given it a lot of thought.

"Yes." Haze fills the silence. "Just be gentle... At first, anyway."

"Of course." My breath stutters in my throat as I manage to catch the word *baby* before it tumbles out of me.

I spend the next few minutes—Hours? Days? I don't give even the remotest shit about time right now—circling, nibbling, munching, and devouring Haze's nipples. I've never spent so much time and energy on such a small, focused part of a man's body before. It's arousing as hell, and I continue jerking myself off. I keep reminding myself to slow my movements down. I don't want either one of us coming until every single detail of Haze's nipples are emblazoned into my memory forever.

I can sense Haze is getting closer, though. His cock sticks out from below his taut stomach. His balls, heavy and full, are bundled tight against his body. I've never seen so much precome streaming out of a cock in my life. He makes the few droplets of come beaded at the head of my cock look like a leaky faucet compared to his Niagara Falls. The clear liquid dribbles down his shaft and pools in the thick patch of pubic hair at the base, making the ashy tips twinkle in the soft light.

He said he can come from nipple play alone. A spark shudders through my cock as I try to visualize what that would look like. I've never seen any kind of hands-free orgasm. I always thought there had to be at least some touch, some friction.

As I continue lapping at his purple nubs, his body rocks, and his lower back twists off the couch.

"More! Harder!"

He's begging now, reduced to a writhing mess as my fingers join my tongue, pinching, stroking, twisting, and tweaking the life out of his hardened nipples. When Haze's body crashes back onto the sofa again, I turn my head just in time to catch the release spilling out of him. Rope after rope of cream drizzles his stomach and chest as his groans fill my ears, encouraging me to follow suit.

I dip my fingers into his release and drench my cock with it, using it as lube. It only takes a few short seconds as my body starts to rock. I feel Haze's fingers cup my face, his plump lips meeting mine as my orgasm washes over me.

I surrender to the blissfulness of it, letting myself ride the waves until they subside. My eyes are squeezed shut, but Haze's lips are still on mine, his smell inside my head, his panting in my ears, his come coating my cock. My senses have never been this overloaded, and I never want this sensation to subside. I don't want to move or open my eyes, afraid this will all have been some sort of splendid dream.

"Are you all right?"

Haze's words break the spell, but at least they confirm that this is indeed real. What we did, did in fact just happen. Nothing can take that away.

I blink my eyes open. My gaze rests on his face: his sweat-drenched forehead, the simmering heat still in his eyes, the gentle upward curve playing at the corners of his mouth.

"You came?" he asks, brushing the backs of his fingers along my cheekbone.

I nod. "Yeah."

"I wish you hadn't. I wanted to make you come."

"Next time?"

He grabs hold of my shirt sleeve, lazily thumbing it. "Yes. But I still feel bad. I want to do something for you."

"Oh, believe me, you have. I don't think I'm ever going to forget how amazing it was to see you come like that. That's crazy. I always thought hands-free orgasms were an urban legend."

I give him a quick kiss. He just smiles, still in a post-sex daze. "Nope. Very real thing."

"I think you should come with a warning," I quip.

"Oh, yeah. And what kind of warning would that be?"

I think about it for a moment. "The warning would read, *Caution: One time is never enough.*"

He throws his head back, laughing. "You make me sound like I'm a drug."

In a way, he is. I can so easily see myself falling for him, becoming addicted to him. His body. His touch. His smell.

"I want to do something for you," he says, his voice raspy. "That was incredible for me. Name it. What do you want from me?"

I tap my finger against his chest. The question leaves my lips without me realizing. "Will you be my date to Gus' wedding?"

12

HAZE

It's a week after my mind-blowing nipple-gasm with Noah, Thursday to be exact, and things are going well. The semester is back in full swing, and I'm excited that it's my final year of study. I still have no clue what I want to do after college, but I have the better part of a year to figure it out.

The training wheels have come off at work. Harmony was an amazing instructor, and because of that, I'm now able to handle the front desk on my own. I unlock the front door and step inside, quickly turning off the alarm code before it starts blaring. I dump my satchel in a locker in the changing room and give myself a quick once-over in the mirror. The puffy bags that found a home under my eyes since returning from London have packed up and moved on. That night I stayed at Noah's was the best night's sleep I'd had in a long time, and it finally cured me of the remaining jet lag.

I smile as I wander down the hallway to the reception area. Thinking about Noah always makes me smile. There's so much I like about the guy that it's kinda hard not to. Let's start with the sex. Holy Jesus fuck. That man has got one seriously talented tongue. When I'd told him that I was able to come just from nipple play, I meant that was how *I* could get myself off. No one else had ever been able to do that for me. Noah took it as a challenge, though, and I am very happy to report it was one that he succeeded at.

Then there's how nice and decent a person he is. I know *nice* and *decent* don't have the same ring as say, *bad boy biker* or *tortured tattoo artist with a hidden heart of gold*, but I've never been attracted to those types of guys. Noah is living proof that a nice guy can be every bit as hot as the stereotypical bad boy.

He mentioned that I should come with a warning label. Yeah, well, so should he. Watching him this past week being friendly to the people he works with, caring about what clients are going through as they bring their pets in to see him, genuinely taking an interest in what's going on around him. Screw heroin, *those* qualities are seriously addictive.

I also need to briefly pay tribute to the man's appearance. He looks the part of the handsome vet to a tee. With his checkered shirts that he sometimes folds the sleeves up on to reveal his lightly hairy forearms—as well as a certain tan leather bracelet—the white lab coat that drapes his strong, broad shoulders, the tight pants he wears that encase his thick, trunk-like legs, and a meaty ass that feels like it's practically begging me to tear into it with my fingers... Or my tongue. I don't mind which.

Finally, there's him inviting me to Gus' wedding. That was unexpected, in the best possible way. It's kinda obvious that we've moved on from the one-night stand category, but it isn't clear where that leaves us. We're colleagues now, so we see each other most days, and we hang out at the bar a few times a week, too. But that only puts us in colleague-land which is still, unfortunately, a few towns over from boyfriend-ville.

And is that where I want things to go with Noah?

...Yeah. It is.

The computer is booting up when the bell above the door chimes. I don't even have to look up to know who it is. "Hello, beautiful people." I chuckle at the excessively loud and over the top entrance Gus makes every Thursday morning. Today, though, in addition to the tray of drinks he's carrying for staff, he's got a certain sexy someone by his side.

"G'morning."

That one simple word from Noah is all it takes for a zap of heat to race up my spine.

"Hello." I greet both men as Gus hands me my almond latte.

"It's Thirsty Thursdaaaay," he roars, giving what is essentially the gay, white, male version of Oprah Winfrey belting out her infamous "You get a car, and you get a car" bit.

"Thanks." I chuckle. "It's a good thing no one is here yet because I have to tell you something."

Gus stops and looks at me. "Yeah?"

I take a quick sip of my coffee, trying to figure out a nice way to put it. The guy is my boss and all, so I have to be tactful. "Um, please don't take this the wrong way, but do you know what Thirsty Thursday actually means?"

Noah barks out a laugh at my question as he and Gus exchange a knowing look. They're friends, and I've noticed they do that a lot. They've developed their own language, their own inside jokes over time. It's nice to see, but I'm clearly missing something here.

Gus turns back to me and says, "Thank you for letting me know." Then his eyes twinkle mischievously as he adds, "Oh, and for the hundred millionth time, can I just say how happy I am that you'll be at my wedding next weekend?"

I laugh. Gus has mentioned it a few...hundred times this past week. And with that, he disappears down the hallway, leaving Noah and me alone.

Noah leans against the counter, his head tipping ever so slightly in my direction. His eyes flicker shut. "What are you—?"

"Patchouli," I answer, assuming he's asking me about my fragrance.

His lips curve up as he shoots me a coy look from behind his thick lashes. "You always smell so damn good. It's..."

"Addictive?"

My heart is thundering in my chest. Frustratingly, Noah and I still hardly ever get any time alone at the clinic, so whenever we do, I hardcore flirt with the guy. What can I say? I like him, and for the first time in longer than I can remember, a feeling has settled in the pit of my stomach. A feeling that's telling me to just go for it.

Noah looks over his shoulder toward the door. It's still early, and his first scheduled appointment isn't for another ten minutes, but that doesn't mean we won't get interrupted by an emergency. As I've discovered working here for the past few weeks, things can go from calm to crazy in the blink of an eye.

His lips twitch. "What are you doing tomorrow night?"

I take another sip of my coffee, eying him. If I didn't know any better, I'd say the guy was a little nervous. I continue with my flirting game. "Dunno," I say with a cheeky grin. "What am I doing tomorrow night?"

His shoulders fall, and the tension across his face eases. He smiles. "Going out on a date with me...I hope?" Once the words leave his lips, he brings up a single red rose to the counter. My eyes shift between his face and the flower. It's such a simple gesture, but man, it feels so freaking amazing.

"A date?" I take the flower from him and bring it to my nose. A delicate rose scent wafts in the air. "Wait, aren't I already going with you to Gus' wedding?"

"Yes, you are. But I've been thinking about it and..." He pauses. "I'd like it if our first date was just us and not at someone's wedding. It's silly, I know—"

"It's not silly. I think it's nice."

Noah breathes out. "Good. Because I'd really like to get to know you better."

I'm smiling so hard, swirling the thornless stem between my fingers. "I'd like that, too."

We fall silent for a few beats. He swallows, and I can see his Adam's apple jouncing in his throat. "I should get ready for my first appointment. Might see you later?"

"Sure thing."

The rest of the morning goes by uneventfully, but the smile that fills my face doesn't fade for a moment. I spend the entire shift feeling like I'm floating on air. Because I had an early start, my workday is over by lunch time. Noah's should be as well—I've pretty much committed his schedule to memory at this point—but as I walk into the staff lounge, I see him standing over the sink, scarfing down a salad. He's still wearing his white overcoat.

"What are you doing?" I ask him.

He finishes chewing his food and swipes the back of his hand across his lips. "Sorry, I'm eating like a pig."

"I wasn't talking about that. I mean, why aren't you leaving? You should be finishing right about now, yeah?"

He gives a clipped nod. "Yeah. Keyword: *should* be. We're short-staffed, and Fulton's surgery ran into some unexpected complications, so he's still in theater, which means someone has to cover his afternoon consultations. It's no big deal."

"Hey." My hand rests on his arm. "It is a big deal. You've been working nonstop. Please make sure you look after yourself, too."

He runs his plate under the water. "Long hours are a part of being a vet. If I wanted to have a nine to five job where I could leave the office right on the dot, I'd be an accountant or something."

He's drying his hands on a dishcloth when I walk up so I'm standing right behind him. He turns around, and we're face to face. I'm using all of my self-control to keep my arms by the sides of my body, even though every cell in me wants to run them up and down his chest.

Whatever I was about to say flies out of my mind, melted by the heated look Noah is pinning me with. He glances over to the door, before pulling me in for a kiss. It's quick and rough and urgent. I close my eyes and kiss him back just as hard. When we pull apart, the skin around his lips is wearing a rosy hue, a remnant of my stubble. I trace my fingers along it.

"Thank you. I appreciate your concern. And thank you for that kiss. That will definitely keep me going for the rest of the day. I might need a top-up tomorrow, though."

I chuckle. "Good thing you'll be seeing me tomorrow night then."

"Good thing, indeed."

~

"The article was brutal," Aunt Jocelyn scoffs.

She's sitting on the couch across from Dad and me in her office, the ice cubes in her drink rattling noisily.

"What article are you talking about, Aunt Jocelyn?" I ask.

"The society ball fundraiser," she answers with an exaggerated eye roll. "The article called me tired and shrill-looking. How does someone *look* shrill?" she asks, sounding both unimpressed and, not that I'd ever point it out to her, shrill.

She doesn't wait for either one of us to answer. "That reporter, Bill Bailey, is a misogynistic pig who has it in for successful women who commit the cardinal sin of turning fifty." She takes a big gulp of her whiskey before continuing. "I swear to god, middle-aged men who look like Walmart catalogue model rejects have no place running the media, much less criticizing women for how they look."

"Hey, I'm a middle-aged man," Dad points out.

"You're not a prick," Aunt Jocelyn counters.

Dad chuckles. "I'll take that as a compliment."

"Next year," Aunt Jocelyn points a perfectly manicured finger at Dad, "you can represent the company at the gala. You'll be able to wear an ill-fitting suit, gain thirty pounds, lose all your hair, and they'll still call you 'an esteemed senior member of the Adams & Daughters law firm.'"

"Is it really that bad?" I ask.

"It's worse. A woman in her fifties just can't win. If I get any work done on my face, I'm desperately clinging to my youth. If I don't do anything, I'm tired and shrill-looking, apparently. If I speak up at a meeting, I'm difficult. If I negotiate too hard, I'm a bitch. And if, on the odd occasion, I lose, I'm considered weak and not up to the task."

Aunt Jocelyn jangles her now empty glass toward me. "Hazey baby, Aunty Jocelyn needs a refill."

I top up her glass. Dad and I are sticking to water since it's only four in the afternoon, while we patiently sit and listen to Aunt Jocelyn rampaging against sexism in the media. Once she's done, I sit up straighter and square my shoulders. "Can I ask you guys something?"

"Of course," Dad replies. "What is it, son?"

I smile at him. We really look nothing alike. Apparently, I got my looks from my mom. Dad has a friendly round face, big brown eyes, and thick brown hair that's only now starting to be infused with some gray.

"Okay, this is a dumb question, I know—"

"There's no such thing," Dad cuts in warmly.

"I know, but this one kinda is."

Tate's advice from a couple of weeks back is still playing on my mind a lot, and if there's anyone I trust for guidance, it's my dad and Aunt Jocelyn. "You know how people say you should follow your heart?"

I see them both nodding. "Well, I guess my question is, how do you actually do that?"

"What do you mean?" Aunt Jocelyn leans forward, resting her drink on the coffee table.

"Well, I agree that it sounds like good advice, but I'm a little stuck on the practical side of things."

There's a moment of silence, before Aunt Jocelyn starts speaking. "At the risk of getting a little too deep for a Thursday afternoon, life isn't about goals, Hazey," she begins softly. "It's like that expression. Humans make plans, and God laughs. Just relax a little, loosen up, and keep on being you. Go with your gut. It'll never steer you wrong. Trust me. Life has a way of making everything fall into place, and things you couldn't have even imagined end up unfolding right in front of you."

There's something about not just what she said, but how she said it, that hits me with a surprising force. I want to ask her more, but Dad starts talking.

"I agree with Jocelyn, son. Don't just focus on external things. Find the feeling, the thing that makes you tingly. That's the sign you're on the right path."

"Tingly?" A smile rises on Aunt Jocelyn's face. "I wouldn't put it in such sappy terms, but I do agree with your father agreeing with me."

All three of us fall quiet until Dad asks, "How's college?"

"It's going well," I reply quickly and silently hope that Dad's question is both the beginning and the end of the conversation about my studies. I know it's a slippery slope into a discussion about my future and, specifically, what I want to do with it. A well-intentioned slippery slope, but still.

"I've actually been in touch with an old friend of mine, Lyon Mandel," he continues.

Aunt Jocelyn tilts her head. "Didn't he go off to L.A. to become some hotshot producer?"

"Exactly." Dad's beaming at me, and I feel like I'm missing something. "He asked to see some of your headshots. Do you have any?"

"Uh, yeah," I reply, cautiously. "I had some taken when I was in London."

"Great. Email them to me, and I'll pass them on to Lyon. He's got a few projects on the go, so you never know what could happen."

"Sure thing. Thanks, Dad."

Aunt Jocelyn starts telling Dad about a difficult client she's dealing with, which allows me to tune out of the conversation. The idea of going off to Hollywood or anywhere else fills me with a low-level dread. I'd miss out on spending time with my family. I'd have to leave Tate, our housemates, and all my friends behind. And I'd have to say goodbye to Noah. I know that whatever is happening with us is only in its early stages, but that just means it's way too soon for it to be ending.

Dad's phone rings, and he excuses himself to take the call. Aunt Jocelyn gets up and drops down onto the couch beside me. "Honey," she says delicately. "I don't mean to upset you, but I want to ask. Your birthday is coming up, so I was wondering if there's anything you want to do?"

I force a smile. "No. Thank you."

Most people don't like birthdays because it's a reminder they're growing older. I don't care about that. I have a much bigger reason for hating the day. "Well, look, if you want to do something small, family only, you just let me know. Okay?"

"Thanks, Aunt Jocelyn. I appreciate it."

She smiles and pats me on my knee. This whole conversation leaves me feeling a funny sort of way, like the tectonic plates of my life are shifting. I just can't quite figure out what the cause of it is. Maybe it's not one big thing, but a whole bunch of little things. As I head home later that evening, I still haven't gotten any closer to figuring things out.

13

NOAH

I manage to leave the clinic on time for a change, which is a good thing. There's no way I want to be late for my first proper date with Haze.

I rush back home to spend some time with Buddy. He doesn't like playing catch anymore. He loses track of the ball, and it unsettles him. He just likes the company, so I simply sit on my back steps and watch Buddy trotting around, happily sniffing everything he can put his nose to.

My thoughts drift to Haze, and I smile. It's funny—when I think about it, everything we've done so far has been kinda back to front. I mean, he was inside of me before I knew his last name. It was only meant to be a one-time thing, and yet even the next day over breakfast, I felt a twinge for something more with him. Then he left the country for six months, and I thought that was it. I'd never see him again. Only for Gus to end up hiring him at the clinic and now we're going on a date.

None of this makes any sense, and yet, at the same time, it feels so right. My attraction to Haze runs deeper than superficial things like his appearance or heavenly scent. He's stirred a curiosity in me. I want to keep finding out more about him, unravel all the pieces that make him who he is. I feel so good when I'm around him, even briefly at work, that I just want to spend more time with the guy. It's exciting, but also a little scary. I haven't felt this way in a very long time.

Buddy plonks himself at my feet. I scratch all of his favorite spots, and he reciprocates with his usual tongue bath in return. I make sure to shower extra thoroughly to get all remnants of him off me. The warm water sluices over my tired, aching muscles. I've been working a lot lately, even by my own standards. Haze is right, I do need to make sure I'm looking after myself. My cock perks up at the mere mention of Haze.

My fingers wrap around my thickening base, and I give it a few tugs. Should I jerk off now to lower my sexual appetite a bit? I've made a reservation at a nice, quiet restaurant by the pier, and I thought if it's still light out when we finish, we could maybe go for a walk along the promenade. Maybe I should pre-jerk off. I'd like to spend at least a portion of the evening on gentlemanly terms.

It's decided then. With one hand working my shaft and the other drifting around to my ass, I shut my eyes and imagine Haze in here with me, running his hands over his smooth chest, playing with his pierced nipples until I make his head drop back. I'd bite into the cords of his throat so hard it leaves marks. Then he'd spin me around, drop to his knees, spread my ass, and tongue-dive into me, driving me wild as he laps at my hole. *Fuck!* My knees tremble as rope after rope of creamy liquid spurts out onto the tiled wall. I finish showering, get dressed, and then spend a few more minutes with Buddy before heading out.

I spot Haze already waiting as I approach the restaurant and silently pat myself on the back for pre-jerking off because if I hadn't, all I'd be seeing is the way his white shirt clings tightly to his chest and the way his black pants hug his round ass. Okay, so I still *see* all of those things, but my urge to jump his bones is a notch or two lower.

"Hello."

"Hi." He shuffles on his feet before giving me a quick peck on the cheek.

"You look beautiful."

He blushes. "Thanks. You're not so bad yourself."

We get seated at a nice table right next to the window, giving us a great view of the people passing by.

"I love people-watching," Haze says excitedly, his eyes already scanning the view.

"Oh, yeah?"

He nods. "I love to create backstories for people. Like, see that young couple over there?" I turn to where he's pointing and see an attractive young couple, walking hand in hand.

"Uh-huh."

"Well, she's clearly more into him than he's into her."

I squint to get a better look. "She's leaning into his touch too much. He's looking around, assessing his options. She's madly in love with him, and he's thinking about finding a girl who's into butt stuff."

We both laugh. "Okay, your turn."

"My turn? For what?"

"Pick someone and make up a story for them."

I glance around. There's plenty of people to choose from strolling on the promenade. People are walking their dogs, jogging, and chatting with friends. "That guy," I say, pointing to a middle-aged guy who looks like an accountant. "He's an accountant," I start off saying, but I'm interrupted by an exaggerated yawn coming from Haze.

"Boring." He's baiting me, I can tell.

"You didn't let me finish." I conjure up all my creative juices and hope for the best. "He's a middle-aged accountant who leads a double life as a..."

Haze leans in closer, and my mind goes to shit. I've got nothing. Literally, nothing, so I just say the first thing I can think of.

"He's a kinky BDSM secret agent action hero."

Haze bursts out laughing. "Whoa. Sounds like he's got a lot going on, then."

"Oh, that's just the beginning." The more I play along with this, the more I find myself relaxing and easing into the conversation. That's the thing about being with Haze. Things always feel so easy, so right.

Once the story of our middle-aged accountant delves into paranormal territory, we call it quits. "Wow, I never thought of myself as the creative type," I observe with a chuckle.

Haze grins happily. "See, there you go. You learned something new about yourself."

I swipe my hand down the front of my shirt and look Haze straight in the eye. "Thank you."

"For what?"

"For agreeing to this date." Haze doesn't say anything, so I go on. "I've been thinking about you and me. How we met. How we're back in each other's lives now... I like being around you."

Our fingers meet in the middle of the table. "I feel exactly the same way."

"You do?"

Haze takes a sip of water. "Yeah. You, um, you do something funny to me."

"Well, I am kinda known for creating amazingly creative backstories about people I've never met."

Haze giggles, and it's the cutest sound I've ever heard. "What I'm trying to say is that when I'm around you, I feel good. I feel like I'm myself."

"That makes me happy."

It does. Especially after what he told me about his ex calling him a chameleon, and meaning it in a bad way, and the trouble he's had settling on a career. "I like that you feel like that with me," I add.

For the first time all evening, Haze turns serious. "It's a little weird, though."

"How do you mean?"

He's thinking about it. I can't tell if he's nervous to tell me or if he doesn't quite know for sure himself. He starts cautiously. "I don't know how much to say. I mean, I don't want you to think I'm some lunatic."

"Haze, I would never think that. And you don't have to tell me anything you don't want to. I'd never pressure you."

That seems to relax him a little. "Okay, thanks. It's just..." He blows out a heavy breath. "I guess the thing about being called a chameleon is that it affects your self-confidence. After a while, I started to believe it, and it was scary to think that I didn't know who I was. But with you, I don't know—I feel like I'm being me, but, like, new parts of me."

"Okay. I'm kind of following, but what do you mean by new parts of you?"

Haze pulls out a strand of hair and twirls it around his finger. "I mean, you bring things out in me. Like, I'm not usually so flirty. Or funny. But with you, I am those things."

I smile. "I have noticed that. You alternate in this really cool way between being out there and serving some serious sass, but then you also get all shy and super cute. I like that."

"Really?"

"Of course. Why wouldn't I?"

"You don't think I'm being disingenuous or fake?"

"I don't know. Are you being disingenuous or fake?"

"No, of course not."

His response is so sharp I can tell he's being honest. "So then, there's no problem, right? See, this is what I meant when I said being a chameleon can be a good thing. Sounds like you're discovering new sides to yourself. That's a wonderful thing."

"You're wonderful."

I feel my cheeks flame. "I mean it," he presses. "What Daniel said to me really messed me up. I don't think you realize how much you've helped me to see things differently. See myself differently."

"As long as you're real and honest and yourself, that's all that matters," I say.

After that, a silence wraps around us. We've fallen into more serious terrain again, which we have a habit of doing. I don't mind, though. We seem to be doing everything out of order. Besides, I'm thirty-four. I'm too old for bullshit and playing games. I want to get to know the real him, not the bullshit, surface-level stuff people usually share when they start seeing someone. I mean, if everyone's so down to earth and enjoys long walks on the beach, why is dating such a minefield? I value honesty and being real. With that in mind, I decide to break the silence.

"Since this is a first proper date, I suppose we should cover some first-date topics, right?"

Haze looks at me curiously. "Like what?"

"Well, you've mentioned your ex, Daniel, a couple of times. Should we start there?"

"Okay," he says slowly. "I'll tell you about my ex if you tell me about yours."

I grin and give a nod. "Deal."

"Daniel was my only long-term relationship. We were together for five years."

"Wow, that's a long time. My longest relationship was three years. When did you guys break up?"

"He broke up with me, geez..." Haze squints and looks up, counting the time in his head. "It'd be over a year and a half ago now."

"Can I ask why you broke up?"

Haze plays with his hair again. I'm starting to notice he does that whenever he's thinking about something. Or hesitant. "He broke up with me because he said that after five years, he didn't know who I was. That even I didn't know who I was. Apparently, I was so busy going along with things that I don't have my own opinions. That whole chameleon thing, that's actually the reason why he broke up with me."

"I'm sorry to hear that."

He shrugs. "He was partly right, but there was more to it than that. Our relationship wasn't working in other ways, either."

I don't say anything, not wanting to invade Haze's privacy. If he wants to tell me, he will. If not, I'm happy to move on to another topic.

"Daniel liked to criticize me for being a chameleon when it suited him. But he also benefited from it. We, uh, had an open relationship."

"Oh, that's cool," I say.

It's not something that would work for me, but I'd never judge others for how they have their relationships.

"No, it wasn't." Haze straightens as he speaks. "I went along with it, but it was never something that felt right for me. It's not what I would want in the future, either." He locks eyes with me when he says that part. "Daniel was a pilot, so he was away a lot, and I'm sure he had a different guy in every city. I did it because he wanted it, and it made him happy. But I never really liked it."

We both exhale at the same time. "Enough about me. Your turn, Noah."

I take a sip of water. "I've had three relationships, and they all ended for the same reason: something better came along."

I do my best to not sound too bitter or hurt as I take a deep dive into the shitshow that has been my love life.

"Michael was my first proper boyfriend. He and I dated in vet school. Once we graduated, he got a placement in South Africa."

"Ouch. Did you try the long-distance thing?"

I shake my head. "I wanted to, but he didn't. In the end, I think he was right. We were so young. It probably would've been more painful than anything else."

"Fair enough," Haze says softly.

"Dustin and I dated for three years. I was working in a clinic on the outskirts of Brookhaven, and he lived in the area. So did his mother. Now look, I love my family, and we're close. We're just not that close that we pop in three, four times a week. Every single week."

Haze snickers. "Yikes."

"Tell me about it. Yet when I pointed this out to him and suggested some boundaries, he created one. Between him and me. Even though I wasn't giving him an ultimatum, he chose his mother."

"Oh, man. That really sucks."

With a huff, I continue, eager to get this over and done with. "Last and definitely least was Graham. We were together for about eighteen months and broke up two and a half years ago. He, uh, he cheated on me."

"I am so sorry. That's horrible."

"Yeah, it is. I guess that's why I haven't dated since. I'm over it now, but I'm still a little...fragile."

"That's completely understandable," Haze says, and there's a soft, genuine smile blooming on his lips.

For some reason, it gives me hope. "Let's never talk about our exes again," I suggest.

Haze laughs. "Done and done!"

At some stage, I'm sure we ordered food and ate it, but I can't remember any of those details. I've been lost in Haze's eyes, his words, his heavenly smell for...holy shit! I look down at my watch. My eyes bulge.

"What is it?"

I look up at Haze. "We've been talking for four hours."

"Uh, yeah." He tips his head to the right. "Look around. We're the last people here."

Thankfully, there's still a little light left outside. "Wanna go for a walk?" I suggest.

Haze smiles. "Sure."

We begin our stroll along the promenade, the late summer air nipping at our thin jackets. "Can I?" I stop myself, suddenly shy for some reason.

"Can you what?"

"Can I hold your hand?"

Without saying a word, Haze entwines his fingers with mine. "I see you have no problem with being out in public," he observes.

"No. I don't. Are you okay with this?"

Haze swipes his thumb over the back of my hand. "I'm fine. I'm not into massive public displays of affection. But that's because that's just not my style. It has nothing to do with being gay. You know?"

"I do. I feel the same."

We smile and continue walking. "Your hands are cold," I say after a few moments. "I think we should warm them up."

A devilish expression lights up his face. "What did you have in mind?"

I try to suppress a smile. "There's a café over there. You up for some hot chocolate?"

"Always."

As we settle into a booth, sitting on the same side, our shoulders and legs touching, I take a sip and savor not just the warm drink, but the moment, too. I wrap my arm around him, and Haze leans into my touch. He smells amazing as always. The slightly lemon-ginger scent wafts over from him and envelops me. It's a bubble I hope will never burst.

We've been talking about everything and nothing tonight. Haze has told me about his fiery Aunt Jocelyn, and she sounds like an incredible—and amusing—woman. He told me a bit more about London, how he liked the city but missed home too much to be able to live there long term. And it turns out he's a massive Beyoncé fan, and I ended up getting a very detailed account into her backstory and music catalogue.

I like listening to Haze talk, but there's been a question I've been meaning to ask. I don't know if there's ever a right time to bring up a difficult subject, but since we've already veered into murky territory once tonight when we drove down Ex-Boyfriend Boulevard, I'm hoping this next detour won't result in a head-on collision.

"How are things with you and your mom? I don't mean to pry. It's just that I've noticed you never talk about her, so I guess I'm just curious, is all. If you don't want to talk about it, please tell me. I won't push."

Haze stiffens under my touch. I release him, and he sits up a little taller, his fingers tapping against the side of his mug. I'm almost about to repeat that he doesn't have to tell me anything when his soft words fill the air. "My mom died right after giving birth to me."

I suck in a breath as pain burrows in my chest. "Oh, Haze. I am so sorry."

He nods, his eyes locked straight ahead. This totally explains why he's never brought her up, and now I feel even worse for being the one to do it. If I had known, there is no way I ever would have mentioned her.

"It was a heart attack." Haze turns to me, and I can see the pain etched in his face. "She suffered a massive cardiac arrest after giving birth, and even though she was in a hospital, the doctors weren't able to revive her."

Tears well in his eyes.

"I'm really sorry." I know I'm repeating myself, but what else is there to say?

"My family came together and really supported Dad and me. Mom was an only child, but Dad has three older sisters. Having them, and my grandparents, made things easier." He stops, the pain etched across his face. "Even though I didn't know her, I still miss her."

"Of course, that's perfectly understandable."

I blink a couple of times, and then the urge to ask a totally random question strikes me. "What was your mom's name?"

His watery eyes stare at me. "Hazel."

I let out a deep breath I'd been holding since this conversation began. "That's—that's beautiful," I say. "That you share a name with her."

There's a bit of both happiness and sadness in his smile. "Aunt Jocelyn is the one who came up with the idea. Dad was a mess, obviously, and he and Mom hadn't picked out a name before I was born. They wanted to see me to get a feel for what name suited me. I think I was nameless for about a week, but then Aunt Jocelyn had a brainwave. Dad loved it, and so I became Haze."

"I've always thought it was a beautiful name, but now I love it even more."

"Thank you."

Haze leans back into me, and I reach around, stroking his hair. We sit like that for a while.

"It's getting late," I finally say, noticing the time on my cellphone.

"Yeah. It is."

Our eyes meet. "Wanna come back to my place?" I ask.

Haze buries his teeth into his lower lip and shakes his head. "No. I want you to come back to mine."

I must look surprised because Haze follows up with, "Why are you looking at me like that?"

"Well, uh, all this time, I've been under the impression that your place doesn't have walls."

Haze giggles. "That impression remains true. We don't have any walls. But I wanna show you something. You game?"

"Sure."

I pay for our drinks, and we walk out of the café, hand in hand, heading back to Haze's no-walls apartment.

14

HAZE

"Celebrity crush?" I ask Noah before quickly adding, "Oh, and take a left here."

Noah taps on the steering wheel as he takes the turn. "Hmm, gimme a sec."

We're heading back to my place, and after some of the topics we covered earlier in the evening, I'm keen to switch to something lighter.

"Chris Hemsworth," Noah declares. "Not just for the body, though, but for that accent, too."

I nod emphatically. "Australian accents are so fucking hot."

Noah chuckles. "And what about you? Who's your celebrity crush?"

"Easy," I say. "Henry Cavill."

"Where do I know that name from?"

I lick my lips. "From the night we met at the bar. He's an actor. I said that you reminded me of him."

"That's right. I thought he played Batman, but turns out he was Superman. I googled him the next day. He's a very attractive man."

"Yeah, he's all right," I say casually. "Got nothing on you, though. Oh, and right here."

Noah braces, but makes the turn. "Thanks for the compliment. It makes up for the terrible navigation."

We laugh.

"Okay, I've got one. Most *embarrassing* celebrity crush?"

"Hmm." Noah pulls up to a red light. "You go first. I'm drawing a blank."

"All right. But remember, this is a judgment-free zone, okay?"

"Got it."

"Does the name Phil Dunphy ring a bell?"

Noah thinks about it as we start driving again. "No," he answers after a while. "Who is he?"

"It's a character from the TV show *Modern Family*. He was the dorky dad."

"Riiight. So you like the actor?"

"Nope. My crush is on the character, not the actor. Phil is this loveable, kinda silly goofball of a dad, but man, I've jerked off a ton to him."

Noah bursts out laughing. "I am going to google him tomorrow."

"Remember." I point my finger at him. "Judgment-free zone. Anyway, it's your turn now."

"Mine's pretty bad," Noah admits. "And I hate, hate, *hate* his politics."

"Oh, god, it's not Trump, is it?"

"Hey, whatever happened to a judgment-free zone?" Noah smirks. "But no, dear lord no, it's not Trump."

We go through a list of other politicians who we ban from the judgment-free register, and thankfully, his crush isn't one of them.

"It's still bad, though," Noah warns. "But... Oh god, I can't believe I'm telling you this. It's George W. Bush."

"Whaaaat? Why?" I shriek.

"I don't know." Even in the darkness of the car, I can see Noah's face turning red. "Like I said, it's not a political thing, but there's something about a Texan, wearing cowboy boots, with that stupid look on his face that he always has. I don't know—it kinda does something for me."

"This has definitely taken an interesting turn. Ooh, speaking of, we should've gone left two blocks ago."

Noah shoots me an unimpressed look, but I can see him grinning. "I'll forgive you for your terrible directions if you forgive me for my awful crush."

"Deal. And while we're at it, let's add this topic to the 'never to be spoken about again' pile."

"Agreed."

A few minutes later, we pull up outside my building. "I'm excited to see your place," Noah says as we make our way out of the car.

I probably shouldn't be, and I'm definitely not doing it to be rude or make fun of the guy, but I can't help but giggle as we walk into my apartment. Noah's got this look on his face like he thinks he's about to step into some alternate universe rather than a converted loft that has no walls. The reality is likely to disappoint him.

"See, no walls. Just curtains," I say, pointing out the rooms we've sectioned off with heavy drapes hanging from the ceiling once we enter.

He's nodding, taking it all in. "What about, uh, the bathroom?"

"That's over there." I point to a small room to the right of the front door. "That does have walls for obvious reasons."

Noah strides over to me. "And where do you sleep?"

I start leading Noah toward my room when Tate pops out of his. "Oh, hey," he says, smiling warmly when he sees us.

"Noah, meet my housemate and best friend, Tate. Tate, this is Noah."

They shake hands. "I finally get to meet *the Noah*."

I shoot Tate a glare that Noah catches, and he starts laughing. "Didn't realize I was a *the*."

They make small talk while I excuse myself and go to the bathroom. When I return, I hear Noah inviting Tate to the bar where we usually have after-work drinks. "You're always more than welcome to join us," Noah tells Tate. "We're a pretty friendly bunch, aren't we, Haze?"

"Yeah. They're not too scary," I reply, and Noah nudges into me playfully.

Tate excuses himself, and we resume the grand tour. First stop: my bedroom. It's actually a pretty decent size. It comfortably fits a king-size bed, a row of cupboards, and dressers, with room for my favorite armchair I had to twist Dad's arm to let me have.

Noah looks around and seems to be taking it all in, not too freaked out by anything. Not that I have anything to compare his reaction to. That's when it dawns on me that I've never brought a guy back to this place before. Daniel visited once, hated it, and swore he'd never come back again.

"How do you, uh, have...intimate relations in here?" Noah asks, his lips twisting in a smirk.

"I don't." I step up next to him and crash my lips into his. He tugs at my hair, drawing a heavy—and way too loud—moan out of me. "Until now, that is."

His eyes flash with something unfamiliar. "Wait. I'm the first guy you've brought back home?"

"Yeah, you are."

"I'm honored."

"You should be."

"Only one problem..." He moves back slightly so we can see each other better. "There's no way I can be quiet when I'm with you. I don't just need walls. I need proper commercial-grade insulation and double-glazed windows when you and I have..."

"Intimate relations?" I offer cheekily.

He cups my ass with his strong hands, pulling me into his body. I can feel his erection through his pants. I press into it with my own. He lets out a low grunt as I slide my fingers along the material outlining his cock. He drops his gaze down. "You're making me leak."

I lean in closer. "You should feel what's happening in my pants."

His eyes flutter. "I've never seen anyone leak as much precome as you do."

"It only happens when I get really turned on. And no one's ever excited me as much as you do."

He moans, swiping his fingers through his hair. "Let's get outta here, then. I need you so fucking much."

"Can I show you something first?"

I hate breaking the moment, and god, there's nothing more that I want than to be balls deep inside him, but this is kinda important. Noah nods and follows me out into the kitchen. I lead him to my setup. It's made up of pots, gas cookers like the ones people take when they go camping, an assortment of bowls, and bottles with all of my oils and fragrances.

He taps his fingers against his chin, his lips stretched in a smile. "So from what I'm seeing here, I assume you're showing me your...meth lab?"

I laugh. "Not even close."

I open up a large Tupperware container, the sharp smells of cedarwood and pine dancing in the air around us. He peers down at my most recent batch of soaps, and it's like a lightbulb goes off in his head. "So *this* is why you always smell so good."

"Not as exciting as a meth lab, but yeah, that explains it."

I scoop up a mini picnic basket and hand it to Noah. Under the piece of cloth lie a number of soaps. "What's this?" he asks.

"Please be honest and tell me if this is a stupid idea, but I'm making a soap basket for Gus and his fiancé. It's a gift for their wedding. Do you think they'll like it?"

Noah's eyes shift between the basket and me a couple of times before he says, "Haze, they will love it. This is such a beautiful and thoughtful gift. I—I can't believe you did this."

He places the basket onto the table and kisses me. I freefall into it, letting his tongue explore the inside of my mouth. We're interrupted by the sound of someone clearing their throat.

"Don't mind me, guys," Tate says, gingerly tiptoeing into the kitchen. "Just wanted to get some juice."

Noah straightens up. I flash him a look, and his eyes widen when he notices the massive bulge he's sporting. He ducks behind a chair to cover himself.

"That's okay," I tell Tate. "We were leaving to go back to Noah's. I just wanted to show him some of my soaps."

Tate grabs the juice out of the fridge. "Haze is one talented boy. Makes the best soaps I've ever used. And if you think they smell good, wait until you see how they leave your skin feeling. So freaking smooth."

I chuckle to myself. "Yeah, well, except for those ones." I point to a pile of the purple lavender soaps that I worked on a while ago.

"I must've gotten some of the calculations wrong because they turned out misshapen and way too oily."

"That's where you are very wrong, my friend." And with that cryptic comment, Tate snags an apple out of the fruit bowl and leaves.

"What did he mean by that?" Noah asks, stepping out from behind the chair.

I shrug. "I have no idea. But who cares? I think we have more pressing matters to attend to."

It's only a ten minute drive to Noah's place. As much as I'd like nothing more than to tear off every piece of fabric standing between me and his body the second we step into his house, Noah has paw-rent duties to fulfill with Buddy. That's after we're both treated to an onslaught of wet, sloppy doggy kisses, of course.

By the time Noah tucks Buddy away for the night and comes out of the shower, my cock is not only achingly hard, it's oozing precome like you wouldn't believe. I'm lying on his bed, resting against the headboard, casually jacking myself off.

"Holy shit," Noah mutters, stepping out of the bathroom completely naked. The light from the bedside lamps illuminates his skin. "Is there anything more beautiful than what I'm looking at?" he asks in a low, deep voice.

"I can think of one thing," I shoot back, smiling. "The guy I'm looking at."

Noah leaps across the room and jumps onto the bed beside me. His lips collide with mine, and the kiss that strikes up between us feels better than magic. I've already pulled out supplies from his nightstand. I position myself on top of him, and his fingers tangle in my hair that's falling by the side of my face.

"I want to fuck you. Is that okay?"

"Yes," he growls back, his green eyes blazing. "I prepped in the shower," he informs me. "So I'm ready for you. Now." The thick need in his voice sends even more precome gushing out of me.

I scooch up the side of his body, pointing my glistening cock at

Noah. His gaze drops to it. His lips smack together noisily. "I want to taste it," he says, not taking his eyes off my leaking slit. "I want to taste *you*."

"Oh, you will. But I have something else in mind. Something even better. Do you trust me?"

He nods, and I wait until he replies with a hungry, "Yes."

I kneel right beside his face and squeeze the tip of my dick, coaxing more precome out of it. I aim my cock at his face, bring it in nice and close, and then swipe the tip along each of his cheeks, coating them with the clear liquid.

"I want to mark you, then fuck you."

The words fall out of the deepest part of me. A part of me that I've never shared with anyone before. "Is that okay?"

"Fuck, yes."

Noah peers up at me through his dark lashes, and the sight of him with my precome smeared on his cheeks is enough to send me over the edge right there and then. I slip a condom on, and even though Noah's prepped himself, I lube up a finger and slide it in gently, just to be on the safe side. The last thing I want to do is hurt him.

I would really love to rim him, but I can see he's too far gone for that. I want to feast on his ass for hours, and Noah is way too impatient for that right now. We'll have to leave that for next time.

"I'm ready," he moans impatiently, "Need your cock inside of me."

Smiling, I give him what he needs. I drop onto my elbows so I can see his face up close as my cock lines up against his entrance. We start kissing, and with one slow, steady movement, I ease myself all the way inside of him. It's the most exquisite feeling, bottoming out inside Noah with my tongue deep inside his mouth.

Noah's fingers claw into my hair, and he gives a gentle tug. I pull out and rut against him. His fingernails dig into my scalp. I do it again, harder and faster. He hisses around my lips. "Fuck, yeah."

Noah's cock is thick and heavy and slapping against his

stomach with every thrust. I grab it by the base, and it feels like fire in my hand. I start jacking him off, matching my hand rhythm to my hips. Our bodies are in sync, moving together in the most beautiful way.

I'm overcome with emotion. Noah looks so beautiful lying underneath me, his eyes closed, surrendering to the bliss. Suddenly, his eyes shoot open. "Fuck, I'm close."

I speed up, jacking his cock hard, rutting into his body with all my force. I can see him losing balance, approaching the edge, and then...falling into the abyss.

"Holy motherfucking...ahhhh!"

Noah wasn't kidding about needing commercial-grade insulation—his cries have probably woken up the entire neighborhood. His body bucks and jerks and twitches for a long time until finally, *finally*, he rides the crest into a deep stillness.

I wipe away the beads of sweat that line his forehead. "Wow," he croaks.

I'm still inside him. My cock pulses.

"I can feel that," he coos softly.

I do it again, on purpose this time, my cock still so achingly hard for him. "It feels beautiful," I whisper.

Noah closes his eyes and nods. He's still sweating quite a lot so I gently blow on his face to help cool him down. After a few minutes, he opens his eyes and cradles my face in his hands. "I want to taste you."

"Are you sure?"

"Yes. Please."

I'd love to come inside him, but after the massive orgasm that just tore through him, I realize that might not be the most comfortable thing for him. Slowly, and as carefully as I can, I pull out. I peel the condom off and scoop my fingers into the pools of come cooling on his belly. I slick my cock with his release. It only takes a few strokes to get me close.

Noah shuffles around on the bed, positioning himself near my cock. He glances up at me, his precome-stained cheeks catching in the light.

"I'm close," I warn.

"I want you."

Then he opens his mouth wide to let me know he really means it. The sight of him like that pushes me over the edge. Noah clamps down on my cock as it explodes, shooting torrents of come straight down his throat. He expertly sucks the crown, coaxing more and more out of me, swallowing it all without any hesitation. The whole time I'm coming, I'm staring at him, transfixed by the beauty of this moment.

"Mmm," he says. He takes my softening cock out of his mouth and admires it for a few seconds. "You taste as good as you look and smell."

I chuckle before quickly dashing into his en suite to grab some towels to clean us up. I catch my reflection in the mirror. I squint at myself. I can't tell how, but I look different somehow. I quickly return to Noah and help clean him up. He tries to take the towel off me.

"I can do it," he offers.

I gently slap his hand away. "No, I'd like to. If that's okay, of course."

Something catches in his chest, but he nods. His eyes don't leave me as I carefully wipe him down and clean up the area around us. Once I'm done, I take the towels and supplies out of the room before snuggling beside Noah.

"Are you cold?" I ask since we're both naked and lying on top of the sheets.

"A little," he replies.

I draw the sheet over us and place the comforter halfway up our bodies. "Better?"

"Yes. Thank you."

Noah looks all dopey, and it's the cutest fucking thing ever.

"I'm still a little dazed," he says with a light chuckle.

I card my fingers through his hair. "That's okay. I am, too. That was..." I'm stuck. How can I possibly find words to describe the intensity and passion that we just shared?

"So," I start, rubbing the back of my hand across his cheeks. "We've covered ex-boyfriends, family, my love of Beyoncé, awkward celebrity crushes..."

"Your horrible navigation skills," Noah chimes in.

I giggle. "That, too. Plus some mind-blowing sex. So, um, I think this officially qualifies as the best first date ever."

"Would you like me to call the Guinness Book of Records, or did you want to do that?"

"Nah-uh." I swoop in, pressing my lips to Noah's. "I'm not sharing this with anyone."

15

NOAH

"I'm cooking sex pasta. I've got strawberries and watermelon. There's some chocolate over there, plus some asparagus and artichokes. Oh, and oysters, too," Gus announces with a series of accompanying hand flourishes.

"What the hell is sex pasta?" I ask.

Chase, Fulton, and Gus' younger brother and best man, David, are milling around in Gus' kitchen.

"Pasta equals carbs, and carbs are a good fuel for sex." Gus wipes his palms down the front of his 'I'm Getting Married Tomorrow' apron that Fulton got for him. "Guys, I'm forty-seven years old. I don't want to have any trouble getting the old fella up tomorrow night."

"Maybe stop referring to him as an old fella?"

"Shut up, Fulton," Gus replies, and Fulton flips him the bird.

"You may also wanna lay easy on the asparagus there. It makes your come taste funky," Chase chips in, quickly tacking on, "At least, that's what Julie's told me."

Fulton flashes me a funny look, but before either one of us can say anything else, David approaches Gus. "There's not a lot of food here, big brother."

"Oh, yeah. That's because this is what *I'm* eating. I've ordered Mexican takeout for you guys."

And right on cue, the doorbell rings. "Fulton, be a dear and get that, would you?" Gus orders with a chuckle. It earns him another middle finger salute, but Fulton obliges.

We clear the coffee table and lay the food out on it. We each find a spot to sit in Gus' massive living room and dig in. "This is much nicer than some crazy bachelor party with strippers," I say, chewing loudly around my chicken quesadilla.

"That's what I thought." Gus wipes his mouth. "I wanted to spend my last night of singlehood with the people I love the most."

"That's really sweet," Fulton says quietly.

"I agree," I say. "It is."

"What's Marco doing?" Chase asks.

"Partying with his friends. I've been told strippers *will* be involved," Gus replies with a dramatic eye roll.

David looks over at his brother. "You don't mind?"

"Nah, I trust him. I'm marrying him, right? What would it say about me if I don't trust the guy I'm about to spend the rest of my life with?"

A funny twinge pokes the insides of my belly at Gus' words. Hmm... I may need to lay off the jalapeños.

We shoot the shit while we eat until Gus decides to change the topic onto...what else? Love.

"So..." He places his plate on the coffee table and reclines in his chair. "Chase and David are both married to lovely ladies, I'm officially off the market in less than twenty-four hours, and that just leaves you two."

Fulton and I glance at each other. Gus goes on. "Now we all know that Fulton is tragically single."

"Correction." Fulton raises a finger. "I think you meant to say *happily* instead of *tragically*."

"Did I, though?" Gus snickers sarcastically to himself. "Which leaves you, Mr. I Can't Do A One-Night Stand Right."

I finish chewing. "Yes?"

Gus' eyes light up. "Ooh, so there is something happening between you and Haze then?"

"We've, uh, been hanging out."

"Yeah, every night for the past two weeks," Fulton teases. "Noah asked Haze out on a date. He gave him a single stem red rose and everything."

Gus flails his arms around. "Shut the front door. You did not?!"

I nod, sighing happily. "Yep. I did."

"A single red rose? Oh my gosh, that's so romantic." Gus clutches his chest, then drops to the floor. "I am on the floor, dying. No, wait. I'm dead. Don't even bother calling the paramedics because I am a goner."

The guys and I laugh at Gus' melodramatic antics.

"Wait. Who's this Haze guy, and what's this about a one-night stand?" David asks, and the guys quickly fill him in.

"The question that remains," Fulton cocks his head to the side and scratches his jaw, "is how many more of the four rules have you broken?"

I roll my eyes, but he's got that animated expression on his face. There's no way to stop the Fulton train when he gets on a roll like this. I settle back into the sofa. Knowing Fulton as well as I do, this could take a while.

"You broke the first rule—don't spend the night—the first night you met him."

"Technically, *he* spent the night with *me.*"

"And as we've discussed at length, Noah Walters, that's not a valid loophole."

"Geez. Judge Judy much," Chase snorts.

Ignoring him, Fulton continues. "Then you broke the second rule by seeing him again."

"Yeah, because he started working at the clinic," I point out. "That's more Gus' fault for hiring him than mine."

"What can I say? The world needs more love." Gus grasps at his chest. "I'm happy to play Cupid in whatever way I can."

"You guys are ganging up on me," I protest jokingly.

"Don't worry, man. I got your back."

"Thanks, Chase. It's nice to know I can rely on one of my friends."

We laugh again. "So now..." Fulton leans forward and squints at me. "The question is, have you shared anything personal?"

Gus gets to his feet. "While you ponder that, I might get us some beers. Yeah?"

"Or something stronger?" I suggest.

David and Chase help Gus clear the plates, leaving me alone with Fulton. "Well," he presses softly. "Have you shared anything personal with him? Or has he shared anything personal with you?"

"Yeah, actually we have. On our first date, things got kinda intense. We shared a lot of stuff, about ex-boyfriends and family." I deliberately leave out the awkward celebrity crush conversation. Not even Fulton knows about that, and I'm perfectly happy keeping it that way. "And we've obviously been talking and getting to know each other better these past few weeks."

"Hmm."

"What are you thinking?" I ask.

"Nothing. I'm just *hmm-ing*."

"Fulton!"

"Fine. I'm just thinking that this is really major for you. I'm happy for you, and more than that, I'm proud of you. It sounds like you're moving on with your life after everything that happened."

Suddenly, the weirdest thing happens. I go from sitting on the couch chatting to my best friend at my good friend's low-key bachelor party to feeling like I've been left dangling upside down at the top of a rollercoaster ride that's come to an abrupt stop.

"Here." Fulton leaps to his feet and hands me a glass of water. "Drink this."

I gulp it down as Fulton bites his lower lip, studying me carefully. "You okay?" he asks, taking the empty glass from me. "What just happened?"

"I think I just had a mini freak-out."

"About what?"

"I just had a thought. About Haze. Things are going so well, we've been loving hanging out together, and I guess I've been so caught up in the niceness and yumminess of it all that I haven't stopped to think about..." My voice trails off.

"Think about what?"

"The future. What if—?" I can feel my chest heating up and not in a good way. "What if Haze leaves me like Michael, Dustin, and Graham did?"

"Hey, hey, hey." Fulton places his hand on my shoulder. "Haze isn't those guys." Fulton's voice is just the right combination of delicate and strong. "Don't let the bad stuff that happened in your past stop good stuff from coming into your future."

"He's studying to be an actor, though. He's not going to stay in Virginia. He'll probably finish his studies and move to L.A. or New York."

"Oh, I'm sorry. Are you a psychic now? Have you spoken to him about any of this?"

I shake my head. "No. It's—it's too soon."

Fulton lets out a sigh. "I think that's the most guy thing you've ever said to me. It's never too soon to talk. Have a chat with him at the wedding tomorrow. This stuff is obviously affecting you..."

I nod, taking a few moments to collect myself. "I hadn't realized, but you're right. It is."

"I'm always right. You should know that by now."

I bump my shoulder against his. "Also," Fulton continues, "not to rush you guys toward anything, but I've got fifty bucks riding on you breaking rule number four and falling in love with him by Thanksgiving."

"Fulton!" I exclaim.

"My money's on Christmas," Chase says, returning into the room. He winks as he hands us our beers.

"I'm old, so I'm more conservative," Gus chimes in with a cackle. "I've got you two together by Valentine's Day."

"You guys." I may be trying to sound like I'm exasperated with my friends, but I'm smiling.

And I don't bother to correct any one of them. Fulton's right—Haze and I do have stuff to talk about. And I'm sure that we will. Soon. But the thought of possibly falling in love with Haze, whether it happens today, tomorrow, or by any of the days the guys mentioned, makes my heart feel like it's about to leap out of my chest.

∾

The wedding ceremony is...unique. I didn't realize that Marco's obsession with all things Elvis would extend to the officiant being dressed up as an Elvis, too, but hey, to each their own. Gus and Marco both look good in their matching tuxes and blue suede shoes. Gus is beaming so hard and looks so fucking happy that it makes me happy. He deserves this.

But I'll be honest. Even while I'm watching the two men exchange vows, my mind is consumed by the man sitting beside me, my hand firmly holding onto his. Haze went all out. Today, he smells like honey, buttermilk, and when I couldn't figure out what the final note of his fragrance was, he told me it was ylang-ylang. I have no idea what the hell that is. All I know is that it makes him smell ylum ylum.

He also looks damn good. He went with a Gus-approved navy blue suit. His hair is tied back in a neat ponytail. The dark colors of the suit bring out the gray flecks in his hazel eyes, and everything about him looks and smells mouth wateringly delicious.

The ceremony takes place outside in a beautiful vineyard. It's only a forty-minute drive from town, but it feels like we could be in the rolling hills of Tuscany. The other great thing about this place is that both the ceremony and reception are taking place here. The reception is only a short stroll away, inside the massive mansion that sits atop a gentle hill in the middle of the two-hundred-acre property.

"You look amazing today. I mean, you look great every day, but this is...extra amazing."

A group of us, mainly staff from the clinic, are standing together in a corner of the reception area. Gus has been telling us all about it since he got engaged. Apparently, the vibe they were going for was throwback 1980s *Miami Vice* meets *The Golden Girls*. All I'm seeing is a lot of cane furniture and servers wearing hideous tangerine suits with shoulder pads. What the female servers are wearing is even worse. But again, to each their own.

"Yeah. Well, you look pretty darn amazing, too. All I can say is,

I'm glad the ceremony didn't take place in a church," Haze says, a smirk tugging at his lips.

I turn to face him. "Why is that?"

He whispers, "Because I'm pretty sure it's a sin to have a boner in church. You made me achingly hard every single time you held my hand."

And fuck if Haze's words don't make me want to scoop him up in my arms and get us the hell outta here. "While I'm only qualified to treat animals, I am also known to be good at addressing the specific ache you're referring to."

"Oh, I'm counting on it." The look Haze shoots me is so hot it could melt the polar ice caps.

Fulton and Chase join us, and thankfully, the world is saved from an end-of-the-world flood for at least one more day.

"Hey, nice tie, man," Haze compliments Fulton.

"Thank you." Fulton proudly pulls it out in front of him for us all to see. "It's knitted."

Haze and I break off into smaller conversations. Fulton starts rambling about his goddamn tie, which is made from merino wool from New Zealand, which I know because he started a text message thread about it last week...and kept updating it until this morning. He intersperses that fascinating conversation with concerns about whether the shrimp and seafood being served are wild-caught or have been harvested.

Next to me, Haze is making small talk with Chase and his wife, Julie. As discreetly as I can, I try to eavesdrop a little on their conversation, which, unless it's about ethics in virtual ethnography, has to be more interesting than mine. That's when my stomach drops. As in, it shoots right out of my body and onto the ground.

I don't catch everything, but Haze is telling them about his dad knowing some hotshot producer in L.A. From what I can make out—it's a little hard to hear; Fulton gets very heated about salmon—it sounds like Haze has got some auditions coming up. In Los Angeles.

It feels like the oxygen has been sucked out of the room. I shove my fingers into the collar of my shirt to loosen it a bit. Luckily, I'm managing to keep the rising panic out of Fulton's view, but shit, *of course* this would happen.

All morning, I've been planning when the best time would be to sit down and talk to Haze about us, our future, and maybe even share some of my worries with him. I decided on after food, but before dancing. But this just makes it all so much more real.

Before I can pull Haze away and fast-track the conversation from pre-dancing to right-the-fuck-now, Gus runs up to the group and huffs out, "Has anyone seen my husband? I've made some last minute changes to our first dance I have to tell him about." He pauses, both to catch his breath and for dramatic effect, I'm guessing. "Not to give away too many spoilers, but I hope you guys still remember the dance moves to *The Macarena*."

I hear a few groans before Chase suggests we break apart to go look for Marco. Fulton cuts in front of me, grabbing Haze, and I hear him muttering something about wild-caught salmon before they head off. I need to talk to Haze, but I also really need to pee. I head the other way, toward the men's room, all the while keeping an eye out for the missing husband.

As I step into the toilet, my heart joins my stomach on the floor. Peeking out from under the cubicle stall are a pair of blue shoes. A pair of blue suede shoes, to be exact. I grit my teeth, my fists balled by the sides of my body. Marco is fucking unbelievable. How dare he do this to one of my best friends...on their wedding day!

I'm about to storm out when a dark thought hits me. If Marco's the kind of guy who would cheat on his husband at their wedding reception, doesn't it make sense that he's also the kind of guy who would lie about it if he ever got caught? I don't want it to be my word against his, so as much as I don't want to do it, I summon every ounce of strength I have and force myself to stay.

The unmistakable sounds of oral sex bounce off the tiled walls. I need evidence. But how? A few seconds later, what I need to do slams into me like a semi. Oh god, I have to take a photo. I scan the men's room. There's one cubicle that's currently being occupied by a cheating scumbag. Beside it are three porcelain urinals. Above them, there's a tiled ledge. I formulate a game plan. I'm going to climb up onto the ledge above the urinals, peek over the top of the cubicle, take the photo, and then get the hell outta here.

I don't want to do it. Every part of me is screaming to turn around, leave, and squeeze every last remnant of this memory out of my mind forever. But then I think of Gus, and how much he deserves to be happy. That's all I want for my friend, and he will never have that while this douchebag is in his life. I have to do it...for Gus.

I take a silent breath, then tiptoe over to the urinals. Gripping the walls for support, I manage to heave myself up onto the ledge. I am definitely going to need to deep-sanitize myself after this, but *I'm thinking of Gus, I'm thinking of Gus, I'm doing this for him.* That's my mantra as I scoot along the narrow ledge until I reach the cubicle wall, my fingers grasping the top of it.

I suck in a breath as I take my first look over the wall. And yeah. Exactly what I thought was happening is happening. Fuck. My fingers are shaking as I fish my cellphone out of my pocket. I click on the camera icon and stick my phone out, but it's kinda hard to get a good view. The guy Marco is blowing is concealing him.

I lean over a little more. Half my body is now hanging over the top of the cubicle. I'm trying to get the blue suede shoes in the shot when two things happen at the same time.

One: I lose my position and feel the balance of my body weight tipping me over the edge of the cubicle wall. "Oh, Jesus," I cry out.

Two: The guy Marco's blowing clearly reaches his point of no return because he lets out a desperate, "Oh, Jesus."

Despite scrambling to stop it, there's no way I can overpower gravity. I'm too far gone, over the edge. And I'm not the only one.

"Shit. Shit. Oh, fuck. Yeah, I'm coming..."

I'm doing my best to hold on, but it's no use. I start skidding headfirst down the cubicle wall.

"Incoming," I cry out as the dude continues yelling, "I'm coming, I'm coming."

I discover a pro tip as I slide headfirst down the inside wall of a toilet cubicle: try landing on a cheating douchebag. They're not good for a lot of things, but they are great at cushioning the fall.

What happens next is a bit of a blur. There's confusion, more yelling, and a whole lot of pain stabbing my neck and right shoulder. The three of us keep hollering as we desperately try to untangle ourselves from each other. I manage to get to my feet and burst out of the confined space. I don't want to spend a second longer than I have to near that asshole Marco.

I rush to the door. Before I open it, I twist around—painfully, my neck is throbbing real bad now—and spit out, "You motherfucker, Marco. You had the best guy in the world, and you ruined it."

I push through the door and am stopped dead in my tracks. The ruckus we created in the men's room has drawn an audience. Gus, Fulton, Chase, and Haze are all staring at me like I'm a zombie from an impending apocalypse. That's kinda fitting, I guess.

"What the hell?" Gus starts as he shoves past the others toward me.

"Don't go in there," I plead to him.

After I say that, the door to the men's room flies open, and we all scatter like a packet of Skittles that have been dropped on the floor. Marco whizzes past us. Gus takes off after him. His wail of, "What have you done?" pierces my heart into a thousand tiny shards.

Fulton and Chase approach the men's room door slowly, like they're a SWAT team moving in on a deranged gunman, and I...I can't take it. I need to get outta there. A surge of adrenaline rushes through me, giving me the boost I need to leg it as far away from there as I possibly can.

16
———

HAZE

There's a loud commotion, and it's coming from the men's bathroom. So I approach cautiously, not sure what the hell is going on. Gus, Fulton, and Chase hear it as well. They move toward it, too. And then suddenly, Noah appears. His face is marked by a heavy scowl, and he's walking crooked.

There's a blur of movement as Gus and his husband run one way, Chase and Fulton inch toward the men's room, and Noah takes off out the door. I scramble past confused-looking guests, following Noah onto the terrace, down the stairs, past where the ceremony was held, and into the green fields.

"Hey, slow down," I shout. "Noah! Wait up!"

I finally close in on him and manage to land my arm on his shoulder. He lets out a loud hiss so I let go. He finally slows down to a jog before he halts completely. Noah drops to the ground and buries his face in his knees. I follow him, sitting close enough so I can be near him, but giving him space if that's what he needs.

He's staring at the grass, breathing heavily, and I can't make out his face. "It was awful." His voice is stripped bare, raw.

"What was?"

I want to reach out and touch him, but because of the way he responded when I touched his shoulder before, I hold back. The last thing I want to do is cause him any physical pain. He's already going through enough by the looks of things.

Noah lifts his head. His eyes have turned dark. He tells me what he walked in on. My stomach twists in disgust as I hear about what Marco was doing. And then my heart catches in my throat, forcing me to cover my mouth, when Noah relays how he tried to get evidence of what was happening.

"Wait! You slid down the cubicle wall? Oh my god. You're probably hurt. We need to get you to the hospital."

He's breathing heavily. All I see is so much pain written across his face. It kills me.

"I'm fine," he mutters.

He sure as heck doesn't sound or look fine. "Are you in pain?"

Noah tries to shrug and winces at the movement. "No. A little. Maybe. I don't know."

I find myself thumbing the top of his hand. "Is this okay?"

His eyes meet mine, and the tiniest smile escapes from his lips. But the longer he looks at me, the glossier his eyes turn. I glance down at our touching hands, and when I look back up again, his emotions start spilling out of his eyes.

I want to reach out and hug him, but I have a terrible feeling he's hurt. I don't know where so I don't know what to do. "Why—why are you crying?" Oh god, I hope he's not in too much pain.

He takes a few moments to collect himself. Then he says, "I just can't believe someone would do that. And to Gus of all people. He's the nicest guy ever. No one ever deserves something like this, but especially not him."

I keep stroking the top of his hand softly. I don't know what to say.

"Love sucks. Men suck," Noah says with a sour bitterness.

"Not all men." I try to catch his attention, but he's staring straight ahead. "Not this one," I add.

Silent tears continue streaming down his face. Something tells me it's more than just the shock of what he witnessed that's stirring within him. Finally, he lets whatever's been trapped inside of him out. "I just give and give, and guys just take and take, until there's nothing left of me... Then they leave. They always fucking leave me."

"Talk to me, Noah. You can tell me anything."

His brow furrows. "Really? Why?"

"Because I want to know everything about you. Even the sad parts. And..." I blow out a breath. Am I really going to say this? Yeah, I am. "Because I want to know how you've been hurt before so that I can make sure I never hurt you that way."

His jaw twitches as he starts to talk. "Love means you put the other person first, you know? But it only works if that's what both people do. I've made that mistake before. I've given all of myself to guys, and they haven't done the same for me. Michael chose his career over me. Dustin chose his mother over me. And Graham, he chose his stupid dick and some twink he picked up at a bar over me."

He wipes his tears away. "I know I'm not perfect. No one is. But why, why can't I find a guy who treats me like I'm important? Like I matter, too?"

I don't know what to say, so I stay silent. I keep rubbing my thumb against the top of his hand. Noah tries to straighten up, but grimaces. The guy is clearly in pain, and I don't know what to do about that, either. I feel so fucking useless right now.

"I think seeing Marco doing...what he was doing back there. It triggered me and brought back a flood of memories for me. I'm sorry, Haze. I'm a mess."

"You have nothing to apologize for," I say, and I mean it. "It's a lot to walk into at any time. Much less after what you've been though, and on your friend's wedding day, no less. Jesus."

"This will break Gus' heart...and fuck." Noah flinches again as he tries to sit up straighter. "I think I've really hurt my neck and shoulder."

It's clear to me that Gus isn't the only one with a broken heart, and while I can't do anything about either one of their hearts, I can do something about Noah's injury. "I am taking you to the hospital. You're hurt. I think you might have been running on adrenaline, but that seems to be wearing off now."

"I think you may be right."

I stand up and stretch out my hands. "Take your time."

He slips his fingers into mine, and I grip them tightly. With a pained "ouch," he peels himself off the ground. The pain seems to be on his right side, so I position myself on his left side, taking some of his body weight as we hobble back toward the mansion.

"Is this okay?" I ask. "Because if it hurts too much, I can call for an ambulance to come to us."

"I can walk," Noah says, and I can see he's fighting back the pain. "I don't want to go in an ambulance. I don't want to make an even bigger scene."

I accept his answer, only because his injury is in the upper half of his body, and he seems to be able to walk fine.

"Thank you." His words whistle in the wind.

"You don't have to thank me." I don't look at him, my focus one hundred percent on getting him into my car and to the hospital as quickly as we can.

I hear him mutter quietly, "Yes, I do," into my shoulder.

I'm pacing frantically in the hallway when the doctor steps out of Noah's room. I practically hurl myself at the man. "Is he okay?"

To my relief, the doctor nods. "He should be all right. He suffered quite a nasty fall, and we're monitoring some swelling around his shoulders. He was in quite a lot of pain, so we put him on a morphine drip to help with that."

"Can I go in and see him?"

"Of course." He pauses, then smiles. "He's quite chatty at the moment. We've taken him off the morphine, but he's still feeling the effects of it. It should wear off soon."

I thank the doctor before heading into the room.

"Hazey baby!"

Noah's sitting up in bed, but it looks like his head is too heavy for his shoulders, his mouth too big for his face. "You caaame!"

"Of course I came." I drag a chair beside his bed. Okay, so he seems to have forgotten that I actually drove him here. Good to know. "How are you feeling?"

"I...feel...floaty."

I chuckle to myself. Well, the doctor did warn me. I grab Noah's hand. He looks down at our joined hands. Then his eyes drift up to meet mine. "I like you, Hazey baby." He throws his head back and barks out a laugh. "Hazey baby. That sounds funny. Can I call you that?"

I smile. "Yeah. You can. My Aunt Jocelyn calls me that, too."

"I wanna meet her."

My smile deepens. "You will. One day."

I can feel Noah's hand tremble in mine. "I will?"

"Of course." I gently rub my fingers along his. "You'll get to meet my family. I'll meet yours. That would be nice, right?"

He nods his head for a very long time. "Can I tell you a secret?"

"Sure." I lean in. "What is it that you want to tell me?"

Noah's eyes cling to mine as he speaks. "I heard you talking at the wedding. I know you're going to leave for Wollyhood."

Wollyhood? It takes me a minute to figure out he probably means Hollywood. Damn, that morphine sure was strong.

"And guess what?" he asks.

My throat tightens. I lean in a little closer. "What?"

Noah lets out a maniacal laugh, which startles me. "I'm going to act like it's okay and that I don't mind. But really, I don't want you to leave me. Shhh..." He smudges his lips with his index finger. "Don't tell anyone."

I swallow hard, but Noah's not finished yet. "I'm going to be actoring, Hazey baby. I'm going to be actoring and pretending like it's okay that you're leaving me." He follows up with more slightly off-kilter laughter.

I drop his hand and stand up, the chair screeching before falling onto the floor behind me. Noah's still looping about "actoring," but all I feel is an oppressive coil wrapping itself around me. I back out of the room, flinging myself into the hallway. My back slams against the wall as white-hot tears stream down my face.

I haven't had time to process any of what's happened today. I mean, right about now, we probably should have been eating one too many slices of wedding cake before one of us asked the other one to dance to a cheesy '80s song.

Gus getting cheated on wasn't part of the plan.

Ending up in the hospital with Noah nursing an injured shoulder wasn't on the cards.

And neither was what Noah just said in there.

I know he's on meds and probably won't remember any of this, but I'll never be able to forget it. Because of course Noah is the kind of man that would sacrifice his own happiness, his own needs for someone else. That's what he's done in every serious relationship he's been in. He gives everything he's got to someone else and gets nothing in return. The unfairness of that rips through me. I cannot even fathom the idea that I could be another person to be added onto that list.

I was waiting for the right moment at the wedding to tell Noah about the phone call I received last night from Dad's producer friend, Lyon. He wants me to fly out to L.A. He's lined up some auditions and wants me to take a few meetings. I only mentioned it to Chase and his wife at the reception because they asked me if I had any exciting acting plans coming up. I didn't go into any specifics. I wanted Noah to be the first to hear it, and now I've fucked that up completely.

"Oh my god, Haze!" Fulton's shriek puts a brake on my downward spiral.

I stab at the tears on my face, doing my best to conceal them. Fulton places his hands on my shoulders and looks me straight in the eyes. "What's happened? Is Noah okay?"

"He's fine," I choke out, realizing how me crying outside Noah's room must appear. "Noah's on meds and has been talking, that's all."

"Oh dear," Fulton groans. "He has a tendency to divulge things whenever he gets a little tipsy."

"Yeah. Tell me about it." I push away the last of the tears and jam my hands into my pockets.

"Wait. He didn't tell you about the time he and I went out to a farm and a cow accidentally sprayed me with anal fissures?"

"Ew. What? No."

Fulton's eyes widen when he realizes he's revealed too much. "Uh...okay. You should probably disregard that."

"Consider it banished from my memory forever."

We step into the room, and Noah's fast asleep now, snoring lightly with his arms by his sides.

I pick up the chair I tipped over. "How's Gus?"

Fulton grabs himself a seat from the corner of the room. "It's all a big pile of mess. I've——I've never seen him like this before."

I scrub my hand down the side of my face. "This has been, hands down, the worst wedding I've ever gone to."

"Same here," Fulton agrees dejectedly.

We sit in silence for a while. "Fulton?"

"Yeah."

I want to ask him a million questions about Noah, but I know it's neither the time nor the place. "Nothing. Don't worry about it."

~

"I am *fine*. You can stop fussing."

"Never," I reply cheerily.

It's the third morning in a row I'm bringing Noah breakfast in bed, and even though it's kinda crazy juggling work, my studies, and looking after him and Buddy, there's no way I wouldn't do it.

"Look." Noah's sitting up in bed, lifting his right shoulder.

"Hey." I aim a stern look his way. "Take it easy."

"I am fine," he repeats. "Nothing is broken or fractured. And the swelling and soreness has gone."

"The doctor still said to try and limit movement for at least five days. You're not out of the woods yet."

I carefully place the tray on his lap. "I'm going to start piling on the pounds if I keep eating like this," he says, digging into the food.

"No complaints here." I smile, sitting at the foot of the bed. "More cushion for the pushing works for me."

I watch him eat, so thankful that he wasn't seriously hurt in the tumble he took. Fulton offered to look after him when they discharged Noah the day after the wedding, but I wanted to do it. I've been spending so much time here that it made sense. Plus, Noah and I needed to talk.

We *still* need to talk.

The first few days were all about making sure Noah was feeling comfortable and settled. Now that I'm confident he is, it's time for me to grow a pair of balls and have the conversation I wanted to have with him at Gus' wedding.

"So," I start, taking a deep breath. "There's something I wanted to talk to you about at the wedding, but never got the chance to."

Noah stops chewing. "Same here, actually."

"Oh. Okay. Do you want to go first?"

He shakes his head. "No. You can."

"Right. So, here's the thing. My dad has an old friend, Lyon. He's some bigshot producer in L.A. Dad told him about me and my studies. Anyway, he sent Lyon my headshots, and the night before the wedding, I got a call from him. He wants me to fly out to L.A. They're casting for some new shows and a couple of movies."

I'm staring at Noah as I speak so I can see the way he slows down his chewing, how deliberate his movement is when he puts his knife and fork down on the plate, and how much effort it's taking for him to plaster a smile onto his face.

"That sounds great. It could be your big break." His words feel like lead balloons in my chest.

"Nothing's certain. It's so competitive that I probably won't even get anything..." My words falter. I want to say, *I don't even know that I want it anymore. I think I want you...* But I don't. Because the part of me that wants a future with Noah is warring with the side of me that wants me to have a future career. And if it's not acting, then what the hell am I meant to be doing with the rest of my life? Thirty is fast approaching, and I feel as lost, confused, and directionless as I was when I graduated high school.

Buddy trots into the room, his tongue lolling out of his mouth.

"Thank you for breakfast. It was delicious."

"No problem." I scoop the tray up and take it to the kitchen just as Buddy makes himself comfortable at Noah's feet. When I return, I pause in the doorway for a moment, and that's when it hits me. I don't know if it's the fact that I've been enjoying looking after Noah and Buddy these past few days, sliding so easily into their lives and slipping into such a comfortable routine. Or if it's the simplicity of a beautiful man lying in bed with his dog curled at his feet. But I can't deny the feeling sweeping over me.

Tingles.

Dad and Aunt Jocelyn were right. It's a feeling you get that makes you know you're on the right path, and I sure as hell am feeling it coursing through my veins right now. It's new, and I've never felt anything like it before, but at the same time, I know exactly what's happening. Leaning against the doorframe to Noah's bedroom, *this* is the exact moment I realize I'm falling for Noah.

He tips his head up and looks at me. "You okay?"

I sit down on the edge of the bed. "Yeah. Fine. Just...thinking. You said you had something you wanted to tell me at the wedding, too?"

Noah's jaw clenches, and he gives a clipped nod. "Uh, yeah."

"I'm all ears."

His gaze drops. "It might be a little redundant now."

"What do you mean?"

He schools his features. "I wanted to talk to you about us. Our future, and if we had one."

My chest tightens. "Why do you think it's redundant to talk about that now?"

He exhales noisily through his nose. "Because you might be off to L.A. to become a star, and my life is here. Buddy and I are pretty cool, but we can't compete with Hollywood."

He looks up, his eyes cutting into me. "Do you want me to stay?"

He opens and shuts his mouth a few times. I stand up and start pacing back and forth. "Why do people always do this?" I ask. "It happens in movies, TV shows, books. There's two people who want to be together, and they just never say it."

"Say what?" Noah asks, his head following my every moment.

"They never tell the other person they don't want them to leave. Noah, I need to know... Do you want me to stay?"

"Yes," Noah answers with literally zero hesitation, making my heart flutter wildly.

"Oh, okay. That's a bit quicker than I expected."

A tiny smile forms on Noah's lips. "I'm just being honest here. Haze, I like you. I really, really, *really* like you. I know it's still early days between us, but my feelings for you are strong and real."

I stop pacing and sit back down on the bed. "I really, really, *really* like you, too." *Actually, I'm pretty sure I'm falling in love with you*, is what I really want to say but manage to restrain myself.

I reach out and cup his left hand in mine, the one that's still wearing the bracelet. Noah lowers his voice. "There's a reason why people in movies, TV shows, and books don't ask the other person to stay."

"What's that?"

"Because it's selfish to make another person not do something they want to do."

"I agree."

Noah's brows pinch together. "You do?"

"Uh-huh. But here's the thing—you're not asking me to do anything. I just wanted to know whether you wanted me to stay. Thank you for being honest."

He looks at me like he can't figure out what's going on. Truth be told, if you asked me right now, what my future holds, I'd be lying if I said I knew. But despite all the uncertainty and confusion, one thing is shining through bright and clear. I'm going to follow my heart.

I may not know the hows, the wheres, or the whats, but I trust the feeling tingling through me, and I know that my future lies with Noah Walters.

17

NOAH

We're back at Gus' place, and the laid back vibe of his bachelor party two weeks earlier feels like an eternity ago. There's no laughter, no joking around, no breezy conversation. Just four depressed men moping in Gus' living room, chewing on half-cold pizza, and barely pretending to be watching the game flickering in the background.

"You know, if this were an episode of *The Golden Girls*, it'd be the most depressing one ever."

"Shut up, Fulton," Gus, Chase, and I say in unison, but not even that can crack a smile out of any of us.

"All right. This is bullshit." I swipe the remote control from the table and switch the game off. "We're all clearly miserable, and instead of drowning our sorrows in booze and bad pizza, we should get this shit out into the open."

All three men look at me. I'm not getting much of a reaction out of any of them, but I don't let that deter me. I press on. "Chase, you go first. What's got you looking so sour?"

He throws down the rest of his slice onto the plate and wipes his hands on his pants. Letting out a hesitant sigh, he says, "Julie and I have been trying to start a family, but...we're having trouble conceiving naturally. We've decided to try IVF."

"I'm so sorry to hear you're having trouble," Fulton says, speaking gently. "I've had friends who had success with IVF. It can work."

Chase doesn't look convinced. "Yeah, it can. It's also expensive as fuck and can take a long time."

We let that settle over us. I've been picking up on small cues for a while now that something was a little off with him. Like how Julie was messaging him more often and how tense he seemed to be in response to her texts. It all makes sense now.

"We're here for you, man," I offer. "Anytime you wanna talk about anything, we're right here."

Chase opens and shuts his mouth a few times, like he's got

something more he wants to add. Finally, he settles on, "Thanks. I know I've clammed up a bit lately. I'll—I'll try to talk more."

Okay, one down, two to go.

"What about you?" I lift my brows at Fulton. He's clearly depressed about something, the key giveaway being the plain gray T-shirt he's wearing. That's never a good sign. "What's bugging you?"

Fulton drops his head. "I had to put down an entire litter of kittens today. They were so abused, so malnourished, that it was the only humane option."

"Fuck, I'm sorry, man," Gus speaks up.

We all know how crazy Fulton is about cats, so it must have been bruising for him. "I just don't understand how people can be so cruel. I mean, if you can't look after an animal, hand it over to an animal shelter. There's no shame in that. Why would someone not do that and instead abuse a poor defenseless animal? I just—I just don't get it."

No one says anything for a while. "We need a proper animal shelter," Fulton declares, taking a pull of his beer.

"There are a couple of smaller ones—" Chase mentions, but Fulton cuts him off.

"No. A proper one," he repeats. "Somewhere that isn't constantly full and turning animals away."

Chase considers it for a moment. "There used to be a big shelter out on Fairview Drive."

"Yeah, but that's been closed for a while," Gus says sadly. "I looked into taking it over, but I just couldn't afford it. Shelters barely break even. Most run at a loss. It's a tough game."

"Well, we need one." Fulton sulks into his drink. "Abused animals are the most vulnerable of all. I can't believe there's no safe place for them."

We sit and share Fulton's pain in silence. Fulton drains the rest of his beer and lets out a loud burp. "I'll be fine, guys. I actually feel a bit better getting that out of me. It was eating me up."

I give him a comforting pat on his back. "It's what we're here for."

Okay, two down, one to go.

"And Gus, how are you doing?" I'm the one to ask since I see Chase and Fulton won't be the ones to do it.

Gus runs his hand through his hair. The guy looks like shit. He hasn't been to work. In fact, I don't think he's left his house since the wedding.

"And I don't mean any offense by this," Fulton says, "but what the fuck are you wearing?"

"It's a slanket," Gus replies with a resigned shrug. "It's a wearable blanket with sleeves."

I lean forward, inspecting the navy blue and plaid slanket more closely. "Are your feet enclosed?" I ask.

Gus lifts a leg in the air, revealing the foot pockets. "Yep, keeps me toasty warm. They say fleece and foot pockets are good for a broken heart."

Gus and Chase continue talking while Fulton inches over toward me. "Let's give Gus a month to grieve. If he hasn't left his house by then and is still wearing slankets, we stage an intervention."

"Agreed," I say with a firm nod.

"How's your shoulder, by the way?"

"Back to normal," I reply, lifting it to demonstrate. "It's like it never happened."

"I'm glad to hear it. You took quite the tumble."

"Tell me about it." I shudder at the memory of what I saw at the wedding, and as much as I dread asking, I can't help but be curious. "Have you heard from Marco?"

Gus shakes his head. "Nope. Nothing from him. His lawyers, on the other hand..."

"Are you fucking serious?" Chase spurts out.

"Deadly." Gus takes a massive swig of his beer. "This is going to get nasty. He wants half of everything. Including the clinic."

"Oh, man," I mutter through gritted teeth. "He won't win."

"No, he won't," Gus concurs as a frown settles on his forehead. "But he can drag this out so that we spend a fortune on legal fees."

"Haze's family owns a law firm. Maybe they can help?" I find myself saying. All three heads twist to face me.

"And how are things with you and Haze?" Gus asks, seeming grateful for the change in topic. "At least one of us has got something good going on in our lives."

"Uh..." I slink back into the couch. "Hold your horses there. Haze is in L.A. right now, going through some auditions. I'm pretty sure he'll land something, pack up and move there, and I'll be able to watch him when we have an Oscars party and be like, 'Yeah, I used to know that guy.'"

Fulton pats my knee. "You don't know he's going to leave."

I know he's trying to be supportive, but I pull back sharply. "Actually, yes I do. I mean, if he doesn't get something now, he'll move when he finishes his studies. Or sometime after that. It's not a case of *if* he leaves, but *when*. Story of my fucking life."

Silence pierces the air. Gus gets his slanketed ass off the couch to fetch more beer, trying to smile warmly as he hands it to me.

"He stayed with you and looked after you after your accident," Chase reminds me. "That's gotta mean something."

"I guess."

"And seriously, you should see the way he lights up whenever you're in the room. It's like the whole world fades to black, and he's only got eyes for you," Gus adds.

I huff out a breath. "Guys, thank you, but stop it, please. I know you're trying to be supportive, but this isn't helping. It only hurts even more when you realize you're on the cusp of losing the person you love."

Fulton gasps. "You love him?"

I take a pull of beer. Shit. Do I? It only takes a few short seconds for the answer to settle over me. "Yeah. I do. I know it's soon—"

"Not that soon," Gus points out. "You met him at the start of the year, and he's been working at the clinic for almost two months now."

"Besides, love doesn't operate on a timeframe. Things happen when they happen. If you love him, you should go for it," Fulton urges.

I draw in a breath. The bigness of what I've just discovered slams into me.

I love Haze Adams.

The tiniest glimmer of hope tugs at my heart. I remember the way Haze looked at me when he asked if I wanted him to stay. I didn't hesitate telling him that I didn't want him to leave, but I was being serious when I said I'd never hold him back or interfere in his dreams.

Did I catch something in his eye, a look like he was going to find a way for us to be together, or did I just imagine it? Would Haze actually give up his dream to be with me? And just as importantly, would I let him do that?

I scan the room. Chase has a slice of pizza hanging out of his mouth. Fulton's scrolling through his phone looking at cat photos, clutching his chest and cooing every few seconds. I turn to Gus just in time to see him pour half a bottle of scotch into the tub of ice cream he's been swaddling like a newborn the entire night. He catches me watching him and lifts a slanketed shoulder in a resigned shrug.

"Geez, this really is the worst episode of *The Golden Girls* ever," I lament.

And for the first time tonight, we actually laugh.

18
HAZE

L.A. was a whirlwind. I was only there for three days, but in that time, I did six on-camera auditions, even more off-camera ones, and met dozens of industry folk. It was all so frantic that it left me no time to just sit and process everything.

At least now I'm back home and doing something I truly love. Actually, that's not entirely true. If I was doing something I truly loved, I'd be in Noah's bed with my tongue buried deep in his ass. But since he's working late today, I do my second favorite thing in the world.

I add a little more purple coloring to the mix, inhaling the fragrances of the new batch I'm making. Fierce Beyoncé beats permeate through the loft. Once I finish up here, I'll quickly head over to Aunt Jocelyn's and then to Noah's place. God, I've missed him so much. We've exchanged texts, but both of our schedules have been so crazy that we haven't spoken in days. It feels like years. It's the longest we've been apart since I started working at the clinic.

I zone out, completely peaceful as I mix and stir and put together this new batch. Funny, I never felt this calm and happy in L.A. Not even once. If only there was some way to make a living from my soaps...

For some reason, Tate has been on my case to do another batch of the purple soaps I made a few weeks ago. They were a total flop—too runny and oily—but for some reason, he keeps on insisting that it wasn't. He also bought me a new mold tray, so when I've got the color right, I pour the warm liquid into the tray. If I had my mind in the gutter, I'd swear the molds kinda look like mid-sized penises.

I hear the front door heave open, and Tate bounds into the kitchen. "Haze." He wraps me up in a bear hug. "Man, I've missed you."

"I've missed you, too."

"So, tell me. Are you a huge star yet? How did it all go?"

I carefully spread a clean dish cloth over the mold tray. "Yeah. I think it went okay."

Tate tilts his head. "Why don't I believe you?"

"Maybe because I don't actually care."

Tate's mouth gapes open, and I admit, my admission catches me by surprise, too.

"Whoa. Where did that come from?"

I shrug. "I don't know. I've struggled for so long to find something that feels like a good fit, and at the end of the day, I'm happiest right here, right now, when I'm making soap."

"So make soap then," Tate rebuffs, like it's the most obvious thing in the world.

"Right. I'm doing my second degree. I have student debt that will take me at least five lifetimes to pay off, and I should just fuck all that to enter the incredibly lucrative world of soap?"

He flashes me a wide grin. "That pretty much sums it up, yeah."

"I don't think that's how the world works."

"Hmm. Well, see, here's what I know about life." Tate wraps an arm around my shoulder. "Expect the unexpected. Finish that batch for me please, and who knows what will happen next?"

I narrow my eyes. "You're up to something."

His lips spill into a wide grin. "Yep. I am."

"So you admit it?"

"Haze, you know me. I have no shame."

I place my hand on my hip. "And when do you plan on telling me about whatever it is you're scheming?"

He eyes the soap tray. "When you make me more of that good stuff."

I don't get it. It makes no sense. Why on earth is Tate so obsessed with a misshapen, way too oily, and greasy batch of soaps that nobody would be interested in buying?

Before I can squeeze any more information out of the guy, he announces he's got a cam session in five minutes and bounces out of the kitchen.

I have a weird sense of déjà vu as I'm recounting my time in L.A. to Aunt Jocelyn in her office. She's kicked off her pumps and is resting her feet on the coffee table, her eyes dissecting me.

"I feel like a failure," I say after basically repeating my earlier conversation with Tate to her. "I'm almost thirty, and despite having had the best dad, the best family, such a privileged start to life, I'm still clueless about something so basic as what I want to do for work."

"Honey, there's nothing wrong with taking some time——"

"No," I interrupt her. "I've taken time. I've taken a whole lot of it. This is me coming out the other side and still having no freaking clue."

She purses her lips. "I'm about to tell you something, Hazey, and you have to swear to me you won't breathe a word of this to your father."

I sit up a little taller in the Chesterfield. "I promise. What is it?"

She smiles and lowers her feet. Her face turns thoughtful. "I was just as lost as you were."

I can feel my brows pinching together. "What? When?"

Her steely eyes meet mine. "The official story goes that after high school, I studied abroad."

"Riiight."

"That's only partly true. While I did study while I was in Europe and got two degrees, I had no idea what I wanted to do with my life. I traveled. I partied. A lot." Even though we're alone in her office with the door closed, she looks around as if to make sure no one can hear.

"It was the summer of 1990," she begins in a hushed tone. "New Kids on the Block were the biggest band on the planet."

I lean in closer. I'm smiling already, even though I have no idea where this story is going.

"I caught their performance in Rotterdam, and let me put it this way, when I say I managed to slip in backstage, I'm not just talking about seeing them after the show."

My mouth falls open. "You slept with one of the band members?"

She looks at me incredulously. "Hazey baby, you know me better than that... Who says it was just one band member?"

We erupt in laughter. "Oh my God, Aunt Jocelyn. You were a badass."

"Were?" She gets to her feet. "You're probably too young to remember, but on Justin Timberlake's first solo album, he had a song called Señorita." Aunt Jocelyn stands right in front of me and lifts up her blouse to reveal a flaming red *Señorita* tattoo on her side.

My eyes widen. "You mean you..."

"Not saying anything." She smiles devilishly, sitting down. "But I'm not *not* saying anything, either."

I roll my eyes at the classic lawyer speak.

"My point is that while it looked like I had my shit together because I was doing degree after degree, on the inside, I was lost and confused and, well, drowning."

I run my fingers through my hair. "I can totally relate."

"Good. Because I don't want you to be alone in this feeling. There is nothing wrong with taking as much time as you need to figure things out. I was completely clueless about what I wanted to do with the rest of my life until..." Her jaw clenches.

"Until?" I prompt.

Aunt Jocelyn fixes us both a drink. She hands it to me, all the while saying nothing until we've both had a sip. "Until your mom died."

"Really?"

She nods, her eyes a little watery. "That woke me up. I had to get my life together. For your dad. For you." She rubs my knee. "For my parents. For the firm. So I came back here and put all those degrees to good use. I took over the firm in my mid-thirties. There really is no age limit on when you're meant to have your life sorted by."

I'm trying to take it all in, but it's a lot. "Wow," is the best I can manage.

"The formula for success is no more complicated than just doing what makes you happy." She takes another sip of her drink. "Stepping up and looking after the people that mean the most to me is what I want to do with my life. There's nothing more that I love in the world. And I still do things on my own terms—that part hasn't changed."

"Aunt Jocelyn," I say, turning to face her. "You're even more badass than I thought you were."

I hear Buddy's excited panting before I even reach the front door. And before I get a chance to knock, it swings wide open. Without thinking, I hurl myself into Noah's arms. Thank god the man has big guns and a steady stance because he scoops me up like it's nothing. Our lips crash together, and somehow, Noah manages to skillfully kick the door shut and carry me into his house with my legs glued to his waist and Buddy prancing around us excitedly.

"God, I've missed you," I murmur into his mouth.

"Ditto." He puts me down. "I don't want to stop kissing you, but..." He lowers his eyes to Buddy. He practically mauls me as I drop to my knees and get covered in his slobbery, wet kisses.

"He's missed you, too. Plus, he's just eaten, so his excitement levels are in overdrive. Wanna come sit out on the porch?"

"Sure."

Buddy leads the way, scampering past us. In the backyard, he sniffs in circles around the bushes, while Noah and I settle onto the stairs. The chill of the autumn night air sneaks through the fabric of my jacket. Noah curls his hand around me, the touch warming me instantly.

"How was L.A.?"

"Warmer than here," I reply.

Noah smiles. I can tell he knows there's more to it than that, but he doesn't press. He never does. And I will tell him all about it, just not right now.

"How's Gus?"

"Not great." Noah's jaw tightens. "It's getting nasty. Marco wrote him a terrible letter, and urgh, let's not talk about it, okay? At least not right now."

"Fine by me. If Gus needs legal help, though, please let me know. My Aunt Jocelyn is a firecracker."

Noah smiles, the skin around his eyes crinkling. "Thank you... Hazey."

We sit in a comfortable silence, watching Buddy hopping around as the darkness of night begins to creep in. "It's getting cold. C'mon, let's go inside," Noah stands but doesn't let go of my hand. "I'll leave the porch light on for Buddy, and he can come in when he's ready."

We walk into the living room, still hand in hand. It's like neither one of us wants to let the other one go. We drop down onto the couch, facing each other. An episode of *This Pet's Got Talent* is playing silently on the TV.

Noah's green eyes pin me with a seriousness I've never seen on him before. "I've been doing some thinking."

My gaze snags on his "So have I."

"I'm just going to come right out and say it." Noah's chest heaves as he takes a deep breath. "I'm falling for you, Haze."

Right at that moment, Buddy runs over and starts licking all over my face. "And I think Buddy feels the same way," Noah jokes.

Once I'm able to wrestle Buddy off me, I lean in toward Noah. "Buddy's a done deal, no question about it, but...I'm falling for you, too."

The smile that fills Noah's face could light up New York City. He cups my face in his hands, and our lips collide in a short, intense burst of a kiss. We pull apart, but our foreheads remain touching. "I have no idea how this is going to work, or what the future holds for us." Noah's voice is stripped raw as he speaks. "But my feelings for you are so real and so strong that I have to trust it."

"I don't know what the future holds, either. But for the first time in...well, ever, I know what I want." I move back slightly so I can look Noah straight in the eye when I say it to him. "I want to be with you. And I'm gonna find a way to make it happen."

His brow creases. "Please don't give up on your dreams for me. I don't want you to have to change who you are ever again."

The beauty of the sentiment behind those words makes my heart clench. Noah's so selfless, it moves me on a deeper soul-level. There's something I need him to know, too. "And please don't ever feel like you're the only one who has to give to make this work. Because I'm here, Noah. I want this as much as you do, and I want to treat you how you deserve to be treated."

Noah's eyes mist. "This is so fucking scary."

I link my arms around his neck. "Tell me about it."

"I've never felt this way before."

"Neither have I. But we'll figure this out. Together. Okay?"

Noah lets out a shaky breath. "Together."

The moment is interrupted by the sound of tongue lapping. We both look down to see Buddy licking Noah's feet. A wicked smile curves Noah's lips. "Are you thinking what I'm thinking?"

Ten minutes later, Buddy is off in doggy dreamland, and his owner is lying on his back with his legs up in the air. Every single cell in my body wants to ravage this beautiful naked man in front of me. Even though it defies every law of physics, somehow I manage to hold back.

I drop down flat on the bed, the tip of my tongue gently caressing Noah's taint. For a change, I'm the one breathing him in, and he smells good enough to eat. Noah has an understated masculine scent that's irresistible.

I stick my tongue out and trace small circles around his hole. "Oh, Hazey baby." His moans fill the bedroom.

"I want to take my time," I say, glancing up at him. "I know you've been working a lot and are probably tired—"

"I'm fine," he interrupts. "Got the energy of a twenty-two-year-old."

I giggle. "Sounds like someone's keen."

He glares down at me. "You have no fucking idea." His thick fingers part his hole open wider for me. "Now dig in."

"Don't have to tell me twice."

I dive into his ass, my tongue in ravage mode. Noah writhes and rocks underneath me as I slurp away at his hole, lavishing it with wet, sloppy licks and kisses. Noah's hands land in my hair. He loves pulling on it, and I love it, too.

"Need more," he pants as I'm making out with his hole. "Need your cock inside me." With an abrupt jerk, Noah snaps his head up. "Actually, wait. No. I need something else right now."

I look up, the taste of Noah's ass imprinted on my lips and face. Noah swings his legs over to the side of the bed and with a practiced ease, flips me over so that I'm the one on my back. With a heated look, Noah lowers himself down onto my—

"Fuuuuuck," I hiss, my hands fisting the sheets. Noah's biting my left nipple. Gently, but with enough firmness to send a shower of sparks raining down my spine. He fondles my other nipple between his thumb and forefinger, toying with the piercing, and man, there is no better feeling in the world.

Noah releases my right nipple. A moan escapes his lips, so I glance down to see what he's doing, and holy fuck, with one hand, Noah's pinching and twisting my left nipple, and with the other, he's fingering himself, his thick digit slipping in and out of his hot, pink hole. If my cock was leaking before, it's positively spurting out a torrent of precome now.

"Noah, you're going to make me blow in less than three seconds if you don't stop. That is the hottest thing I have ever seen."

With one final deeper twist, he releases my nipples and frees his fingers from his ass. "Wouldn't want that now, would we?"

He climbs past me and rifles through the drawer in his nightstand. He pulls out his jumbo-sized lube and a condom and expertly rolls it over my cock. "Wow, you're really hard," he observes with a wicked grin.

"Uh, yeah. You on my nipples with your fingers in your ass is permanently emblazoned in my memory."

He chuckles as he spreads a generous slathering of lube over my cock. Keeping his eyes trained on me, he straddles me. Never breaking eye contact, he slowly lowers himself onto my cock. I can see the fullness of the stretch break out across his features. His breathing deepens, his cheeks puffing out, the slight grimace that tugs on his lips, and then...we bottom out, and I witness the blissfulness wash over him.

With a guttural moan, he adjusts his knees and begins to bounce up and down on my dick. I bring my hands to his nipples, tweaking them gently. "You like this?" I ask as he starts to increase the pace.

"Yeah. It feels good. But your cock in my ass feels better."

I smile. "Good to know."

Noah's rocking his hips, and fuck, he clamps his ass around my cock so tight I have to focus on my breathing to not ruin the moment by coming too soon. I trace my fingers over his stomach, pinching into the soft flesh. I rub the insides of his thighs that are coated with a sprinkling of light hairs. And then I grab his cock, jerking it hard and rough. Noah's head falls back.

"You like that, huh?"

"Oh, yeah."

The sight of this beautiful, caring, sensitive, funny man bouncing up and down as my cock plunges deeper and deeper into him becomes too much. I can feel my balls tighten, my orgasm building.

"I'm getting close," I whisper.

"Same. Keep jacking me off. Let's come at the same time."

I let out a snort. "That doesn't happen in real life."

He drops his eyes to meet mine, and there's something deep dancing behind them. "We can make it happen."

And fuck, right at that moment, Noah's release spurts from his cock while my orgasm tears through me. It's a cacophony of grunts and "oh fucks," but the really crazy, beautiful thing? We never take our eyes off each other. The whole time our bodies are rocking in sheer ecstasy, we stay connected.

For the first time in my entire life, a deep knowing fills me. I'd told Noah we'd figure this out together, but those are just words. Now, as the intensity of the orgasm we just shared together slowly subsides, the words are gone, replaced by a deep, soul-level understanding.

I don't have to give up my dreams for Noah because Noah *is* my dream.

19
NOAH

The last two weeks have been like living in a blissful bubble I never want to burst. Haze and I both have busy lives, but we've managed to fall into this really lovely, really settled routine.

When we're not working, or he's studying, Haze is at my place because, you know, it has walls. We don't necessarily do anything super exciting. We just enjoy spending time together. It doesn't matter if we're playing with Buddy, cooking up some dinner, or I'm subjecting the poor guy to old seasons of *This Pet's Got Talent*. For the first time in a really long time, something interesting is happening: I love my life again.

Don't get me wrong. I've always *liked* my life. I have a dream job, amazing friends and colleagues, and I'm close with my family, but now, because of Haze, I'm *loving* it again. I didn't realize just how dull things had gotten over the past few years since my relationship with Graham ended. I guess that's why I threw myself into work and avoided dating, apps, and one-night stands.

Until I had my first one... There's no way I could have predicted any of this would happen with Haze, but I'm so glad it has. I've never been happier in my entire life.

I'm wrapping up my consultation with Mr. Roberts and his adorable seven-year-old son, Alastair. They picked up their Great Dane pup, Duke, from the breeder yesterday and have brought him in for a vet check. It's always a good idea to get a puppy checked out as soon as possible after getting it to make sure there are no serious issues.

Alastair's bright blue eyes shining with excitement reminds me of what I was like at that age. Getting your first puppy is an experience you never forget, but it's the million and one questions that Alastair's peppering me with that makes me see his love of animals is something extra special. Who knows? Maybe he'll end up becoming a vet one day, too.

"Gentlemen," I say, carefully keeping a firm grip on the pup. "It looks like Duke is perfectly healthy."

They both smile as Alastair leaps up from his chair and starts stroking Duke. He is an adorable puppy, I have to admit, all limbs with ears that drop almost to the ground and a deep rich blue-gray color.

"How often can I comb him?" Alastair asks.

"Now, now." Mr. Roberts joins his son at the table. "I'm sure Dr. Walters is a very busy man. He's already given us a lot of information, and the rest I'm sure we can find online."

"I don't mind, really." I look down at Alastair's happy face. "While he's still a puppy, you can comb him, very gently, once every few days. When he grows up, once a week will be fine."

I face Mr. Roberts. "If you care about your carpet, regular brushing will help with shedding. A lot."

The man chuckles. "Thanks, Noah. I really appreciate everything."

"No problem. We're here anytime you need us. And if you have any more questions, please don't hesitate to give us a call. You can't believe everything you read online."

I watch as Alastair props himself up on a chair and, with all the care in the world, gently lifts Duke and places him into his travel cart, before Mr. Roberts locks it and carries it out of the room. I follow them down the hallway to say my goodbye in the waiting room. It has absolutely nothing to do with my desire to see the gorgeous guy sitting behind the reception desk. Nope, not at all.

Haze notices me and smiles, unleashing a calm, happy feeling through me. We both finish our shift in fifteen minutes. Haze is such a natural with people, charming them with his easy confidence and genuine friendliness. It's something I'll never get sick of seeing, and yeah, I do often find myself lingering in the reception area until after the client leaves, hoping to sneak a cheeky kiss.

Once Mr. Roberts, Alastair, and Duke are out the door, I slip behind the counter and am on Haze like white on rice. I've obviously checked to make sure no one is around and the waiting room is empty, because professionalism and all that, but as I pull him into a kiss, everything else in the world fades away.

"I got you an early birthday present," I murmur against his sweet lips.

He brings me in even closer, lashing my mouth with his tongue, before pulling away and asking, "Oh yeah? What is it? Or are you going to torture me and not tell me?"

I chuckle. "I could never torture you. Well, not in a bad way. Let's just say this kind of torture is one I think you'll like very, very much."

"Is that so?"

I nod earnestly. "Uh-huh. Just let me finish typing up my notes, and barring any last-minute emergencies, we can leave soon. Okay?"

Fifteen minutes later, Haze's fingers are tapping against my thigh on the drive back to my place. Well, technically, they're tapping a little higher than my thigh, his long fingers trailing a ring of circles in my bulge. My dick is so hard I'm surprised it hasn't torn a hole through my pants. Thankfully, there's not much traffic. Despite the general inability of men to do more than one thing at a time, I'm gripping the steering wheel tight and paying extra attention to the road. The relief I feel pulling into the driveway is indescribable. We jump out of the car and rush inside to be met with a tornado of dog licks and excited yelps.

"I'll take care of Buddy, feed him, take him outside," Haze yelps out in between having his face slobbered. "You go upstairs and get to work on that early birthday present of mine."

Haze stands up, and I bury my face into his neck, inhaling his scent as deeply as I can. "Mmm. I like it when you get all bossy."

"Stop tempting me. Now, go!"

I have the world's shortest shower and get the bedroom all set up. I left the house after Haze this morning, so I've prepared the room, setting candles everywhere. I dash around, lighting them all. I've finally learned that ylang-ylang is an essential oil that produces a slightly sweet and floral aroma. I light a tealight candle in an essential oil burner and add a few drops of the stuff into it. I also learned that ylang-ylang is associated with feelings of euphoria. Not that we need any help in that department, but I hope Haze likes it, anyway.

Speaking of Haze, I quickly grab his early birthday gift and hide it under the pillows. I can hear his footsteps coming down the hallway, so I jump onto the bed to assume the position he loves to see me in. On my back, legs in the air, playing with my hole.

"Holy fuck," Haze says as he swings the door open. "That's it. I'm done. Creamed my jeans."

I start laughing. "Creamed my jeans? Those are some seriously unsexy words."

Haze huffs out a laugh while stripping his clothes off in record time. His body lands on top of mine, the weight of it sending a rapid rush of heat through me, lighting up my insides.

"I want you inside me." I can hear the need dripping from my voice, but I don't care. Being with Haze is giving me a newfound confidence to tell him what I need. I know he doesn't judge me for it.

"Done and done."

He dives down, and I let out a moan the instant his tongue lands on my hole, lapping at it furiously. We're clearly not taking our time today. I whimper as his tongue drives deeper into me, melting me like ice cream on a hot summer's day. As much as I'm loving what he's doing, I need more.

"I need you. I need your cock inside of me. Right now."

Haze smiles and nods. "Now who's being bossy?" he teases, tearing open a condom I've laid out on the bed and sheathes his cock.

"I've prepped already," I say a little too excitedly.

Don't get me wrong, I love it when Haze takes his time, but right now, I need him inside of me so that I can bring out his early birthday present.

With a light chuckle, he gets his cock into position. It never fails to excite me that he can enter me hands-free. I feel the crown of his cock nestling in my taint and then with a gentle thrust...

"Ahhh."

Haze finds the magic spot. With his eyes trained on me, he slides his cock deeper inside. I interlace my fingers around his neck, and he bottoms out.

"God, you feel incredible."

"Yeah, well, I want to make you feel even more incredible." I reach my hand under the pillow.

The corner of his eyebrow flicks up. "What is that?" he asks.

"These," I say, lifting the two black clamps closer to him so he can get a better look, "are vibrating nipple clamps. There's no way I can reach your nipples with my tongue while you're fucking me, so I thought these might be good. Wanna try?"

Haze flashes a massive smile. "Fuck, yeah."

He stays still as I attach the first clamp on his right nipple. "Is this okay?"

Haze closes his eyes and takes a deep breath in. "Yep. Just need a moment to adjust."

I wait patiently, giving him all the time he needs. "There's no rush."

His eyes flicker open. "Thank you. I'm ready for the next one."

With as much care as possible, I attach the other clamp to his left nipple. After just one deep exhale, Haze points to a small black box beside me. "And what's that?"

I pick it up so he can see it better. "This is the controller. It has five settings from light to very heavy. Would you like to control it or—"

"You." Haze's voice comes out deeper than I've ever heard, and I can feel his cock throbbing inside of me. "But I have to warn you, this might make me come super quick."

I smile. "I'm perfectly fine with that."

"I'm going to turn it on, just at the low setting," I say to him, letting him see exactly what I'm doing. "Please tell me if you want me to turn it off, and I will. Straight away. It's also safe for you to just take the clamps off at any stage, too. Okay?"

Haze bobs his head, loose strands of hair bouncing around his shoulders. "This is the best early birthday present ever."

I grin. "We haven't even started to use it."

And with that, I turn it on, and holy shit, Haze's whole body starts trembling.

"Fuck, fuck, fuck," he pants.

My fingers fumble with the controller, and I quickly switch it off.

Haze glares at me. "What are you doing?"

"Sorry. I thought you were in pain."

He licks his lips and then ducks his head, treating me to a kiss. "Yeah, I was. But it's the good kind of pain. Trust me, I'll let you know if it ever gets too much."

"Oh, okay."

"And..."

"Yes, Haze?"

"Thanks for looking out for me."

"No problem. I'm going to switch it back on, okay?"

Haze closes his eyes and nods. With the flick of a switch, his body jerks and trembles again. I can see his Adam's apple thrashing about in his throat, but after a few moments, he settles. I don't know how many nerve endings the human body has, but it looks like every single one of them is lighting Haze up from the inside.

I feel his hips start to rock against me. I wrap my fingers around my dick and start jacking off. By the way Haze is responding to the stimulation, I can tell he's close.

He increases his speed. "More." The word escapes from the side of his mouth. "Turn it up."

I do as he commands, and it sends him to a whole new level. He falls down and slams his mouth into mine, canting and bucking against my body. The gentle hum of the nipple clamps gets drowned out by the most filthy-sounding groans coming from...shit, I can't even tell who's making the noises, me or him.

"I'm gonna come," he cries out.

I watch as his body twists and contorts in the most incredible ways. I turn the machine off as soon as he's done and gently unpin the clamps from his nipples. He collapses in a heap beside me.

"Did you come?" he croaks out.

"No. Not yet."

Summoning all his energy, Haze glides himself down to my cock and swallows it all in one smooth movement. A few seconds later, I can feel one of his fingers enter me. Then another, Holy hell, then another.

My back arches off the bed as I flood Haze's mouth with my release. He devours it all, not spilling a drop. I tap his shoulders and indicate I want him beside me. Haze scooches up the bed and nestles into my chest. I stroke his hair and breathe in deeply, filling myself with the smell of him.

"So you enjoyed your early birthday present, I take it?"

"Uh, that would be a one thousand percent yes."

"I'm glad." I continue gently threading my fingers through his golden strands. "And what about your actual birthday next week? Will you be having a party?"

Instantly, Haze's body stiffens against mine and not in a good way. "No." His voice is so low I can barely hear it. "I've never had a birthday party."

"Why not?" The question escapes my lips right as the answer hits me like a slap in the face. "Oh, shit. I'm so sorry. I've got post-sex brain."

Haze wiggles away from me, and we both sit up against the headboard. "It's weird enough on its own that my birthday is also the anniversary of my mom's death. The thought of a party just feels...wrong."

"I can completely understand. What do you normally do on the day?"

Haze scratches along the base of his neck and gives a little shrug. "Depends. When I was a kid, we used to have a family dinner that week, not on the day itself, and that was a chance for everyone to give me a present. When I got older, I started going to the cemetery, but that would just bum me out for the rest of the day."

His eyes turn watery, but he keeps speaking. "I don't want to have a massive party and, like, get wasted or anything, but I guess I would like to do something. It would have to be super chill, low-key...but I don't know what that looks like. So every year when my family asks me what I want for my birthday, I say the same thing."

"Which is?"

A sad smile forms on his lips. "Nothing."

"Oh, Hazey..."

He folds into me, and I hold him tight, his hot tears soaking my chest. I stroke the length of his back as quiet sobs fall from him. Right there, in that moment, I decide to give Haze the birthday he deserves.

Two days later, I find myself in an impressive corner office downtown, shaking hands with an equally impressive-looking lady. Not a hair out of place. Her makeup is exquisite. Her white power suit pops even more, courtesy of a chunky orange necklace.

"He talks about you all the time, Ms. Adams," I say as we shake hands.

"Please, call me Jocelyn. All good things, I hope."

"Yeah... Mostly," I joke and hold my breath, hoping she gets it. If she's as feisty as Haze says, she will. I'm hoping she'll appreciate my attempt at humor.

She studies me intently for a few moments, assessing me, before breaking out into a warm smile. "Well, good." She gestures toward the brown couches in the center of her office. "Because if you want the more interesting stuff, you should come straight to the source. Hazey won't give you all the juicy stuff...but I will."

Her eyes light up when she talks, and even though she and Haze don't share many physical characteristics, they both have that same kind of genuineness and warmth. I feel at ease with her already.

"I hope you don't mind me contacting you out of the blue like this."

"Not at all. Haze may have mentioned you one or two...hundred times."

A happy feeling washes over me as I begin explaining my idea to her. She doesn't say a lot, but I can hear her humming along every so often. It doesn't take that long to explain my idea to her, and when I'm done, she nods approvingly.

"I like what you've come up with, Noah. More importantly, I think Haze will like it, too. Leave it with me."

We go over a few of the finer details, and as I'm standing in the elevator, I rub my hands in glee. I know it's a bit of a risk, but I really, *really* hope Haze will love it.

20

HAZE

"Thanks for dropping me off," I say as Noah pulls up out the front of my building. It's the day before my birthday, and this has become part of our normal morning routine. Even though I'm spending all my spare time at his house, most of my day-to-day stuff is still at my place. I appreciate it even more because I know he's got a busy morning ahead of him. Not only is he starting work soon, but he also needs to pick up some meds for Buddy, who got a sore tummy last night. That means he'll need to dash back home, give Buddy his pill, before heading into the clinic.

Noah cuts the engine and turns to me. "Of course, Hazey. I'm not going to let you take the bus to get home. That'd make me a monster."

I giggle. "I don't think me catching public transport qualifies to make you a monster, but I do appreciate the ride. I really hope Buddy will be okay."

Noah smiles warmly. "He should be. It's nothing too serious. He probably just chomped on something he shouldn't have in the garden yesterday."

"Keep me updated please. I want to know how he's getting on."

"I will."

Something's shifted between us since I broke down in his arms, talking about my birthday, a few nights ago. Noah's always been kind, caring, and attentive, but he's somehow managed to step it up a notch. I gotta say, I love the feeling of being with someone who treats me so well. I only hope I'm giving Noah everything he deserves as well.

"Thank you," I repeat. My tone is more serious this time.

He reaches for my hand across the console, knitting our fingers together. "For what?"

I glance out the window. It's still early, but a few people are out and about, bundled up in winter jackets, steam puffing out of their mouths or from the foam cups they're carrying.

"For dropping me off when you have a million things to do. For being an all-round amazing person. For making me feel so safe and warm. For allowing me to be myself when I'm with you." I take a breath. "For making me feel...tingly."

"Aww, baby. That's so sweet." Noah's fingers squeeze tightly around mine. "And just for the record, you make me feel tingly, too."

"Tingly is good."

Noah's head lifts, sunlight splashing across his face. "Tingly is *very* good."

Heat ignites inside of me at the sudden, yet very welcome, change in direction. I giggle, giving him an all-too-chaste kiss, and step out of the car. A few moments later, I lean against the wall in the elevator, smiling. I can't believe this is my life. It's been a few months since I started working at the clinic, and the time Noah and I have spent together has been the most incredible thing ever. I still have to pinch myself sometimes that we're in each other's lives at all. That was so not the deal when we first met.

The doors to the elevator open, and I step out. I try to recall the four one-night stand rules Noah had when we met, but all I remember is the first one, *don't spend the night*, which we broke straight away, and the last rule, *don't fall in love*, which I'm breaking with every breath I take.

I meant what I told Noah in the car. When I'm with him, I feel like I can be myself. I don't know how he does it. Heck, I don't think it's any one particular thing that he does, but ever since we first laid eyes on each other, he's managed to bring me out. The real me. And man, as much as I'm falling for Noah, I'm totally digging discovering who I am, too.

I call out when I open the front door, but no one responds. I don't have classes until the afternoon, so I decide to kill a few hours by making some soap. I had the thought it might be a nice idea to make a batch for the vets and nurses at the clinic. I've never met a more hardworking group of people in my life. It's only a small gesture, but I hope they like it.

Since I've got the place to myself, I decide to crank some Queen

Bey beats as I get to work. I prep the kitchen table by covering it with newspapers and laying out all the base oils, creams, and fragrances. Before I can decide what specific blend I'm going to make today, my cellphone rings. I pick it up. It's an out-of-town number.

"Hello."

"Haze Adams, you are about to become a star!"

Oh, shit. My stomach drops. It's Lyon from L.A. A very happy-sounding Lyon. I step away from my soapmaking station and drape myself across the kitchen counter. I feel the blood drain from my face as Lyon starts yammering away at a million miles an hour.

I've secured a role. It's not the lead, but the lead character's best friend. It's a new scripted sitcom being billed as *Sex and the City* meets *Queer as Folk* for disgruntled millennials and depressed Gen-Z-ers.

"Oh."

Lyon keeps on babbling away. I'm still listening, but now that I've got the gist of it, I'm not really taking it in any more. I place the phone on the counter and hit the speaker icon. Lyon's exuberance fills the kitchen. If we had walls, his excitement would be bouncing right off them. Meanwhile, I can barely muster the strength to stand.

When he finally runs out of puff, he asks me a question which I've completely missed, only catching the end of it.

"Sorry? When can I do what?"

"Get out here? Pronto would be preferable. Quit your studies. Quit your job, and whatever else you've got going on in your life, and get your ass out here to L.A."

His words are like balled-up fists slamming into my chest. "Quit?" I eke out.

"Uh, yeah." I hear him snicker. "Hollywood isn't going to come to you."

I scrub my palm down the side of my face. "Uh, okay. When do you need to know by?"

"Know what by?" His tone shifts, growing low and guarded.

"My—my decision," I stammer. "How long do I have to think about this?"

A deafening silence follows. "What is there to think about here?"

Uh, how about all of the things in my life that I don't want to quit? Like my work. Like where I live. Like my family. Like Tate and my friends... Like Noah. Okay, *especially* Noah.

When I don't say anything, Lyon breaks the silence with a pointed reminder. "This is an incredible opportunity for you. This role will get your foot firmly in the door. After this, you'll have a profile to go on to bigger and better things." He pauses for a beat. "Is that what you're worried about? That you didn't get the lead role?"

"No. It's not that," I somehow manage to wrangle the words out. "It's definitely not that. I'm sorry, Lyon, but I'll have to think about this. I need some time."

"You have ten minutes." He hangs up before I can say anything.

It takes me a few minutes before I can even move. I'm in shock, as much about getting a role on a sitcom as I am about the fact that my gut is lurching with a heavy dread that feels so, *so* wrong. It's the complete opposite to how I was feeling only minutes ago in the car with Noah, or even as I was getting ready to make a batch of soaps. There's no *tingly-ness* here.

All I'm left with is a heavy feeling bubbling up from my stomach and into my throat, making me feel like I'm about to heave. I start pacing up and down the length of the kitchen, gripping my phone tightly.

It's happening.

The thing that I both wanted and feared the most is actually happening. It feels like worlds are colliding as the various options and scenarios flash before my eyes.

I take the role and move to L.A. The show is a huge success. Like Lyon said, it's a stepping stone to bigger and better things. I get more work. Get cast on another show. Maybe work my way up to shooting some movies in the summer. I become famous. Rich. I buy a house in the hills. Win awards. Travel the world…

I'm trying to psych myself up here, reminding myself that this is an amazing opportunity, one I should be wanting. I scrub the side of my face. So why does it feel so wrong? Why am I left with this stone-cold ice block of dread and doubt? If this is what I genuinely, truly want, then why is it taking so much effort to convince myself of it?

The truth is, I don't want it. Not just a life in L.A. but a career in performance. I've just been too afraid to call it out, scared that it's another notch to add to my growing list of things that I started but never finished. I've felt this way for some time, maybe even before London, but something's different now.

Previously, I could bury my feelings under reasonable-sounding excuses like *you've still got time to figure it out* or *you don't have to make any decisions until you graduate.* But for whatever reason, that doesn't cut it anymore. I've gotten to the point where I don't believe what I've been telling myself anymore.

My phone vibrates in my hand. It's a text from Noah. I open it. It's a selfie of a smiling Noah crouching down next to Buddy. The text reads: ***Someone was a very good boy and took his meds. Missing you already. Buddy says licks.***

Seeing Noah smiling, Buddy next to him, those simple words, it makes me come undone. Goosebumps shoot down my arms as I reply with trembling fingers: ***Miss you both too.***

I shake my hair out before calling Lyon back. He answers on the first ring. "Lyon. I've made my decision."

Half an hour later, I'm immersed in a world of melting oils and heavenly smells. My emotions feel like they're floating in the ether. I'm in my Zen place, but obviously, the decision I just made is dominating my thoughts.

Don't get me wrong. I one hundred percent know that I made the right decision in rejecting the role. No question about that. I guess I'm just in that in-between space of closing one door and being on the precipice of stepping through the next. I feel confused and worried and anxious, but I also feel something else. And it comes down to one silly word.

Tingly.

I don't know how I know, but I can feel that everything is going to work out well. I'm going to be all right.

I hear the front door open, and Tate strides in carrying a bag of bagels. He drops them onto the counter and exclaims, "Oh my goodness! Are my eyes deceiving me? Is that——is that Haze Adams I see standing before me? It's been so long."

When I don't react to his teasing, Tate makes his way over to the table and gently nudges into me. "Hey. You okay?"

That snaps me out of whatever daze I've just been in. "I got the part."

"Oh my god! That's amazing. Congrat——wait. This is good news, right?"

With a soft smile, I tell him, "I turned it down."

"Oh. Okay. Can I ask why?" There's no judgment in his voice, just curiosity.

"Because it's not what I want and..." I suck in a deep breath. "For the first time in my life, I actually do know what I want."

"Which is?"

I grab my phone from the table and show him the selfie of Noah and Buddy. "This."

Tate scratches his chin. "That is one good-looking dog."

We burst out laughing. He leans his hip against the table, his eyes bright and friendly. "I am so happy for you."

"You don't think I've just made the biggest mistake ever and will regret this decision for the rest of my life?"

He hands me back the phone. "Do *you* think that?"

"No fucking way," I reply with no hesitation.

"Well, then, that's all that matters." He places his hand on my shoulder. "Take it from a wildly successful cam model who is used to dealing with people's sex-negativity and kink-shaming. Life is not about what anyone else says, thinks, or wants for you. It's about doing what *you* want. And for the first time since I've known you, it sounds like you're figuring out what that is."

"I am. I really am."

"Soooo... Speaking of things that we want," Tate begins, almost a little coyly as he eyes off my soapmaking supplies scattered across the table. "Any chance you could make me another purple batch, please?"

I shake my head in disbelief. "Okay. Enough is enough. Why do you keep asking me to make soaps for you? And why are you obsessed with the purple batch? They didn't turn out right. They're too oily and slippery, and they don't keep their shape."

Tate lifts a finger in the air, his eyes gleaming devilishly. "Be right back." He jogs out of the room, and when he returns a few seconds later, he's got his laptop tucked under his arm.

"So." We both sit down at the table. "Do you remember the ice bucket challenge a couple of years ago?"

I think about it. "Kinda. That was that online thing where people had a bucket of ice dumped over them to raise money and awareness for a charity?"

"Yeah. That's right." Tate opens his laptop as a smirk engulfs his lips. "So now, think of my ass as the bucket and your soap as the ice."

I'm used to weird shit falling out of the guy's mouth, but this is next-level, even for him. "I have absolutely zero idea what you're talking about right now, Tate."

"Here, look at this. This is from my 4FansOnly, so it contains some explicit nudity. If you're uncomfortable, please let me know."

I wave my hand. "I'm fine."

Tate drags his laptop in front of me, and when I see what he was referring to, my mouth falls open. "What—what am I even looking at here?"

"It all started when you made that first batch of purple soaps that you said you got all wrong."

"I did. The texture and consistency weren't right," I point out. "You wouldn't be able to wash yourself with them. They were too oily. Remember how you tried to pick one up and it slipped out of your hands?"

Tate's face lights up. "Exactly!"

I'm confused. "Exactly what? Why is a bad batch of soaps a good thing?"

Tate sticks out his left hand, palm up. "Soap." He sticks out his right hand, also palm facing up. "Lube." He clasps his hands together. "Soap lube."

"Mmhmm." I'm still not fully getting it, though.

"There's one more piece to this puzzle," Tate adds.

"This very X-rated puzzle," I throw in.

He snorts. "Right. Remember how you were also pissed because the soaps came out looking funny?"

"Yeah. They kinda looked like small dicks."

"Exactly! I don't have three hands to demonstrate, so just do your best to follow along. I'll be sure to speak slowly."

I roll my eyes, giggling. "Go on."

"Dildo... Lube... Soap."

I blink. I blink some more. "So you're telling me... Wait. What are you telling me?"

Tate lets out an impatient huff, but goes on. "Remember that client who wanted me to shoot stuff out of my ass?"

"How could I forget?"

"Well, your dildo lube soap was perfect for that. Right size, right smoothness, right oiliness. Right everything. When I showered after that session, I couldn't help but notice how great my ass smelled."

"That makes sense. The soap bars are fragranced, and I guess because I only use natural, high-quality ingredients, there wasn't any sting?"

"None whatsoever," Tate confirms, his eyes alight, like he's on the verge of revealing some amazing, life-altering discovery. "Haze, every guy who's a bottom wants one thing. Okay, two things. They want a top who can take them to pound town like they mean it."

I flick an eyebrow. "Pound town?"

Tate ignores me. "And they also want to make sure that they're one hundred percent fresh down there. You've inadvertently stumbled upon a genius idea—a dildo-shaped, lubey, soapy product that will give bottoms all over the world that extra bit of assurance."

I have no idea what my face looks like right now, but I'm pretty sure my expression is set to WTF mode. "I—I don't know whether I should be scared or jumping up and down for joy right now."

"Option B," Tate assures me, flashing me a huge grin. "The reason I've been hounding you for more soaps is because I started my own, X-rated version of the ice bucket challenge. I posted some videos using dildo lube soap shooting out of my ass, making sure to espouse the wonderful added benefits of it leaving your ass smelling fresh as a daisy. I made sure to tag other models and influencers. I sent them your soap. Then they did a video, tagged their friends, and it snowballed from there."

"What size snowball are we talking about here?"

Tate stops himself. "Oh man, if I wasn't so into the story I'm telling you right now, I'd answer that question in the most explicit way possible."

I giggle some more. "Duly noted."

"The non-explicit answer is that #dildolubesoap has been trending on 4FansOnly for the last three weeks. That's unheard of. Most hashtags fade away after a day or two. This has exploded. It's gone viral. Big time."

I play with a loose strand of hair. "Holy shit."

"But likes, follows, and tags don't pay the bills. Am I right?"

"Right," I agree cautiously, mentally bracing myself for whatever Tate is going to throw at me next.

"Soooo, I created an online shop and set up a preorder page. I listed each bar of soap at fifty bucks."

"Fifty bucks?" I exclaim.

"I don't know if that's good or bad?"

"That's highway robbery. You could sell the soaps for ten bucks and still turn a profit."

He shrugs. "Sorry. I didn't want to underprice them, that's all. We can adjust the price later. Anyway..."

He pulls the laptop back and taps away furiously for a few seconds before sliding it in front of me again. My eyes bulge. "There are four thousand preorders here, Tate," I gasp.

"Yep. At fifty bucks a pop, that's a cool two hundred grand in your hand." Tate's face explodes with laughter and happiness. "I know this is a lot, and yes, it's out there and hella X-rated, but don't you get it?"

"Get what?"

"You love making soap. It makes you so happy. And maybe now you can give it a shot. This can be your new dream."

Tate rambles on about some of the finer points, but he doesn't need to convince me. I already know that the crazy bastard might be onto something.

How?

One word.

It starts with *T* and ends in *ingles*.

21

NOAH

I finish typing the last of my consult notes for the day and glance over at the time. It's five to six, and by some miracle, it looks like I'll be getting out on time today. You know you've been working too much when a nine-hour workday seems short.

I chug down the rest of my iced latte before throwing it in the trash. I'm going to need my energy because as long as today has been, I have another challenge ahead of me tonight: I need to keep Haze out until midnight. Once the clock strikes twelve, it officially becomes his thirtieth birthday, and he gets to see the surprise his Aunt Jocelyn and I have planned for him. I cross my fingers, toes, and everything else that's crossable, hoping that everything goes according to plan.

I got changed earlier, so I quickly duck into the staff lounge for a quick round of goodbyes. I spy Fulton staring out the window. He's working the late shift today. "Hey, I'm off."

He spins around. "Cool. I'll see you tonight. At midnight?"

I bring my hands to the side of my face, crossing my fingers. "Yep."

"It'll be fine," Fulton says reassuringly. "More than fine. It'll be beautiful. Haze will love it."

"I hope so." I'm about to say goodbye, when I decide to ask, "Any word from Gus?"

Fulton's lips tighten. "I spoke to him earlier today. He sends his apologies. He's still not up for leaving the house. Looks like we might have to stage that intervention, after all."

"Shit."

I hate hearing that Gus is still cut up about what happened at the wedding, and yeah, I feel guilty, too, that I've been spending all my time with Haze and neglecting my friend. As if reading my mind, Fulton jumps in. "Don't stress about it. Tonight, you're doing something amazing for Haze. Maybe we can find some time in the next few days and check in on Gus?"

I give a firm nod. "That sounds good. Let's do that. All right, I'm off."

"See you at midnight."

I make my way down the corridor to the waiting room. It's a bustling menagerie of dogs, cats, and other animals, but all I see is the guy sitting in the corner. Well, first I smell him, of course. That spicy-citrus scent of his is one of my favorites. He brought over a big batch of it to my place, and I love it. Even when Haze isn't there, his smell lingers everywhere.

I didn't tell him where we're going or even what we'll be doing tonight. I was as vague as I could be without arousing any suspicion. I hope it's worked because truth be told, once we have dinner, I have no idea how we're going to spend the rest of the evening without going to my place before midnight.

Haze is wearing a light gray T-shirt and faded blue jeans. My breath hitches in my throat the way it always does whenever I lay my eyes on him. His hair is out, framing his handsome features beautifully. He smiles and gets up when he sees me.

"Well, hello."

"Hello yourself," he replies, kissing me.

The noise and chaos of the waiting room fades into nothingness. Haze's lips have the power to do that. In fact, Haze's talented mouth has the power to do a whole lot more than that, too.

"Mr. Piddles?"

Haze and I turn to see Fulton calling his next appointment. A young hipster couple rise to their feet, their cute little furball Maltese nestled in the guy's tattooed arm as Fulton ushers them into the consult room. A giggle escapes from Haze.

"What's so funny?" I ask.

Haze leans in. "I'll tell you one of my favorite things about working here. It's when one of the vets comes out into the waiting room. You all look serious and professional with your white lab coats, and then you yell out, 'Fluffy' or 'Mr. Piddles.' It cracks me up."

I let out a chuckle. "Gus wanted the clinic to be animal-focused. That's why we use the animal's name."

"I think it's adorable."

I help Haze put his jacket on. "Does that mean you think I'm adorable?"

He flicks me a look over his shoulder. "What do you think?"

My chest warms, and once Haze is dressed, I sling my backpack over my shoulder and hold the door open for him. We venture out into the cold evening air, and at least the blast perks me up a bit. It's only a short walk to the Mexican restaurant that's become one of our favorite places to eat. I tell Haze about my day as we make our way over, fingers threaded.

We find an empty booth, and Haze hunkers down beside me. I like it when he does that. As much as I like looking across the table at him, having him next to me, within touching distance, is even better. We order our usual. That's when I notice Haze drumming his fingers on his thigh. He swallows loudly. "I have some news to tell you. Two things, actually."

My face must tense up because when Haze gazes over at me, he adds, "It's nothing bad, don't worry. It's just big and a little crazy. And by a little crazy, I mean a lot crazy. I've spent the whole day trying to figure it all out in my own head."

"Hazey." I rub my hand along his denim. "It's okay. Take your time."

"Thanks." He closes his eyes, and the words whoosh out of his mouth. "I got a call this morning after you dropped me off. It was from the producer I met with when I went to L.A."

My shoulders stiffen, but I do my best to keep my face neutral. "And what did he say?"

Haze's eyes grow serious. "He said I scored a role on a new TV show."

I force a smile, trying my best to ignore the million little stabs pricking the insides of my chest. "Congratulations. That's wonderful news."

"I turned it down."

My mouth flies open. "Wh—why?"

"Do you remember when you dropped me off this morning and we were talking in the car?"

I nod. "Yeah."

"Remember, *tingly*?"

"Yeah?" I'm still confused.

Haze smiles, and there's a calmness behind it that I've never seen on him before. "When I'm with you, I feel tingly. When I'm making my soaps, I feel tingly." He pauses, twisting his hair between his fingers. "Which brings me onto my second piece of news."

"Uh-huh."

If my mouth flung open over his revelation about declining the role, then when he tells me about Tate's idea for dildo lube soap, my mouth is stretched so wide you could probably fly a Boeing 737 into it.

"So, whaddya think?" he asks, once he's done telling me about it.

"I'm thinking I should've ordered something stronger than a diet Coke," I joke. "But you know what, I actually think it's a great idea. One, because it means you get to do what you love, something that makes you tingly. And two, because as a guy who identifies as a bottom, I'd be placing an order for a bulk supply."

"To go with your gallon of lube," Haze teases.

"Sure, make fun of me, but we're on our third tub," I remind him.

Haze giggles, but then something weighty settles over him. He opens and closes his mouth a couple of times. I squeeze his thigh, silently assuring him he can take all the time he needs. His voice is small when he does speak. "Noah, this is the first time in my life that I feel... I don't even know what the right word is. Certain, maybe? When it comes to my future, I actually know what I want. I want you, and I want to give this business a shot."

My stomach is doing somersaults, backflips, and a whole goddamn gymnastics routine at this point. "You have no idea how happy I am for you."

I mean it with all my heart. I want nothing but the best for him, and even if that meant he had to pack up and move to L.A., I wouldn't have stood in the way of his dreams. Sure, it would have killed me, but Haze's happiness means everything to me.

"And I have to admit, completely selfishly, I am so glad you chose dildo lube soap and me."

Haze's eyes find mine again as I feel his fingers grip around the back of my neck. "No. I chose you first, *before* the dildo lube soap. Tate came in and told me about it after I'd declined the role."

I can't believe it. I feel like I've been hit by a truck and wrapped up in a warm cocoon all at the same time. I try talking, but no words come out. A tightness squeezes its way from my chest, up my neck, and makes its way to my eyes, which overflow with tears.

"You—you chose me?"

Haze presses our foreheads together as his tears join mine, spilling all around us. "Yes," he breathes out shakily.

"I've got a chicken enchilada, two beef burritos, and a mixed plate of tacos."

The server's voice shatters the moment. We peel off each other, hastily wiping our faces.

"Thanks," I manage to mutter.

"This is...a lot," I say, picking up a fish taco.

"You mean all this food or what we were just talking about?"

I snicker. "Both, I guess. I'm so glad we're able to talk honestly and openly. That's a really rare thing."

Haze bites into his burrito. "Tell me about it."

We make our way through the mountain of food we've ordered. I tell Haze more about my day. Fulton's shirt saying, **It's all fun and games until someone ends up in a cone**, and Harmony accidentally breaking a coffee mug pale in comparison to the day he's had.

As we eat, my heart is still thundering in my chest. I have to confess that for a moment there, he had me worried. It was like coming face to face with your greatest fear. The thought of losing

Haze is too much to bear. With every mouthful of Mexican, my resolution grows stronger.

First, I have to somehow make it to midnight to give Haze his birthday surprise. Then I have my own special birthday present to give him. I've been sure it's something I've wanted to do for a while now, but after hearing him choosing me, fuck, it cements my feelings for him even more.

I'm not a clingy guy. I believe that love works best when it's two well-rounded individuals coming together to lift each other up, not two incomplete people needing to find fulfillment or validation by being with someone. But I can't deny that hearing Haze say that he chose me feels like the best thing ever.

It makes me even more determined to treat him right, give him everything that he deserves. Because for the first time in my life, I'm finally with a person who will treat me exactly the same way in return.

Now all I have to do is figure out how the heck we're gonna spend the next five hours.

Why does time have to be such a royal pain in the ass?

When you want it to slow down so that you can savor a moment, it seems to fly. The older you get, the faster the years go by. And on the odd occasion when you want it to hurry up so that you can get to something you've been planning for and are incredibly nervous about, it slows down to a snail's pace.

It's half past eleven, and after Mexican, we got a hot chocolate and whiled away some time at a cute little cafe, then browsed the aisles in an open-till-late bookstore. Next, I introduced Haze to my favorite dessert place, and now, since I've totally run out of time-killing ideas, we find ourselves at our usual, after-work bar.

Haze lets out another yawn as he props himself up against the counter in an effort to stay awake and upright. This yawn is longer and louder than the five that have come before it. He taps his fingers impatiently. "Why are we doing this?"

"Doing what?" I pull my drink to my lips, hoping to cover the white lies I've had to tell him all night in an attempt to deflect his questions about why we're not going home like we normally would. I just need to milk this whole distraction routine for another thirty minutes. Less, actually, if you count the ten minutes it takes to drive from the bar to my place.

"Ooh, I've got something for you." I rifle through my backpack.

Haze eyes me suspiciously. "I've been wondering why you were carrying that around all night."

I hand him the present. "I know it's not technically your birthday for another half an hour, but it's from Fulton." I don't mention how he gave it to me this morning and told me to use it in case I was running out of excuses to keep Haze out until midnight.

Haze holds my gaze for a moment, then shrugs and takes the gift from me. "No complaints here."

He rips it open and unfolds the T-shirt. It's got **Beyoncé wasn't built in a day**, written across it with a silhouette of the singer behind it. I lean forward. "Do you like it?"

"I love it." Haze looks genuinely pleased with it. "You know I love her, and I really dig the message, too. I'll be sure to text him tomorrow to say thanks." He lets out another yawn, covering it with the back of his hand. His eyes have gone watery, and the poor guy looks positively—and adorably—dopey.

I glance over at the clock behind the bar. It's twenty to midnight. "Come on. Let's go back to my place." After I settle the tab and we leave the bar, I silently pray for every single red light possible.

22

HAZE

We leave the bar and drive to Noah's place in silence. A slow silence. Geez, guess I'd never noticed before how much of a stickler Noah is for sticking to the speed limit, so much so that I'd swear he was driving a few miles under it.

He's been acting a little funny tonight, although I can't quite put my finger on it. Mainly because I'm tired and emotionally drained from the day. I'm surprised Noah isn't yawning yet. He's had a much busier, even longer day than I have.

I've had a great night with him, I really have. The food at dinner was delicious as always, but what was even better was getting the chance to tell Noah about everything that happened today. I'd been tossing up all afternoon whether or not to pay him a visit at the clinic. It was killing me keeping it inside. But I decided against it. I know how busy he is at work, so I didn't want to throw all of this onto him there, and also, well, it turned out to be good to have some time alone to let it really sink in.

Once I came down off the adrenaline high, I ran a bath and let the reality wash over me. I'd said no to a potentially life-changing offer, and still, as I soaked and yep, listened to Queen Bey, I felt a soul-level sureness that I'd made the right decision. In a way, having a few hours to myself helped because the more time passed, the more my assuredness grew.

The only thing I was left nervous about was Noah's reaction. He's not the kind of guy to ever hold someone back from pursuing what they want in life. He's too decent, kind, and selfless to do that. I wanted to make it clear to him that even though he obviously factored into my decision, I was ultimately doing this because I wanted to do it.

I know I've made the right choice. I'm sitting next to the most wonderful man I have ever met and there's no way on earth I'd give this up, give him up, for anything. I have never felt as free, as happy, as...*me* as when I'm with him.

I was both glad and relieved at Noah's reaction to my news about L.A...as well as about the dildo lube soap. That one, even I'm going to need some time to totally wrap my brain around. If someone told me that *this* is the pivot my life would take, even twenty-four hours ago, I would've laughed in their face. But what was that quote Aunt Jocelyn had said, something about people making plans and God laughing? This moment is very that.

I lean against the headrest and let out a contented sigh.

"We're almost home."

I'm too in my head to notice the tight grip Noah has on the wheel as we crawl our way through the near-deserted streets. Or the stiffness in his shoulders as we walk up the driveway once we reach his place. And I come *this close* to missing that when we reach his front porch, we're not met by the excited yelps and scratches of...

I frown. "Hey... Where's Buddy?"

A flash of—is that guilt?—sweeps across Noah's face. He fumbles urgently with his keys, like they're on fire or something, all the time not saying a word. The keys jangle loudly as he jams them into the lock. Once the door opens, that's when I know something is definitely up. There's no Buddy leaping out at us. Noah gestures for me to enter first, and as I brush past him, he whispers into my ear, "I hope this is okay."

We go inside, and my heart shoots up to my mouth. The entire living room is lit up in candles, and my whole family is there. Friends, too, as well as some of the staff from the vet clinic. The TV has been moved, and along that wall, there's a massive photo of my mom, taken when she was heavily pregnant with me. Her smile beams peacefully over all of us.

Noah's hand presses against the small of my back as I take it all in. "I knew a surprise party would be inappropriate, but I wanted you to have something special. I'm so sorry for your loss, but I'm so thankful you're in my life."

I hug Noah harder than I've ever hugged anyone in my life. "I hope this is okay," he repeats, and that's when I lose it, tears streaking down my face and falling off my chin.

I nod. "Yes. This is perfect. Thank you."

When we pull apart, my family has moved closer to us, and I take turns hugging my dad, cousins, and aunts. Aunt Jocelyn is the last one I get to.

"Why do I have a feeling you had something to do with this?" I sputter into her ear.

"It was all Noah's idea. I just helped him out with some of the logistics. He's a keeper, Hazey."

And don't I know it.

Music starts to play softly in the background. I recognize those first few chords instantly.

It's Beyoncé.

Halo.

I find myself standing with Dad next to a table that has an assortment of finger food laid out on it. "She would have been so proud of you, son," he says, wrapping his arm around my shoulder. "Just like I am."

He wraps me up in a big hug. "Thanks, Dad."

I see a few of the guys from the clinic approach, so I introduce Fulton and Chase to my father. We all chat for a few minutes, before Dad excuses himself.

"By the way, thanks for the T-shirt, Fulton."

A funny look crosses his face. "Oh, so Noah gave it to you?"

"Uh, yeah. Wasn't that why you gave it to him?"

Fulton grins. "It was his to use in case of an emergency. I told him to give it to you if he was having trouble keeping you away from the house and needed to buy some more time."

"Noah's a terrible liar," Chase chimes in. "We were worried he'd blow the cover tonight if you straight out asked him why you were staying out so late."

"Ah, I see. Good thing I never asked, then."

The guys nod, and I get Noah's funny behavior tonight. It all makes sense. The long dinner. The hot chocolate. Meandering through a bookstore. Having a nightcap at the bar. No overly excited retriever waiting at the front door. Which reminds me...

"Hey, where's Buddy?"

Fulton smacks the side of his face. "Oh, shit. He's still in the laundry room. I'll let him out."

A few moments later, Buddy scampers into the room going into sniff and lick overdrive. As Fulton returns, Tate comes over and gives me a hug. I introduce him to Fulton and Chase. I make a mental note to invite Tate to come to the bar and hang out with the vet crew. I know Noah invited him when he came over to the loft, but we haven't had a chance to organize anything yet. Judging by how well he's getting along with the guys, it's a no-brainer, really.

"Where's Gus?" I ask.

Fulton's eyebrows crease. "He sends birthday wishes as well as an apology that he couldn't be here tonight. He still isn't ready to leave the house."

"Oh, I'm so sorry to hear that. Tell him thanks and that I look forward to seeing him at the clinic whenever he's ready to come back."

"I'll be sure to do that."

I see Fulton elbow Chase, and before I know what's happening, Tate grips my arms, the music gets cut, and my father walks out of the kitchen, balancing a massive cake lit with what looks like a million candles. Then something happens that I've never experienced before. People start singing, "Happy birthday to you..." To me. They're singing it to me.

Shit. What am I meant to do? I feel flushed and awkward, and I suddenly have no idea what to do with my arms. Until a strong hand curls around my waist, that is. It's Noah. His face is shining in the candlelight. He winks, but doesn't stop singing. He's actually got quite a good voice.

"Hip hip, hooray!"

It's not until Aunt Jocelyn walks up on my other side and

whispers, "Time to blow out the candles, birthday boy," that I manage to tear my gaze away from Noah.

Oh. Right. Yeah, that bit.

"Make a wish," someone cries out.

I hunch over the cake, make my first-ever birthday wish, and with a massive huff, blow out every single candle on that cake.

"Happy birthday, son." Dad rubs my back and hands me a knife. "Just make sure you don't touch the bottom."

I take the knife, but I'm confused. "Wait. If I can't touch the bottom, how am I meant to slice the cake?"

I hear a few people giggling good-naturedly as Aunt Jocelyn explains the intricacies of the ceremonial first slice. Thankfully, she also offers to take over the real cake cutting from me afterward. We get into a good rhythm. She carves, and I dish it out, making sure everyone in the room gets a plate.

And even though I didn't do it deliberately, it seems that I've left the best 'til last. But when I reach Noah, and he instinctively curls his arms around my waist, I set the plate aside and pull him into a kiss. A simple one. Just lips resting on lips, the touch sweet and tender.

"Thank you for tonight," I murmur into his lips.

"You're welcome," he hums right back.

I pull apart, happy I can still taste him on my lips. I cup his face in my hands. We stay frozen for a few seconds, our candle-infused eyes locked on each other. Noah drops his chin knowingly before reaching for something behind him.

His voice drops until it's barely more than a whisper. "I realize that we've been doing this relationship back to front, but somehow, it doesn't feel wrong, does it?"

I shake my head. "No, it doesn't. It just feels like...us."

Noah nods. That's when I notice he's choking back tears. Before I can say anything, he shoves a rectangular-shaped box toward me. "Here. Seems like it might be a good time to give you this."

My eyes dart between the box I'm holding and Noah's face that I can't quite read at the moment. When I finally open it, I gasp when I spot what's inside.

"It's a boyfriend bracelet," Noah explains as I carefully take out the black leather bracelet. It's beautifully crafted with thin white stitching running along the edge and a stainless steel metal clasp in the middle.

I hear Noah inhaling sharply. "I don't know if a boyfriend bracelet is even a thing, but...do you like it and...would you like to be my boyfriend?"

My eyes glisten. "Yes," I breathe.

"To which question?" Noah sounds a little nervous.

"To both," I quickly reassure him. "Yes, I love the bracelet, and fuck, yes, I want to be your boyfriend."

Relief washes over Noah's face. "Oh, thank god. Otherwise that inscription would have been awkward as hell."

"Inscription?"

I bring the bracelet up to my eyes to get a better view when Noah grabs my arm.

"Remember, we do things all out of order and on our own timeframe, okay? If it's too much or too soon, you just let me know."

Noah is still nervous. If anything, he's more nervous now than he was a few moments before. It doesn't make any sense.

"Okaaay." I gaze down at the bracelet, and even in the dim lighting of the room, I can see the five words engraved on the underside of the metal clasp.

I love you, Hazey baby

My whole body tingles from the top of my head to the tips of my toes. I throw myself into Noah's arms, and it's a good thing the guy thinks quick and has Hemsworth-sized guns because he scoops me up and cradles me in his warmth.

"I love you, too, Noah Walters."

23

NOAH

"Whoa, whoa, whoa. Back it up. Dildo lube *what?*" Fulton chokes out.

The poor guy just took a sip of his drink right as Tate started his big announcement. Good thing he managed to not spill any of it over his ***I like big mutts and I cannot lie*** T-shirt.

I clap Fulton across the back to help with his coughing fit. Once it subsides, Tate checks to make sure he's okay before repeating, "Dildo lube soap." He produces a sausage-shaped, purple bar of soap and places it onto the table for everyone to see.

Fulton, Chase, Tate, Haze, and I are in our usual spot, in our usual bar, but there is nothing usual about the conversation that's about to unfold.

Oh, and Gus is making his first public appearance tonight, too. He's been pretty quiet so far, mainly keeping to himself and only speaking when someone says something to him, but it's good to see him out of the house and wearing an outfit that doesn't have feet pockets.

It's been a week since Tate met the crew at Haze's subdued birthday celebration, but he's clearly comfortable sharing the news about Haze's new business venture. Speaking of, my *boyfriend* is currently sitting right beside me, snuggling his lemongrass-and-ginger-scented body into me.

My boyfriend.

I don't think I will ever get tired of those two words.

I know we've only been official for a week, but I can't describe how happy I am. I took a chance and gave my heart to the most wonderful person I've ever met. I trust him with it, and I know he'll never hurt me.

Fulton's sitting on my other side and has regained his ability to speak. "And what, pray tell, is dildo lube soap?"

Tate's eyes dart around the booth. For the first time, I can see his usually confident demeanor give way to a slight hesitancy. "Is everyone here okay with adult content?"

We all nod. "And does anyone here have a problem talking

about gay sex explicitly?" Tate asks, his gaze lingering on Chase, the only straight guy in the group.

A chorus of "no" and "nopes" circles around the booth.

I glance over at Chase since I know what's coming. "This is gonna get kinda graphic, Chase."

He drains his beer. "So? I'm down."

"It involves...butt stuff."

"Butt stuff isn't limited to any one orientation," Fulton is quick to point out to me.

"Yeah, I know. Of course. I get that. I just want to make sure everyone is comfortable," I reply.

"We are," Chase says almost a little too excitedly. He turns to Tate. "Now get on with it."

"Right." With a brisk nod, Tate's swagger returns. "Once upon a time, two princes, who were also best friends and housemates, lived in a magical loft with no walls. One prince was a long-haired sweet angel named Prince Haze——"

"Also known as Hazey baby to some," I mutter into Haze's ear and bring him in for a kiss.

"Just to you." He smiles against my lips.

Tate clears his throat. "And the other prince was a top one percent content creator on 4FansOnly, and his name was the Poly Prince."

"This is going to be the most X-rated fairy tale you guys have ever heard," Haze interjects, and everyone laughs. Yes, even Gus, for the first time tonight.

"Anyway," Tate goes on. "Prince Haze happened to be a wonderful soap maker. One day, he produced a batch of soap that wasn't quite right. It was a little too hard in the center and a little too oily around the edges."

Fulton lifts a brow. "I sense we're veering into 'Goldilocks and the Three Bears' territory."

"Kinda," I agree with a smirk. "Just with different kinds of bears."

Tate keeps going. "Prince Haze left the batch out on the counter, but the unsuspecting Poly Prince didn't realize anything was wrong with it. So when he showered to, uh, prepare for his upcoming magical scene, he wanted to make sure he was extra fresh...down you know where."

"I'm suddenly liking this story a lot more." Fulton perks up and leans in closer. "Bottom prep is a real thing, even though no one ever talks about it openly."

"Amen to that, brother," Tate says with a gleam in his eye before resuming his story. "When the Poly Prince used Prince Haze's soap, he couldn't get a handle on it. Literally. The soap was so oily he couldn't properly grip it. It reminded the Poly Prince of lube. That's when a crazy idea took hold of him. He looked at the soap in his hand. Not only was it slippery, it also reminded him of, well, a small dildo. So..."

Tate takes a breath, and as I glance around the table, I find all the guys hanging on Tate's every word. Even Chase. Actually, *especially* Chase.

"...the Poly Prince shoved it in his ass."

Fulton's glasses practically fog up. "And?" he asks, pushing them further up his nose.

"With just the teeniest push, it squirted right out. It felt good, and it helped give the Poly Prince a little extra bounce in his step. And that was the moment he discovered..." Tate drums his fingers against the side of the table. "Dildo lube soap."

"Wow," Gus says after a few moments of stunned silence.

"That's just the first half of the story. Tell them what happened next," Haze prompts.

Tate snickers. "Well, I shot a few videos using the dildo lube soap."

"There's a market for that?" Chase's voice is laced with a curious edge.

"There's a market for *everything*," Tate responds knowingly. "Believe me. I've probably seen a good chunk of it. The videos started to get traction, so I pestered Haze to make some more of the stuff. I then set up an online challenge where I tagged other influencers and creators, sent them a batch, and encouraged them to post videos. Long story short, it went viral, it trended, and I started taking preorders that blew up. So there's definitely demand there."

"I think this is genius," Fulton states. "For too long, bottom prep has been something that's considered shameful or embarrassing, which makes no sense. All it does is make people who do it feel bad for no reason, like they have to hide it or pretend it doesn't happen. I think this will be a great way of starting conversations and opening—"

"Legs?" Gus jokes.

"Minds, I was going to say," Fulton smirks.

"We've come up with a name and slogan, too," Haze adds. "The acronym for dildo lube soap is DLS, so we're going to call it..."

He glances over at Tate, and they say it together. "Get fresh with DLS!"

Tate throws in an animated hand flourish for good measure, and it earns a round of applause from the table. Everyone seems to be reacting positively. Even Gus. I look at him and notice his gaze lingering on Tate. When I glance over in his direction a few moments later, his eyes are still on Tate. Hmm.

After that, everyone starts chatting away amongst themselves. Fulton turns to Haze and me. "So this DLS, this is a real thing?"

"Yep. Sure is," Haze answers brightly. "I've spent the last week working on setting up a proper website and doing all the fun paperwork and registration stuff you need to do when you start a new business. I've always loved making soap. I just never in my wildest imagination thought I'd be able to make a career out of it."

"I'm really happy for you, Haze," Fulton says, and I can hear that he genuinely means it.

Haze smiles at him. "Thank you. I couldn't have done this without Tate. Heck, I would never have come up with this idea in a million years. And he's done such a great job of generating interest. The stuff is gonna fly out the door faster than it'll fly out of people's asses."

We laugh. Chase leans over and joins the conversation. "So, no Hollywood then?"

Haze shakes his head firmly. "Nope. It didn't feel right. The whole time I was in L.A., it felt like I was dragging myself to auditions and meetings, going through the motions without any of the positive, feel-good stuff you should be feeling when you do what you're meant to be doing with your life."

"I hear ya," Chase acknowledges. "I feel that way about my work. I think we all do."

Fulton and I murmur in agreement.

"I'm glad you've found something you love to do that makes you happy," Chase adds. "But you are still going to keep working at the clinic, right?"

"Of course, yes," Haze says. "I love it there. It's the best job I've ever had. I'm going to defer studies for a year so that I have time to focus on the business. But yeah, you're not getting rid of me that easily."

"Good. I'm glad," Chase says with a grin.

"Hey, where did Tate go?" Fulton asks suddenly.

I glance around the booth. "And has anyone seen Gus?"

Fulton's eyebrows skyrocket. "Wait a minute...you don't think those two—"

"I see them over there, standing by the bar," Chase cuts in.

"You can relax." I give Fulton's shoulder a clap. "As if something would ever happen between those two. Gus is still recovering from the nightmare wedding, and from what Haze tells me, Tate isn't the relationship type."

Haze confirms, nodding. "Tate's poly. I don't know if he's ever dated just one person before."

"So there you go. Nothing could ever happen between those two because even once Gus is ready to start dating again, he's strictly a one-man kinda guy. He wants the husband, the kids, the whole white picket fence thing."

"Whereas Tate's poly and proud," Haze mentions. "And I don't see that changing any time soon."

"What about you?" I ask, lowering my voice. Haze and Chase have continued talking, so I take a moment to check in with my best friend. "Are you open to dating?"

He waves me off with a "Pfft," but I can see the dark storm clouds gathering behind his eyes. Fulton's whole face pinches, and he looks at me with the same hurt and pain I've seen in him almost every time we talk about the prospect of him dating.

"I'd like to find someone, but..." He runs a hand through his hair and blows out a heavy breath. "Harry."

I wince. Fuck.

Harry's not a human or an animal, but is nevertheless a constant presence in Fulton's life, holding him back from finding the love and happiness I so badly want for my best friend.

The guys return with drinks, and we spend the next few hours talking, laughing, and drinking. My fingers find Haze's many times during the night. Every time we touch, it fills me with warmth and joy and love.

Gus is the first one to start yawning, but pretty soon, all the guys are. They get up to leave. I tug at Haze's arm and suggest, "Maybe we can stay for one more?"

He licks his lips and smiles. "Sure."

As the guys shrug on their jackets, scarves, and gloves, Fulton stops wrapping his bright pink and purple polka-dot scarf around his neck and breaks out into a shit-eating grin.

"Ooh, I almost forgot. You two owe me fifty bucks," he says to Gus and Chase. "I won the bet. I guessed these guys would get together before Thanksgiving."

Gus and Chase grumble and throw some faux-dirty looks at Haze and me as they fork over the cash to a smiling Fulton. He waves it in the air. "I'm donating this to an animal shelter."

"G'night." I wave them off, watching them as they weave their way through the bar until they disappear.

"Why did you want to stay?" Haze asks, gripping my hand in his.

I point toward the pool table. A group of four college-aged guys have been playing there all night. "It's crazy to think that I was sitting right here, and you were standing right over there, and now we're..."

"Sitting together over here," Haze teases.

"You know what I mean."

He nods, thoughtfully. "Yeah. I do."

"It was only meant to be a one-night stand." I chuckle, rubbing my fingers against his. "And look what you made me do. I broke all the rules and fell head over heels in love with you."

A smile forms at the corners of his mouth. "I'm not complaining."

"Neither am I." I raise our linked hands and kiss the back of his. "I'm so excited about our future."

"Same. You make me so happy. I'm never leaving you. For as long as you want me, I'm gonna be right here."

"Then you'd better be ready for the long haul. Because I am never letting you go, Hazey baby."

EPILOGUE

Six-month anniversary...

HAZE

"I feel terrible," I say dejectedly.

"Well, then, stop it. You have nothing to feel terrible about."

I can hear the warmth and genuineness in Noah's voice, but I can't see him to save myself. There's mountain-high piles of boxes littered throughout the entire kitchen. We even had to take a curtain down to extend the area because there's just not enough room. Five months after our proper official launch, DLS demand is definitely outpacing supply.

I trundle past the boxes and the three kitchen tables I've added, all jam-packed with oils, creams, and bases, to find Noah on his knees, carefully taping up a box.

"Noah," I say when I get to him.

"Yes."

He drops the tape and grips my calves, the touch soothing me instantly. He gazes up, and man, those piercing green eyes of his flood me with so much warmth every time I look into them.

My bottom lip quivers. "I'm so sorry this is how we're spending our six-month anniversary."

"Hey, hey, hey." Noah climbs up off the floor and cradles my face. He gently grazes my stubble, and the friction feels soothing.

"Let's have a break. You're probably tired, right?"

I nod. I've been working sixteen-hour days for so long I've lost count of what day it is. Well, I remembered that today was our six-month anniversary, but that's mainly because Fulton texted me two days ago and suggested we think about celebrating half anniversaries, too. He's a big fan of that apparently. Noah told me Fulton celebrates his half-birthday every year since his actual birthday falls on Christmas Day.

Noah leads me into the living room, and we both flop down on the couch. We shuffle until we're lying on our sides facing each other, our legs tangled. Noah gently rubs his bare feet over the top of mine.

"How are you not tired?" I say. "You work just as much as me."

Noah smiles softly. "Guess I'm used to it. Besides, I love what I do so I don't really notice the time. I just wish I still had a sexy receptionist to ogle every time I came out into the waiting room."

I nuzzle into his neck and giggle. Yeah, about that. The original plan was for me to stay on at Vet Shop Boys until the business took off. No one, least of all me, expected it to take off so fast, so soon. Gus was great about it, of course, and threw me a massive sendoff party. Luckily, I still get to see everyone when I manage to tear myself from my soaps and make it to the bar occasionally.

"It's just so hard. There's so much work. It never seems to end."

"That's why I'm here. I'm going to help you get through it. The first year is always the hardest when you start a new business. It *will* get easier."

"Thank you. I needed to hear that." I huddle even closer to him, closing any tiny gaps between our bodies. "I just feel guilty that we're packing dildo lube soap on our six-month anniversary. It's hardly romantic."

"We're together, baby. Every second I spend with you is romantic and wonderful and precious to me."

Tears well in my eyes right as my stomach lets out a loud grumble. "How did I get so lucky?"

Noah's lips stretch. "I'm the lucky one. And..." He fumbles around behind him, checking something on his cell phone. "In just under three minutes, we'll both be even luckier."

"Huh? What do you mean?"

"I ordered Mexican. I figured you probably haven't eaten all day."

He shoots me a look, and I avert his gaze, trying to conceal my guilt from him. I just get so wrapped up in what I'm doing that time flies and I forget to eat.

"I don't want you wasting away." Noah's fingers find the hem of my shirt. "I love all these muscles too much for you to lose them."

"Oh, is that right?"

Our lips meet just as there's a knock at the door. Noah leaps to answer it. Five minutes later, we're sitting on a blanket on the floor, with a veritable Mexican feast spread out in front of us.

Noah's turned thoughtful. I can tell. His giveaway is that he starts chewing slower. He's building up to something.

"Anything on your mind?" I prod softly.

"Actually, yes, there is." Noah puts his burrito down and licks his fingers clean, taking his time.

"How do you feel if we keep doing this?" he finally asks.

"Which part?" I smirk. "Both of us working crazy hours or eating food on the floor?"

A faint smile plays at Noah's lips. "No. I mean, if we keep celebrating our half anniversary. I know we're borrowing Fulton's idea, but I think it could really work for us."

I take the last bite of my taco and wipe my hands on a napkin. "Work for us? How?"

Noah slides his fingers along my arm. "I asked you to be my boyfriend on your birthday, so technically that's our anniversary. Your birthday also marks the day of your mom passing. That's a lot of things colliding on that one day. I don't want you to feel overwhelmed each year on a day that's meant to be a celebration."

My chest floods with warmth. This is so classic Noah. Thoughtful. Sensitive. Downright amazing. "What do you have in mind?"

"Well..." He reaches for my fingers and entwines them with his. "Here's my plan. Just so you know, you have complete veto over everything."

I grin. "Noted."

"How about we celebrate our half-year anniversary starting tonight? Then, your birthday is your day. The people who love and care about you will have an opportunity to shower you with gifts and spoil you. About your mom, I was thinking of maybe celebrating her birthday. It might be nice to honor the life she had on the day she came into this world, rather than the day she left it. How does that sound?"

I don't know when it happened, but at some point as Noah was talking, I started crying.

"It sounds like you're the most incredible, supportive, thoughtful person in the whole entire world. It's a beautiful plan. I love it."

"Really?" He lowers his head so that he's staring directly into my eyes, gently thumbing away the tears off my cheeks. "I'm so happy to hear that because this is about finding what works for you. I hope you know you don't have to agree with anything just to make me happy."

And there it is. The words that heal me every time he utters them.

Whether it's choosing what we watch on TV, or how we spend our first anniversary together, Noah doesn't just love me for who I am—he encourages me to be even more of who I am. No shame, no apologies, just this open-ended invitation to dig deeper into myself to uncover all the new and exciting parts of who I am that I haven't discovered yet.

I crumple into his body, and he strokes my back soothingly. "Thank you." It's barely more than a whisper. He doesn't respond. All I feel is his strong hand rubbing up and down my back.

I've always hated not knowing what I wanted to do with my life, hated being called a chameleon. That word had been weaponized and used against me to make me feel bad, like there was something wrong with me for not having my shit figured out by some randomly assigned time in my life.

Who says you're meant to know what you want to do with the rest of your life by the time you graduate from high school?

Who says your first degree has to be the career you enter and stick with for the rest of your life?

Who says there's a correct order when it comes to falling in love, certain steps that need to be followed in a particular way?

I never imagined my life would turn out the way it has. I now see so clearly that I was torturing myself and drowning in self-imposed pressure by trying to figure it out. Dad and Aunt Jocelyn were right, and I often remind myself of the advice they gave me. Following your heart is about focusing on your feelings, not on external things you can't control. And when you do trust what you feel, life takes you in the most beautiful and weird and completely unexpected directions possible.

I can't even begin to describe how good it feels to wake up every morning next to Noah and feel tingles. And no, I'm not just talking about what he does to my nipples...that's usually more of a nighttime thing.

I could never in my wildest dreams have predicted that this would be my life. Running a successful X-rated soap business, co-paw-renting a golden retriever who licks me to death every time I see him, having wonderful new and old friends and family who support me in whatever choices I make, and of course, sharing it all with the most incredible man in the world by my side.

All the threads I've been pulling at my whole life are coming together now, weaving into this beautiful, rich, colorful tapestry that is my life. Maybe I've been in touch with my feelings for longer than I give myself credit for, but being with Noah gives me the space and the safety I need to keep going.

To keep trusting myself.

To keep pushing myself forward.

I don't know what I did to deserve him, but I really am the luckiest guy in the world. And I can't wait to spend the rest of my life with him.

Oh, and there's another thing I've learned over these past few months.

I *am* a chameleon.

And I fucking own it.

One-and-a-half-year anniversary...

NOAH

"This is amazing." I slide the glass door open, letting the salty air of the Gulf of Mexico whoosh into the oceanfront villa.

"No, *you're* amazing. Happy one-and-a-half-year anniversary."

We step out onto the balcony, the sunshine hitting my face as Haze wraps his arms around my waist. I knew he was up to something. He's almost as bad at lying as I am. But this? A surprise week-long vacation at a luxury resort in Florida. Wow. I'm blown away.

"This must have cost you a fortune."

He nuzzles against the back of my shoulder. "Yeah, it did. Good thing I earn a fortune."

I smile. That would be an understatement. Haze pulls in more in one month than I make in an entire year. And I couldn't be happier for him. DLS has blown up with articles in *Buzzfeed, Vice,* and *The Huffington Post* cementing it as a must-have sex item.

Haze has had to hire a crew of staff, and he's leased out a massive warehouse a ten minute drive from my place. Actually, I should say, *our* place. He moved in with me right after our six-month anniversary. I was over the moon the day he moved in, but that paled in comparison to the other little guy in our lives: Buddy. It's like he knew what was happening, seeing all the boxes being carted inside that Saturday morning. He gave Haze the biggest licking of his life.

That night, Haze gave me a good licking, too. And judging by the hardness pressing up against my ass, there's a good chance I'm in for one now, too.

"You. Bed. Now," Haze grunts into my ear.

My smile grows. "It's like you were reading my mind."

We dash into the incredible main bedroom. Seriously, the room is the size of our entire house, but I don't have the attention span to pay attention to any of the details. We're here for a week. I'm sure I'll have time to appreciate them later. Our clothes land on the floor so quickly it's possible we've set a new world record.

I lick my lips. "How do you want me?"

"You know *exactly* how I want you."

Warmth floods every part of my body. I do. I give my boyfriend what he wants, climbing onto the massive bed and flipping onto my back. With practiced ease, I hook my elbows behind my knees.

I take a breath and remind myself that I get to spend my life with this incredible man. He's replaced the dusty gray film that had settled over my life with vibrant colors of love, trust, and security.

Yes, it's been a hard slog. Getting Haze's business off the ground meant a lot of sacrifices. He's had to give up his studies, his work at the clinic, and it's also meant working late and most weekends. I pitch in whenever and wherever I can, but his success is all his. I'm more than happy to be the man behind the man.

Haze crawls along the bed, his lithe body sleek and graceful like a panther in the moments before it pounces on its prey. Luckily for me, that prey is my ass. Haze's head ducks as his mouth ghosts my ass. I can only feel his warm breath against me, but god, even that's enough to send shivers shooting up my spine.

Suddenly and with no warning, he spreads my ass and spears his tongue into my hole. I fist the sheets, hissing, "Holy fuck."

He pulls back and tips his head up to meet my gaze, his eyes glimmering. "Is this okay?"

I swear, for as long as I live, I will never, ever get tired of hearing those three words from him. Sharing my life with someone who makes me feel special, takes my needs into account, and prioritizes me in the same way I prioritize him... I always hoped to have a relationship like that. And now I do.

"I am so much better than okay," I reply. "I'm okay like you wouldn't believe."

A smirk teases his lips. "Oh, I think I have an idea."

And with that, he dives back in, burying himself in my ass, eliciting pleasure and bliss out of me I didn't think was humanly possible.

After a few minutes, hours, months—seriously, there's no way of telling how much time has passed—I gesture for him to come up for air. He helps me lower my legs before crawling his way up my body. I spin him so he's on his back and launch into my own tongue lashing, my lips finding his left nipple piercing, my fingers tweaking his right.

"Oh, Noah." It's Haze's turn to turn into a quivering mess as I nibble, pinch, twist, and tweak both of his sensitive nubs. We still do the electro thing every once in a while, but nothing beats skin on skin, lips on nipples contact.

After I've taken him to the brink—I lost count after the fourteenth time he begged for me to slow down so he wouldn't come hands free—my eyes find his, and I murmur, "Fuck me, baby."

We're long past the stage of using condoms. We both got tested, and we're monogamous, so now we get to fuck bare. And there's no better feeling in the world. Haze pulls lube out of who knows where and slathers it over his cock and my entrance.

"You don't want a finger?"

I shake my head violently against the pillow. "Nope. Need your cock. Now."

Haze drops his body down, and I reach around, pulling out his ponytail so his hair falls all around his face. He lowers down onto his elbows, our mouths melding in a deep, passionate kiss. I feel the crown of his cock at my hole. Fuck, I love that he can get inside me without using hands.

He kisses me harder as he begins to enter me. My heart rate speeds up as I'm overcome by that delicious stretch. It's raw. It's deep. It's one of the most beautiful feelings in the world. Haze is fully inside me, and as always, he stills and pulls off my lips. "Is this okay?"

I do what I always do—play with a stray strand of hair and say, "Yes, Hazey baby."

He smiles and rolls his hips, slowly and gently at first. He's balled his fists up by the sides of my body, the muscles in his arms flexing with his steadying movement.

"I want you to know how much I love you."

"I know that. I love you, too."

His pace increases, rutting into my body harder now.

"And I also want you to know that I couldn't have done any of this without you."

I open my mouth to protest, but he keeps going. "And before you say your usual thing about how this is all me and you're just playing a supporting role, I want you to know that I value the time and the energy you've spent to help me with the business and also...the way you've inspired me to find myself."

"Of course. I'd do anything for you."

We've fallen into a steady rhythm. The sounds of waves crashing onto the shore flit into the room, floating around our words.

"I want to be there for you as much as you've been there for me."

"You are." I cup his face in my hands. "You look after Buddy when I have to work late. You make me smell almost as good as you do with an endless supply of beautiful soaps. You make me dinner and sit through endless repeats of *This Pet's Got Talent*. You love me and look after me in all the right ways. But most importantly of all...you stayed."

Haze closes his eyes, the smile etched on his lips. He increases the tempo even more. Having a part of him inside me feels so good. Having him in my life feels even better. My heart is so full, so close to bursting, knowing that I've given my trust, my love to a man who treats me so well and won't leave me for something—or someone—else.

I want to spend my forever with this man.

Haze wraps his fingers around my cock and starts stroking. With a fevered pitch, he slams into my body, and I can feel him unload inside of me. With just a few more strokes, I follow soon after.

I glance out the windows. We arrived at the resort just after lunch. It's pitch black outside now. "I think we've been fucking for hours," I observe with a chuckle.

Haze carefully pulls out of me and reaches for the towel at the foot of the bed. As he's cleaning me up, he nods. "And this is just day one. I'm sure there's plenty to do and see around here, but I am more than happy to stay holed up in this room all week."

"Holed, hey?" I tease.

And with a giggle, he disposes of the towel and the lube and nestles into me.

I sigh a contented sigh, and for some weird, totally random reason, as I'm lying there, naked and spent after a whole day of mind-blowing sex, it hits me. The idea for the perfect way to propose to Haze...

Two months later...

"God, I'm going to embarrass myself on a scale I never have before."

Fulton places a hand on my shoulder. I turn away from the mirror, where I've been waging a losing battle with a way too tight T-shirt and face him. "Relax. Gus, Chase, and I will be right behind you. Literally," he adds the last word with a giggle.

Chase walks past us, arm outstretched and flicking his wrist sharply. "I still don't think I've got it," he grumbles to himself.

I lean in toward Fulton, tugging at the tight material barely concealing my stomach. "This is way too small."

He shoots me a hopeless look. "Hey, I did my best. This outfit isn't designed for people of our size, or in other words, men. You know my friend Melinda?"

"Yeah."

"Turns out she's a whiz with a sewing machine, but..." Fulton's voice trails off.

"But what?"

"She's a seamstress, not a magician," Fulton explains. "Besides, you look hot. You are serving total Dad-bod realness with a touch of vet-xtravaganza."

I peer back into the mirror, unconvinced. We're backstage at our usual bar. Up until the day after Haze and I got back from our sexcation—sorry, I mean vacation—in Florida, I didn't even know this area existed.

That's the day I spoke to the owner and made a special request. I booked out the entire place. It cost me an arm and a leg, but that wasn't the hardest part. No, the grueling, muscle-killing, panic-inducing rehearsals that have followed over the past eight weeks were the real tough bit.

I admit, when Haze showed me the Beyoncé *Single Ladies* video, I liked it, but didn't think too much more of it. I mean, it's cool that it's all shot in black and white, and I liked the simplicity of the dancing. Or at least, what I *thought* was simple dancing. Because when you're cramming in a dance rehearsal after pulling a fourteen-hour day, a simple left-leg kick, right-wrist twist combo feels more complicated than performing a femoral head ostectomy.

I tug at the hem of my—geez, what would you even call what I'm wearing? Fulton managed to snag some skin-tight black outfits with the right kinds of cut-outs in the shoulders and legs for us to wear. Like he said, they're designed for women. While I appreciate his friend's efforts to "mannify" them, I feel like I am one dance step away from having the most humiliating wardrobe malfunction possible.

"He's here." Gus rushes up behind me. "I have confirmation that Haze Adams is in the building."

A smirk twists Fulton's lips. "And how do you know that, Gus?"

"Tate texted me," he replies with a shrug. "What? We exchanged numbers so that we could text each other to make tonight...special."

Chase joins us, and as the four of us stand in a circle, I say, "I just want to thank you guys so much. I couldn't do this without you."

"Hey, anything for love," Gus says and offers me the warmest smile I've seen from him in a long time.

"We love you, man," Chase throws in. "We'd do anything for you."

"Yeah. And doing *this* proves it," Fulton mutters dryly.

"I love you guys, too."

"All right, are we finished with feelings?" Gus asks, straightening up and fiddling with his outfit. "Are you ready, Noah?"

I do a final once-over in the mirror before giving a determined nod. My heart is banging furiously in my chest, and my mouth went dry a few hours ago. Thankfully, Fulton grabs me by the hand and leads me down a narrow corridor. It doesn't take long to reach the side of the small stage area.

I peer out onto the crowded dance floor. My heart rate spikes even more. Okay, maybe that wasn't the smartest idea. Every single person that matters to me in my life is here tonight. Even my sister flew in from Phoenix to be here.

But it's one person who's responsible for the bundle of nerves coiled in my stomach.

I hope I don't stuff it up for him.

I hope he likes it.

And I sure as fuck hope he says yes.

A voice from somewhere counts down as Fulton gently pushes

me toward the edge of the stage, as he, Gus, and Chase follow a close step behind me.

"And three, two, one..."

Three minutes and eighteen seconds later, I am drenched in sweat and possibly a candidate for early hip surgery. My lungs are on fire, and my face is probably tomato-red, but I don't care about any of that right now.

With a single spotlight beaming down on me, my backup dancers have exited stage right and I'm alone on the stage, down on bended knee.

I see Tate shove a surprised and confused-looking Haze onto the stage. He's cupping his hands over his mouth so I can't get a good read of what's going on with him. His eyes are watery, like he's been crying.

Shit, it wasn't that bad, was it?

He reaches me, and I stare up into his beautiful face. He takes hold of my shoulder, instantly steadying me. "Haze Adams, since the night we met, I knew you were special. It was only meant to be a one-night stand, but instead, you turned out to be the one. The one I want to spend the rest of my life with. Will you—will you marry me?"

I hear a breathy "yes," and then I have no idea what happens next. A thunderous roar erupts, and I'd like to think my adoring fans flood the stage and crowd surf me over to the bar. What probably happened was Haze had to take most of my body weight as I took step after painful step, plonking my ass down on a stool which I have no intention of moving from for the rest of the night.

After every last person has come over, wrapping us in hugs and excited cries of congratulations, Haze and I finally have a moment alone.

"That was incredible." He wipes my still-sweating forehead down with a napkin.

"You really had no idea?"

He smiles. "No. I mean, I heard you humming Beyoncé around

the house. I just thought my great taste in music was finally rubbing off on you."

I let out a low chuckle. "I certainly have more of an appreciation for choreography."

"I can't believe you organized all of this. You're incredible. I'm the luckiest guy in the world."

"See, that's where you're wrong," I say, nudging against his body. "I am."

I really was.

I took a chance and decided to love again. Letting someone in is one of the scariest things in the world. You give them all of you—your trust, your love, your heart. But when you find the right one, that person sees those things as the precious gifts that they are, they cherish them, and they value and nurture them. And most of all, they return it.

Love really is a two-way street.

I lean in and press my lips to Haze's. Our paths were only meant to cross for a few hours, and yet, here we are, on the brink of a lifetime together.

"I love you so much, Noah," he murmurs.

"I love you, too, Hazey baby."

THE END

ABOUT CASEY COX

A dash of feels... A sprinkle of LOLs... A generous pinch of quirky, fun, and unique characters chasing their happily ever after... Combine it all, stir vigorously, and what do you get?... A Casey Cox contemporary MM romance!

Casey lives on the east coast of Australia, loves the beach, is obsessed with donuts, and is the proud paw-rent of two utterly adorable French Bulldogs, Ralphie and Lilly.

For more information about Casey, please visit -
www.caseycoxbooks.com

www.ingramcontent.com/pod-product-compliance
Lightning Source LLC
Chambersburg PA
CBHW031059020726
47495CB00007B/1963